DRAGON'S KNIGHT
BY CAROL L. DENNIS

POPULAR LIBRARY

An Imprint of Warner Books, Inc.

A Warner Communications Company

POPULAR LIBRARY EDITION

Popular Library®, the fanciful P design, and Questar® are registered
trademarks of Warner Books, Inc.

Cover illustration by Janny Wurtz

Popular Library books are published by
Warner Books, Inc.
666 Fifth Avenue
New York, N.Y. 10103

Ⓦ A Warner Communications Company

Printed in the United States of America

First Printing: January, 1989

10 9 8 7 6 5 4 3 2 1

To Mother, who thinks
I can do anything.

Carol Dennis

PROLOGUE

Four beings of pure energy joined in a preordained meeting, shaping a vast hall from the dust of interstellar space. Then, simply because they had the power to do so, they recreated the forms they had once worn.

"The time for vengeance is at hand," Oron, a tall golden plume of light, intoned in the minds of the others.

"There is a threat to the young Bright Ones. We must keep vigil," agreed Cronal, the second Watcher, smoothing his star-pale beard with an aged hand.

"Is there no other avenue open to us?" The Lady, the only female Watcher, stood lapped in silver. Her lucent skin and shining hair glowed, as did her robe. Her argent eyes looked sadly at the first two speakers. "Can we not hold our hand yet a while? No race grows strong enough to join us without making some errors. Let us give the Keepers and Wyrd more time to contain the evil one who has sprung up among them." Her soft words echoed telepathically with hope and patience.

"Yess," hissed the dragonoid shape that was Drakon, "we must allow the Keepers more time, lest we repeat the mistake made by Wyrd and destroy what we mean only to protect. Wyrd has tried to expiate his guilt by serving lesser races. He has worn the form of a dragon bracelet for centuries. He will work with the humans to contain this threat to the Bright Ones. He has never forgotten that his experiments with the Old One's gates destroyed a Bright One."

1

"The Bright Ones are few; the humans are many. I will defend the young ones," Oron said.

"Would they want that protection at the price of a whole world's destruction, Oron?" the silver Watcher asked quietly.

The golden plume wavered, indecision written in a shifting column. "Perhaps not, Lady."

"Realm is an important gate. Once closed, hundreds of worlds will be shut off from communication with one another," Drakon inserted into the silence. "This action will sacrifice many opportunities for trade and mental growth if those worlds must exist alone."

"In my visions of the future, I note that our brother Wyrd will play a part," Cronal added.

"Are we agreed to wait before making final judgment?" Drakon asked, his red eyes flashing.

"Yes," Cronal said. "The Keepers deserve a chance to save their worlds."

"I, too, would watch before acting." The Lady smiled her approval.

"Then I will wait also—but I watch! If there is an endangered Bright One and no one else to save it, I shall cast the uncontrolled gate and the planet that holds it into the Black Universe. There it will never threaten another Bright One," Oron said in a voice which mirrored the cold between the stars. He winked out with no further ceremony.

"Oh, dear," the Lady sighed.

"Oron has little patience with those of flesh and blood," Cronal said. "His kind never knew the burdens of a physical body; therefore, his race has the greatest kinship with the Bright Ones who approach the energy form he inhabited before he joined us on this plane."

"Wyrd has successfully aided younger races before this crisis. Let us place our faith in him once more," Drakon said, bowing his head before taking wing and fading silently into ruby dust.

"And what of us, old friend?" the Lady asked Cronal.

"We shall do as we have done for eons, my Lady. We shall watch." The hand he raised in blessing faded gradually as the Lady he addressed became a million silvery motes which scattered into Otherwhere.

CHAPTER ONE

"I'm bored!" Mirza announced to her friend Ebony.

The huge black dragon perched on the tower above, but her long snaky neck allowed her to drape herself down the building and rest her head on the window ledge of the tower room where Mirza stood.

Mirza pushed her red hair back and looked out the tower window.

"Where are the children?" Ebony asked in mindspeech.

"Argen is with Librisald, the old librarian, down in the book storage area of the university library," she said. "They are trying to catalog the books the Old Ones stored there."

"That task should keep him safely busy," Ebony said, "considering there must be fifty rooms packed floor to ceiling with books."

"Now, how did you find that out?" Mirza looked at the dragon. "Oh, I know. Seren is off with Fafnoddle, poking around on Realm. I bet he told the Faf, and then Faf told you."

"It would be difficult for two dragons bonded as we are to keep secrets," Ebony said, and ruffled her scales with satisfaction. "And where is your little daughter? She is younger than the twins and must take more care."

"She's staying with Grandma Cibby in her cottage in the woods." Mirza paced restlessly. "So here I am without a matronly care. Instead of doing something exciting or interesting with my vacation, I'm just standing here."

"You'll think of something," Ebony told her. "I must return

3

to the cave. First Egg's little sister is ready to hatch any day now and I want to be there."

"How is First Egg?"

"He's at the awkward stage. He pokes his nose into everything and refuses to study. I wish he were more like your Argen. Someday he will be wise—for a human," Ebony added. "First Egg may have to be bespelled into a cavern for a few centuries with the *Dragon Chronicles*."

"Oh, surely not," Mirza said.

"You sound just like his father. Dragons will be dragons, he says. He's sure the boy will finally settle down and be a credit to the family. Although how that will happen with that old rogue Fafnir pouring wild tales into his ears, I can't imagine."

Mirza smiled, remembering the ancient dragon who had been a terror to all during his prime. Somehow she didn't see First Egg ever being that violent. Times had changed. Since the dragons had been allies during the Great War against the Shadowlord, most people on Realm accepted them. "Seren is pretty adventuresome himself. I don't know why they aren't together now."

"Probably because my foolish husband is out skylarking with Seren like a youngster himself. Come to see me at the cave," she invited with a show of teeth that passed for a smile in dragonkind.

Mirza watched the black dragon vanish into the sky. "Now that looks like fun," she muttered to herself. She swiftly changed herself into a large hawk, fluffed her feathers, and sailed out the window. A few short wingbeats took her to the other side of the university where the library was. She landed on the window ledge and hopped onto the floor before changing back into her human form. She paced through the huge, deserted room. Usually only Andronan, her grandfather, the Head Keeper, used the Room of the Book of Worlds.

The Book of Worlds, a creation of the Old Ones, kept a constant record of the happenings on all of the worlds that contained gates to alternate earths. Mirza went to the stand that held the giant book and began idly turning pages, skimming the news. She stopped as a footnote caught her attention.

"Rogue gate?" she muttered. Now that interested her. She

knew of no one capable of manipulating the energies involved in gate creation besides herself and one other—the Shadowlord. All of the resident Keepers on the various worlds served by the gates watched constantly for the presence of the evil mage. His continued existence endangered Bright Ones and younger races as well. No one reported any trace of the wizard. Now, Mirza realized she had probably located their enemy. She didn't want to be responsible for a false alarm. She decided she would use the master gate at Realm to look into their gate on the planet. What was its name? Achaea. She knew about the planet although she had never visited it herself. Achaea was the home world of the beings that earthlings knew as the Greek gods. It would be a fascinating place to search, she was certain.

She hurried to the courtyard of Realmgate, smiling and returning the greetings students and faculty offered her as she passed through the many corridors. Since winning the great battle she and her husband Jarl had fought with the Shadowlord, most of the students studying to be Keepers knew her. The Shadowlord had almost destroyed the Bright One that nested in the sun of Realm. If she and Jarl had not stopped him, the Bright One would have died within the sun and the resultant nova would have destroyed Realm. As she wished the twentieth student a cheerful "May the Bright Ones smile upon you!" she reflected that anonymity had its advantages.

The long stone corridors would have been forbidding except that the ancient builders had added large windows which looked out on beautiful gardens filled with wondrous plants from all the alternate worlds that the gates served.

Mirza moved from the cool shadow of the corridor into the bright light of the courtyard where the gate pulsed, waiting the will of a traveler to choose a destination.

"Hello, milady," the assigned Keeper of the gate said, smiling at Mirza. His wrinkled face lit up. Mirza was a favorite of his. He had known her since she was a child.

"May the Bright Ones be with you, Guardy," Mirza replied. "Is it all right if I use the gate?"

"Of course," he assured her. "In what way may I assist your trip?"

"Oh, I'm not actually taking a trip. I just want to look in on a few places."

"You'll be here for some time?"

"Yes, I think so."

"Then perhaps you would finish my watch for me. There are a few minutes left before the end of my vigil, but I have some errands to do."

"That's fine with me. I'll keep watch until I'm relieved. If any strange animal or being blunders through the gate by accident, I'll give him forgetfulness and send him home. You go ahead," Mirza said.

"Thank you."

"No problem," Mirza replied, and then wondered if Guardy had understood the Earth slang she used.

"Of course there's not a problem, milady," Guardy said. "I would not leave my post if there were."

"It's just an expression. On the world where I live now, people say that when they mean everything is all right."

"That's fine then." He waved and walked quickly to the exit.

Mirza could hardly wait. She moved to the observation square and positioned herself safely in its center. The star-shaped mosaic that outlined the gate itself flickered, then adjusted itself to the planet Achaea as Mirza thought about the scenes she wished to view. The gate could offer views of many places easily, but each gate had only one location where travelers could move between worlds.

When Mirza looked on the landscape the gate offered to her view, she thought how much it resembled the country Greece on Earth. Sleepy villages, olive groves, and herds of goats and sheep dotted the countryside. She grew aware that the quality of the light shifted strangely. That meant there was a disturbed Bright One in the sun of Achaea. She decided to take one more peek to double check her findings before she went to tell Andronan. If a Bright One was in trouble, they would probably need both Jarl and Wyrd. She thought about Achaea's great Isle of Atlan, a kingdom of great majesty and power. Everything seemed normal from a distance. She wanted a closer look, so she concentrated on a grey fortress on the northern end of the island.

The gate pulsed wildly, emitted a high keening noise, and created a great wind that sucked her from her vantage point.

"Rogue gate!" Mirza called a warning, realizing no one would hear her even as she disappeared.

The gate at Realm returned to normal seconds before the appointed Keeper entered. "Hmmm," he muttered to himself. "Guardy isn't here. It's not like him to leave early." He glanced around the empty courtyard. "Oh, well, no harm done," he said softly to himself as he sat on the stone bench to guard the portal of the gate.

CHAPTER TWO

Jarl Koenig missed his family. Only a week earlier his wife Mirza had volunteered to take the children on a visit to her home back on Realm. He stared blankly at the computer screen. The silence in the house irritated him. Jarl accepted the idea that his wife had special powers which some would call magical. After twelve years of married life, he still found something strange about Mirza's method of going home. Her relatives lived on an alternate earth accessible only by using a gate. The Old Ones had created a system of gates between worlds using a science so advanced that it resembled magic. The artifacts of the Old Ones—still functioning, for the most part—showed Jarl how far twentieth century technology had yet to go before it could rival that of the gate's designers.

He glanced down at the dragon-shaped bracelet on his

wrist. "What the—" he muttered aloud. Something had awakened the pseudolife of Wyrd. The dragon's coils tightened, a sure sign that something was about to happen.

The dragon's words formed in his mind. "Ssomeone comes."

"Who comes?" Jarl said aloud. He could communicate with his golden bracelet mentally, but he still preferred to speak when he had the opportunity. Mindspeech was only one of the talents that had developed since he became the wearer of the bracelet. Some of his abilities seemed so strange to him he still had trouble believing what he could do.

"Fafnir," Wyrd answered.

"The Dragon Fafnir?" Jarl pictured his huge saurian friend materializing under the ancient oak tree in the forest behind his house. The tree was the gate between Earth and Realm, Mirza's home. If his nosy neighbor Mrs. Dzingleski saw the dragon, he mused, she might stop being so infernally curious about his business. Then he imagined the monumental task of convincing her she had not seen what she had seen. This brought his errant sense of humor to a halt. He hurried out the back door, wondering where he was going to put the dragon now that he had arrived on earth. It was near Halloween. Perhaps he could convince anyone who saw Fafnir that he was some kind of animated monster for a mythical business promotion.

The small bushes at the edge of the clearing disappeared behind him as he entered the main part of the forest. Actually, it was small, as forests go. The grove was necessary to protect the location of the old oak, the focal point for the magic of the gate on earth.

"Fafnir," he called softly. Somehow it didn't seem proper to yell in the Forest of the Gate. "Where is he, Wyrd?"

"Not here."

"I can see that for myself. Fafnir is too big to play hide-and-seek. Where has he gone?"

An amused chuckle was his answer.

Jarl knew from experience that when Wyrd decided to be enigmatic, he might as well forget his question. If Wyrd, his bracelet, answered anything during a secrecy fit, the remark was so cryptic it made no sense at the time.

Jarl retraced his steps, noticing the patterns the leaves made on the bright moonlight that bathed the forest floor. The dragon had probably flown directly to the house. Jarl picked up his pace as he smelled toasting marshmallows. Had the children returned with Fafnir? He entered his back yard through the swinging gate that Mirza insisted on to keep the children safe. He thought the gate was a good idea, but he felt it protected his neighbors more than it protected Seren, Argen, and Lealor. A witch's children were pretty durable. His lower jaw dropped as he viewed the scene.

In the light of a brisk blaze, First Egg, the grandson of his dragon friend from Realm, was carefully toasting marshmallows—one on each talon. The pony-sized reptile enjoyed the warmth. The jack-o'-lantern grin on his face indicated huge satisfaction. The inky spaces at the front of his formidable mouth awaited his adult fangs, which would grow in soon. He was teething early. First Egg was only seventy, and Jarl knew that dragons weren't mature until they reached one hundred. Jarl's twins, being human, were only twelve years old, but time on Realm moved differently. The gates twisted the skeins of time, as well as space. Sometimes when he returned to Earth, the date was the same as when he left—which was impossible, he always told himself, thinking of his adventures during the absence from home.

"First Egg!"

"Uncle Jarl!" The dragon hissed happily, turning to face Jarl so rapidly he forgot about the fiery marshmallow stuck on his forked tail. He pounded his tail on the ground, preparing to run to his human friend.

Whoosh! The dry leaves that littered the yard caught fire. Jarl dodged the awkward embrace of the sticky dragon and raced for the hose, which he directed on the fire. First Egg watched with salad-plate eyes, alternately cheering Jarl and licking marshmallow from his claws.

Jarl directed a mental probe to his bracelet: "I thought you told me Fafnir was here."

A gleeful chuckle ticked Jarl's mind. "Sso I did."

First Egg busily raked smoldering leaves into the center of the yard where a small blaze still flickered unsteadily. Jarl relentlessly turned the hose on the fire. The look on the dragon's face was ludicrous.

"I want to toast more marshmallows!" First Egg said like a petulant kindergartner.

"Not tonight, First Egg," Jarl said, surveying the beleafed and sooty dragon with disgust.

"I'm not First Egg anymore."

"Why not?"

"Because I've got a baby sister ready to hatch at home. I'm all grown."

"Have I lost count somewhere? As your godfather, shouldn't I have been part of your naming day?"

"I decided to call myself Fafnir, after my grandfather."

"Sorry, Wyrd," Jarl muttered. "I thought you were kidding."

The bracelet winked a lazy eye at him before closing both emerald slits for a nap.

"Well, First—I mean, Fafnir," Jarl said, "I didn't even send you the traditional piece of gold to begin your hoard."

"Oh, that's all right. I'll get some gold from here," Fafnir announced confidently.

"From where?" Jarl's eyes widened. He smelled trouble. Dragons were notoriously stubborn. He hoped he could talk this one out of whatever scale-brained idea he had.

"My granddragon told me about the gold on this world. Now that the other dragons have moved to Realm, all I have to do is take it from the humans who stole—" Here he pressed a claw over his lips. "Sorry," he apologized. "From the humans who got it from our hordes in the first place."

"Where will you find it?" Jarl repeated his question.

"Fort Knox, Uncle Jarl," Fafnir answered. "Don't you even know where your world's own hoard is? Grandfather told me everything."

Jarl swallowed, took a deep breath, and counted to ten mentally. He reached nine before he saw the lights of a car coming up the road. All he needed now was Leocadia Dzingleski to show up, snooping for gossip. "Time to come in, Fafnir," he said with commendable panache, turning the hose on the dragon. Tiny bits of soot and leaves washed into the grass of the yard.

"That's cold," Fafnir hissed, exhaling a warm draft of air to dry himself.

Jarl noted the temperature of the exhalation. Yes, Fafnir was definitely maturing. Any day now he'd be belching flame and destruction all over the place. Jarl hoped he could convince his guest to return to his home as fast as possible. He didn't approve of children smoking, and he certainly didn't want a newly flamed dragon lighting up his home.

"I'm cold, Uncle Jarl."

"Fafnir, I'm not your uncle. Besides, I feel old when you call me uncle. Just call me Jarl."

"My mother told me it wasn't polite to call my elders by their first names." The little dragon's righteous nod aggravated Jarl.

"All right, but you're actually older than I am."

"I am?" Fafnir's head shot closer to Jarl as the dragon peered at his human friend.

"Yes, you are." Jarl gritted his teeth. "Come along. I want you in the house before the neighbors park their car and see you." Not for the first time Jarl damned the luck that caused the Dzingleskis to buy the land next to him. When the previous owner died, Jarl had been in Realm. He returned to find the land subdivided into plots which cost an exorbitant sum. Jarl would have been surrounded by neighbors except that his land adjoined a national forest on two sides.

He needed the privacy. Mirza, his Realm-born wife, was not only a witch, but a shape-shifter. While ordinary husbands lectured their wives on not wearing their nighties in front of unshaded windows, Jarl had to contend with a wife who liked to take strolls sky-clad. Somehow, that sounded much better to Jarl than stark naked. The first few years of their marriage they had no neighbors, so it didn't matter. Later, one of the little neighborhood girls swore she had taken a ride on a real unicorn, and another neighborhood boy said he saw a winged lady dancing in the woods. Then Mirza had to cease her excursions.

Jarl closed the kitchen door with a sigh of relief. Fafnir barely made it into the house. He stood looking at his guest, wondering how he would keep him entertained until he could send him home. A sharp knock on his front door interrupted his reverie.

"You stay here until I call you," he told Fafnir. The dragon opened the refrigerator as Jarl hurried to the front part of the house. Thank goodness Mirza had left enough food prepared for an army—it ought to hold the dragon for a while, anyway.

"Hello," Jarl said, opening the door. Mrs. D. stood in the doorway in full panoply. She had swathed herself in clothes she deemed suitable for what she referred to as a "cultural evening." This meant her long-suffering husband had driven her into the city to the opera or theater.

Her inquisitive eyes swept around as much of the room as she could see through the half-opened door. "Homer and I smelled smoke. Is something on fire?"

"I had a little trouble earlier when I burned some leaves. Everything is under control now. I was just getting ready to go to bed."

His visitor's sharp gasp was his first intimation that "things" were not under control. As he glanced behind him, the door swung completely open. Fafnir stood in the hallway, an apple pie balanced on one talon. A fleck of whipped dairy product sat jauntily on one nostril.

"May I eat this?" the dragon asked.

Jarl's head nodded an affirmative while his mind broke the speed of light, thinking how he was going to explain Fafnir to his fainting neighbor as he caught her.

CHAPTER
THREE

Jarl looked down at the huge woman who sagged in his arms. "Don't just stand there, Fafnir! Come and help me get her on the couch."

"You told me—" the dragon began in righteous tones.

"Never mind what I told you." Jarl almost snarled the words. "My back is breaking, and if she ever gets stretched out on the floor, we'll need a derrick to lift her."

"It's a nice clean floor, Uncle Jarl—"

"And don't call me Uncle!" Jarl dragged his neighbor's dead weight over to the couch and draped her unconscious form there.

"What's this?" The dragon offered Jarl a folded sheet of paper.

Jarl glanced over his shoulder. "Fafnir, I don't have time to read to you. I've got to decide what to tell Mr. Dzingleski. He's parking the car now, but he'll soon be at my door. How do I explain this?" He gestured to the prone form on the couch.

"This has a picture of a dragon on it! It's not a very good picture, of course . . ."

"A dragon? Let me see that." Jarl snatched at the paper, which turned out to be a program from a Wagner opera. "The Ring cycle! This is the answer to my problem."

When the knocking on the door started, Fafnir moved to open it.

"No, Fafnir. You go hide in the kitchen and don't come out—no matter what happens. This man mustn't see you." Jarl hustled the puzzled dragon into the kitchen and hurried to open the front door.

Mr. Dzingleski stood in the doorway, a look of inquiry on his face. "I wondered if my wife was here," he began in his soft voice. "She wanted to check about the smell of burning leaves, you know. Ever since she joined the volunteer fire department, she's been really alert to fires." His voice trailed off as Jarl motioned him to enter.

The first thing he noticed was the recumbent form of his wife. "Oh, dear," he whispered, as if he feared waking her. "What happened?" He stood in the center of the room watching his wife.

"She's probably just overwrought. What with all those speaking engagements to local groups about fire safety," Jarl said lamely. His neighbor was such an ineffectual person that it made Jarl feel awkward. He had no doubt as to who was the boss of the family next door. If Mr. Dzingleski were the one on the couch, the administration of smelling salts and the calling of the emergency ambulance by Leocadia would be history by this time.

His neighbor approached the couch gingerly. "Leocadia, my dear," he began in his soft voice as the huge body stirred, then sat up.

"What in the world," she said, correcting her unladylike posture immediately. "The last thing I remember—" Her eyes widened. "I saw a—" Her confident voice faltered as she glanced around the room. "I mean, for a moment there, I thought I saw—" She paused.

Jarl watched the changes come over her face as she remembered clearly what she had seen. He smiled comfortingly. "Yes?" he offered.

"I—I—"

Mr. Dzingleski stared. He obviously had never seen his wife at a loss for words. "Perhaps we should go home, my dear," he said quietly. "All that rousing music, valkyries and dragons—" He stepped back as she lumbered to her feet.

"Dragons," she muttered, looking at the long hall that led to the kitchen.

"Wagner's very heady stuff," Jarl said. "I have strange dreams after seing his operas. I guess my imagination runs away with me."

"Yes," she agreed. "There's no telling what the imagination of a truly sensitive patron of the arts might create after an evening at the opera."

"Come, Leocadia. We are keeping Mr. Koenig from his rest." He gently shepherded his wife to the door. As proof of how shaken she was, she said not another word, but went quietly.

"Good night," Mr. Dzingleski said for the pair of them as they exited the room.

"Good night," Jarl echoed into the soft dark before he closed the door behind them. He saw Fafnir peering from the shadowy hall. "Well, I'm glad that's over."

"Is it safe to come in now?" the dragon asked.

"Sure."

"Why did I have to hide? The man seemed very nice. He wasn't an evil wizard or anything, was he?"

"Fafnir, haven't you learned anything about modern Earth?"

"Well, there is some stuff written in my father's books, but they're so boring! He told me to read about Earth so that someday I could come to visit you." The dragon gave a self-satisfied smirk. "I didn't have to wait for him to bring me, did I? I came all by myself!" Fafnir thumped the floor with his tail. In his enthusiasm, he was apt to forget how large he was.

Jarl jumped to the rescue of a lamp that tottered from the force of the small gale the dragon had raised expressing his pleasure at the trick he had played on his father.

"And just what do you think your father will have to say when he learns you have used the gate to travel here without his permission or an invitation to come?" Jarl asked, hoping some sensible thoughts might keep the rest of his furniture from imminent destruction.

"Oh, kippers! I never thought about that. You aren't mad at me because I just popped in to see you, are you?" The dragon's eyes filled with tears.

"No, no," Jarl hastened to reassure him before he drenched the carpet past redemption. "Come on. Let's go to the kitchen and see what we have to eat." Jarl herded his uninvited guest down the hall.

"I'm glad you're not mad at me," the dragon said, wiping his eyes on a tea towel that was quite inadequate for the mopping exercise.

Jarl rummaged in a drawer until he found a large terry cloth dish towel. "Here," he said, handing it to Fafnir. "I'm not angry at you, of course, but it is always a good idea to check before you visit someone."

"When I decided to come, I just flew to the gate and used it." The dragon hung his head.

"Don't you remember how Mirza had to cast a spell on you so people would see you as a human the last time you were here?"

"Now I do. It's so hard to keep in mind what a strange place you live in. Imagine! A whole world that thinks dragons are only legends! People here must be pretty stupid. We dragons have always liked to travel. When the Old Ones opened the gate system between worlds, practically every dragon who was important traveled through them. It says so in the *Dragon Chronicles*."

"Didn't your *Dragon Chronicles* also tell how you dragons joined the other magical creatures that moved to Realm when men started turning to science instead of magic?"

"I haven't read everything in our history books. They're so boring. I skipped around, here and there, reading anything that interested me."

"I wouldn't let your mother find out how you've studied them," Jarl warned. "She takes the past very seriously."

"Why would any dragon find all those old boring tales interesting? Besides, my mother can quote for hours. I guess before my granddragon died, she made my mother memorize almost all of the *Dragon Chronicles*. Mother said that was how they kept young dragons out of mischief—" A horrified look passed over his face. "Jarl." He inhaled a great amount of air. The top slice of the bologna Jarl was using to make a sandwich flew through the air and plastered itself over Fafnir's nearest nostril. His pink dragon tongue licked it off and jammed it in his mouth. He chomped once, then continued. "Do you think she'll make me learn it all by heart, too, because I came here without her permission?"

"Perhaps. I really can't say. What do you suppose your father is going to do?" Jarl asked the question with clinical detachment. He thought some punishment was in order. He shuddered to think what would happen if Fafnir started dropping in on them with no warning. That would strain even Mirza's magic skill—try to keep the neighbors from finding out about Fafnir then!

There were always hordes of kids running in and out of the house to Mirza's magic cookie jar that was always full of fresh cookies. The refrigerator that she enchanted to be full of fruit juice and fresh milk, no matter how often thirsty children opened it, made their house a prime stop for the youth of the neighborhood. The neighborhood mothers probably hated his wife. They must think she spent most of every day baking and shopping.

Fafnir opened a frozen package of croissants. He delicately stuck one to each claw, and then flamed them briefly. His tongue raked the strawberry filling from one before he tossed it into his mouth and swallowed.

"Do I have to think about what my father will do? I'd rather have Auntie Mirza come home with me and help me explain. Then maybe he won't turn me into a jar of coralberry jam."

Jarl smiled. He couldn't help it. Fafnir would make the largest jar of coralberry jam anyone had ever seen. He'd heard Fafnoddle threaten his son with just such a transformation in moments of stress. Ebony, his wife, wouldn't let him smoke in the home cave. She said it made her feel ill. So Fafnoddle found himself forced to express his feelings verbally.

"Well, can she?"

"Can she what?" Jarl asked between bites of his sandwich.

"Can she come with me to help explain?"

"She who?" Jarl had lost the thread of the conversation as he watched Fafnir spear giant dills with his tongue. Jarl hoped pickles and strawberry croissants wouldn't disagree with his guest. He had no idea how to soothe a dragon with a stomach-ache.

"Aren't you listening to me?"

"Yes, but who are you talking about?"

"Auntie Mirza, of course."

"Mirza's not here. She's back on Realm with the children."

"No she's not. I looked for her before I came. I can't find her."

"She has to be there! She wouldn't leave Realm without telling me. I'm to join her there tomorrow."

"I tell you, she's not there. I looked. I thought she'd come home for a while. That's why I decided I'd visit and pick up a little gold from Fort Knox, then return with the start of my hoard. I knew she'd help me."

"You must not have looked everywhere. She's probably turned herself into a unicorn or something and is traveling around incognito."

"I know I'm right. Mother said she hasn't been able to contact Mirza and mindspeak for two days. So she must have gone someplace."

Jarl knew about the special bond that his wife and Fafnir's mother had formed. *If Ebony couldn't reach Mirza, then she was not on Realm.*

"How exciting!" Fafnir said, wrapping his tongue around the pickle jar and holding it close to his saucer-sized eye to make sure he had not missed any pickles.

Jarl automatically cleared away the mess in the kitchen as he puzzled over the situation. "Exciting?" he finally asked when the dragon's comment registered.

"Why, yes. It's not every day that someone disappears. Especially an adept like Auntie Mirza. I just bet that dreadful Shadowlord has his cowl in it somewhere. Aren't you worried, Uncle Jarl?"

Jarl, too busy being concerned, didn't even bother to correct the dragon. "We'd better use the gate and return to Realm."

"Before I get a chance to find any gold for my horde?" Fafnir wailed his disappointment. "We have to go now?"

"Now!" Jarl said firmly.

CHAPTER
FOUR

Jarl and the dragon stood beneath the great oak that marked the gate's position on Earth.

"Are you ready, Fafnir?" Jarl asked.

"Couldn't I fly someplace close and pick up just a few gold items?"

"Absolutely not," Jarl said in his firmest voice. He had no way to enforce his preferences on Fafnir. Jarl wanted to have him safe in Realm before the young dragon figured it out. He hoped he would never have to cover up the presence of a live dragon on earth. With Mirza's help, they might manage. She had a very innovative mind. Alone, he shuddered to think what might happen. You could always discredit what people said about what they saw, but most places where Fafnir could find gold readily had security cameras. How could you fool a photographic negative? Now that he had managed to distract the dragon from his Fort Knox idea, he wanted them safe on Realm before Faf thought of it again.

"Visualize the star at the university on Realm," he commanded. He hoped the dragon would follow his advice. If Fafnir decided to be cute, no telling what place he might envision. While Fafnoddle and Ebony were friends, they were like most parents. They would probably hold Jarl responsible if anything happened to their little darling, although only a dragon could consider anything as large as Fafnir "little."

Then seeing that Fafnir had closed his eyes, Jarl made the appropriate magical passes to activate the gate.

After a brief moment of vertigo, Jarl opened his eyes. They were both safe in the great Courtyard of the Gate. Jarl heaved a sigh of relief. Now, if he could just get Fafnir to return home of his own volition. He turned to the dragon and said, "It's important that you go home now."

"Do I have to? Things are just starting to get interesting."

Jarl was astounded to notice that young Dragons wheedled exactly like young humans. He hoped child psychology worked on dragons too. He decided to try.

"Well," he began, "I suppose you may stay—but you'll have to explain to Andronan about using the gate without his permission."

"Couldn't you do that for me?" The dragon's eyes widened. If there was one human he was in awe of, it was Andronan, the Master Keeper.

"I could if you weren't here. However, if you insist on staying, then you'll have to talk to Andronan yourself. In fact, he should be ready to see us any minute. I had Wyrd call him as soon as we got here. He's waiting in his study for us."

"Please explain to him for me that I really had to get home. My mother will be worrying about me, I'm sure," the dragon said dutifully.

"Very well. By the way, here is a piece of gold for your hoard. This way, you didn't waste the trip." Jarl handed the dragon a gold coin that he had palmed from Seren's coin collection before they left Earth.

"Oh, thank you! Now I'm officially an adult!"

"Weren't you before? You said you were."

"Not quite. The first real piece of gold a dragonette gets turns him into an adult officially."

"Congratulations, then," Jarl called as Fafnir rose into the air. For a brief moment, Jarl wondered if he had broken dragon protocol. He had a feeling there should have been some type of ceremony with Ebony and Fafnoddle present. He didn't have their permission, either. Then he shrugged his shoulders, greeted the gatewatcher politely, and hurried up the steps to Andronan's study.

*   *   *

"Come in, Jarl," Andronan called, just as Jarl reached the door to his study. How the old Keeper always knew when someone stood outside his room had always puzzled Jarl. Jarl's bracelet alerted him to company, but the old mage had nothing but his magic talent to tell him of visitors. Of course, there were still things Andronan did that Jarl could not duplicate even with Wyrd's aid.

He strode through the door, noting that Andronan was sitting in the tilt-back chair Jarl had created for him some years earlier. That was one innovation that he had taught Andronan. He wondered if there was any other way in which he really affected Realm. The land seemed changeless. Since they had defeated the Shadowlord, no major threat had developed in any civilized portion of the country. He smiled at Mirza's grandfather.

"It's always good to see you, Jarl. I don't know where Mirza could be. She's never missed greeting you when you arrived here before," he said. A slight frown, almost lost in the wrinkles, briefly marred his ancient face.

"There's nothing to worry about, but I did come to check on my family," Jarl replied.

"Oh, they're all fine. Argen and Librisald are thick as a bookshelf jammed with those old dust catchers they love to peer at together."

The old man's tone sounded slightly mocking, but Jarl knew what a bibliophile Andronan was himself. Indeed, Andronan had carried the young Koenigs with him on visits to the library on more than one occasion. Seren and Lealor enjoyed making houses with the old volumes. Argen would sit patiently in a corner, leafing through books carefully in hopes of finding a picture or two. He never seemed to tire of the library.

As the children grew older, Lealor became an animal lover. She spent as much time as possible in the woods which were so abundant on Realm. Jarl never worried because he knew that Rory, his leprechaun friend, kept an Irish eye out for her. He had appeared more than once with Jarl's daughter riding leprechaunback. It said a great deal about the bond between the two. Few existed on Realm who had ever touched Rory, but in the tiny hands of Lealor, he became almost gentle.

Most knew the leprechaun as a feisty, fiery-tongued individualist who hurled imaginative invective as easily as he gulped whiskey. They would have to see the sight more than once to believe it.

Jarl smiled to himself as he pictured his eldest, Seren. The boy and the dragons on Realm had taken to each other instinctively. Before Jarl thought Seren was old enough to ride horses on Earth, Seren and Fafnoddle had been sailing around on Realm updrafts. "Just checking things over," as Fafnoddle explained calmly when a horrified Jarl first saw his small son kicking his heels and shouting, "Faster, Faf, faster!" Seren would be all right so long as he stuck with the dragons. Jarl quailed mentally as he considered what young Fafnir and Seren could think up together. Maybe a word or two with Fafnoddle might save both sets of parents hours of concern. With a son like young Fafnir, Jarl imagined Faf's scales would tarnish centuries earlier than normal.

Jarl continued the conversation. "I wasn't thinking of the children this time. I had an unexpected visit from Fafnir—the dragon we used to call First Egg—" Jarl explained, knowing Andronan probably thought he meant the young dragon's grandfather, Fafnir.

Old Fafnir was the dragon Jarl met on Realm during his first visit. He might never have met Fafnoddle, Fafnir's son, if it hadn't been for Jarl's promise to make Fafnoddle go with him to rescue Mirza. Things had certainly changed! While Fafnoddle was still a vegetarian, his pacifist tendencies had totally disappeared since the battle with the Shadowlord's Dark Legions. Old Fafnir, delighted with his son's prowess, loved telling how his son and Ebony had seared demons into fine ash to protect Realm.

Andronan nodded to show he understood. Jarl said, "Young Fafnir said Mirza was not on Realm."

"Are you sure?" Andronan stood. "Let us go to the gate and ask the keeper there if anyone has seen Mirza leave. She always tells me if she plans to go gallivanting."

Although Andronan usually talked just like everyone else, occasionally his great age showed when he used some charmingly dated word or expression. Jarl filed "gallivanting" away in his mind. Somehow, the term was exactly right for the restless flitting his wife had a tendency to do when she became bored. On Earth, membership in a half dozen volunteer groups kept her busy. Jarl wondered what she had done on Realm before he married her. He had never thought to ask.

They passed through the corridors to the gravity wells which served as elevators in the university. Andronan acknowledged the reverential bowed heads with his kindly smile as they passed the students and faculty who thronged the halls. Jarl raised his hand in greeting as he saw people he knew.

They crossed the well threshold and sank decorously to the ground floor. Jarl wished he could understand the engineering skills the Old Ones had used to create the wells. No moving parts were evident. Whatever form of energy powered the wells still worked perfectly. Jarl thought it might be some use of solar power, but he had never been able to find the book that explained the system. Librisald had been cataloging books all his life and still had not reached the end of the tomes the Old Ones had left behind. Jarl had seen the stacks of the library. There were over fifty rooms remaining, piled from floor to ceiling. No one expected Librisald to live long enough to complete the cataloging. Argen was already a help, but he didn't read enough languages to be very efficient. When his son grew older and came to the university to study, Jarl knew what he would become. Seren's voice echoed in his father's memory: "There's no hope for Argen. He even smells musty like those old books he and Librisald carry around all the time. Phew."

Andronan led the way out of the gravity well into the beautiful courtyard. There, the Realmgate pulsed with a soft radiance among flowers and trees of such colors, shapes, and scents they almost defied description.

He approached the current Keeper who watched the gate.

"Have you seen my granddaughter, Mirza?" Andronan asked.

"No, sir," the young Keeper answered with the traditional nod of respect. "Guardy was talking about seeing her here the other day," he added.

"We will stand watch for you. Please find Guardy and ask him to join us here." The politely worded request had all the force of a royal command, to judge from the Keeper's hurried exit.

In a very short while Guardy entered the courtyard, followed by the younger Keeper. "How may I serve you, Andronan?" he asked.

"We wondered if you saw Mirza leave Realm by the gate the other day."

"She was here, looking into one of the worlds, but there was no warning she intended going anywhere," Guardy told them. "She came almost at the end of my watch. Why, she even volunteered to finish my vigil for me," he added as he recalled the afternoon.

"When you left, Mirza was still here, using the gate to look into another world?" Jarl asked.

"That's correct. Right here." Guardy nodded as his finger pointed out the spot.

"Did you know which world she was watching?"

Guardy said, "No, I didn't think to ask."

"Who had the watch after you that day?" Andronan questioned.

"Why, it was Vigan, the young Keeper you sent after me."

Andronan gestured for Vigan to approach. "Very well, Guardy. You may return to your studies now, if you wish."

"I'll just stay, if you don't mind. Is there some problem about Mirza? I well remember what shenanigans she could pull when she was a girl."

Andronan gave the old keeper a mock look of disapproval. "As do I, and I also remember who helped rectify her minor mistakes and mitigate the punishment for some of the catastrophes she almost caused, old friend."

Guardy chuckled softly. "Me and every other Keeper on Realm," he said, being deliberately ungrammatical.

Andronan and Jarl turned their attention to Vigan. "Do not fear, my son," the Master Keeper said kindly. "Did you see what world my granddaughter Mirza watched the other day?"

"No, I never saw her. I remember the day because I passed Guardy as I reported for my turn as Watcher. I thought it was odd that no one was on duty, but it was only a matter of minutes. I knew Guardy wouldn't leave his station unless all was well."

"Then we'll have a long search. There are thousands of worlds that have gates. Without a clue, it may take days to find out where she went." Jarl glanced at his bracelet, but Wyrd said nothing. Wyrd had never been exactly talkative. However, in the past, the dragon had helped many times. As Jarl gained control of the powers that Wyrd possessed, the dragon intruded less and less into human affairs, seemingly content to be an ornament on Jarl's wrist.

"She may be in danger and have need of you. We must find out which world drew her interest." Andronan smoothed his beard as he thought out loud.

"Excuse me, but I may be able to be of some assistance." Vigan's interruption surprised them all.

Andronan's raised eyebrows encouraged him to continue. "Ruel, one of my friends, saw a bird fly from the window where the *Book of Worlds* is. He said it flew here to the Court of the Gate. There is neither food nor water here. Perhaps the Lady Mirza shape-shifted herself and came here. Might she not have left some clue in the room?"

"It's the only lead we have." Jarl started out of the courtyard with no further ceremony.

"We thank you both for your assistance," Andronan said to the two Keepers before he, too, headed for the room where the *Book of Worlds* lay opened.

CHAPTER
FIVE

Jarl waited impatiently for Andronan to join him at the shaft which would bear them to the upper levels of the building.

"If we are fortunate, Mirza left the *Book of Worlds* open to the page where she was reading, Jarl."

"I can't imagine why she would leave without telling someone. After all, the children are here. It isn't like her to go off without letting someone know."

"If she was in as great a hurry as we think, she may well have left the book open," Andronan said, as he left the shaft slightly ahead of Jarl. The room they wanted was only a short distance down the corridor.

When they entered the room, they saw the *Book of Worlds* resting on its lectern—and it was open. Jarl's sense of relief was palpable. Andronan and Jarl both noticed the name of the place at almost the same moment: Achaea. Even as they gazed, a footnote was being added to the bottom of the entry on the page.

"A rogue gate is being used?" Jarl said, puzzled. "Who would take the risk of using a rogue gate?"

"The Sshadowlord," hissed Wyrd.

Jarl was skeptical. "Why would anyone want to create a gate on a planet ruled by the ancient Greek gods? If I remember my mythology correctly, the old gods of Greece didn't think much of mortals who meddled with godlike powers. It doesn't make sense that Mirza would rush off to help Zeus and Company." Jarl paced around the room as if he needed to be taking some kind of action.

"I know why she may have gone so hurriedly. Look at the addition to the footnote." Andronan's long index finger pointed to the lines he meant.

"That says the gate is becoming unstable. It's sure to unbalance the nearby star. Does it harbor a Bright One?"

"Yes. The worlds where gates are possible all have stars which host Bright Ones. The Old Ones probably understood why this is so, and several of our most intellectual mage/keepers are studying the issue. Yet we do not understand." Andronan shook his head. "The universe is so large, and our minds are so small. One lifetime is scarcely enough to begin to unravel the secrets that wait for us on this plane."

"I'll need to check on the children. I don't like to leave them, but Mirza could be in danger. The last thing I need is to try to watch the kids and look for Mirza at the same time. I'm not sure they'll be safe here. Perhaps I should take them home to Earth."

"Surely they would be safer on Realm. We understand magic and Lealor, at least, has magical powers. On Earth most people do not believe in magic and wouldn't know what to do to counteract it if she forgot and shape-shifted or misspoke a spell," cautioned Andronan.

"That's right. I'll have to make arrangements for the children to stay on Realm. I don't like to bother any of my friends here—"

"It is no bother. You locate the children, and I'll be responsible for them while they are here. The children's visits are far too short as it is. It will be good for the Keepers to have some lively young ones about the place again."

While Jarl appreciated the offer, he had his doubts about allowing the children to run wild on Realm with only the Keepers to act as watchmen. The younger Keepers needed to continue their studies, and the older Keepers were immersed in various projects and might well forget the children for days on end. Just as Jarl was about to make his decision, Wyrd spoke in their minds.

"I will arrange protection for the children."

Jarl was about to question his magic talisman, but Andronan said quietly, "We would appreciate that. We know that the Shadowlord feels no compunction about involving innocent family members in his plans. We have not been able to find any trace of him in all these years. I often have a feeling that he takes an interest in what we are doing." Jarl looked as if he intended to ask a question, but Andronan answered it before he had the chance. "I have never been able to trace him by any means at my disposal."

"We would appreciate your help." Jarl hated to admit it, but he still had many things to learn about the powers that those familiar with the gates could summon. He could now accomplish many feats that he previously believed to be impossible. Jarl knew enough to realize that no matter how much it humbled his pride, he probably would need all the help he could get. If Wyrd said he could protect the children, then he undoubtedly was capable of doing something to keep them safe.

"To create the protection, I must be near the children." Wyrd's strange, gemlike eyes glittered, a sure sign some paranormal or magical thinking was occurring. "Excuse us, Andronan. We go." With these words Jarl felt the familiar jarring wrench and moment of vertigo that always accompanied Wyrd's version of traveling. It reminded Jarl of the gate trips. However, it was impossible to believe that a small bracelet could unleash or control the vast powers of a gate at will.

Jarl glanced around him. They were upstairs in one of the large rooms of the library. The piles of dusty books, layer on layer, made clear the origin of the librarians' term, stacks. The high windows illuminated the room. A stray beam of light accented millions of dust motes stirred up by Argen, his son. He staggered along under a miniature mountain of books.

"That is you under there, isn't it?" Jarl asked, taking the top foot of books away to reveal his son's flushed face.

"Hi, Dad. What are you doing here? Librisald was just talking about you yesterday. I'm helping him catalog. I've finally learned the Old Ones' numbering system, so I'm pretty sure these books are a set."

Jarl glanced at the spines of the books. "You're right. You'll be about three feet closer to finishing the cataloging when Librisald tells you where these belong."

"It's so frustrating. All I really am is a go-fer."

"A gopher? I realize you dig around a lot, but I don't think you really deserve to consider yourself a rodent," Jarl teased.

"You missed a pun. G-o-f-e-r, Dad. Get it? I 'go fer' this book and then I 'go fer' another. Argen's grin made him seem younger than he actually was.

"I got it, but I wish I hadn't. Your mother's gone through the gate to Achaea, and Andronan and I believe that she may need a little help. Before I go, I want to make sure there is protection for my children, including you, my son."

"Seren and I are old enough to manage on our own. Lealor's the only one you have to worry about."

"Nevertheless, Wyrd has offered to give you a little extra protection, and he wants to see you."

"Me?" Argen's eyes rounded. Their father never spoke of his relationship with Wyrd, but many of the people on Realm told tales of the eldritch power Wyrd could summon to aid Jarl.

"Do not fear." Wyrd's voice echoed in Argen's and Jarl's minds. "You will appreciate my gift."

A silver glow began to emanate from Wyrd's scales. It grew to basketball size, then began to shrink until there was only a silver band pulsating in the air. Then the band slowly flew to Argen and settled gently on his wrist.

Argen looked down. A silver replica of Wyrd rested on his arm. Within a few seconds, it felt as if it had been there forever. "Wow," Argen breathed.

"Not Wow. My name is Nyct," the voice of Argen's bracelet said in his mind.

"Nyct," Argen repeated dutifully. He looked at his father. "Its name is Nyct," he told him.

Jarl, who up to this moment had no idea of the method Wyrd would use to give his children protection, looked a little bemused.

An audible hiss came from the silver bracelet. "I am not a thing," he told Argen. "Please refer to me as 'he' or use my name."

"Sorry," Argen managed.

"Apology accepted," Nyct answered.

"Dad, are you sure—"

"This is my son." Wyrd's voice reached all three of his

listeners. "I had not thought to ever have another, but now I make you a partner, so you shall not face adversity alone."

"Thank you. I'm honored," Argen managed to say, rising to the occasion.

"You are considering the disadvantages of wearing a talisman. You are young to bear the burden, but you have not thought about the advantages of your new partner," Wyrd said, in the softest tones Jarl had ever heard him use.

"Advantages?" Argen repeated.

Jarl remembered his feelings when he first came to Realm. He also remembered how dumb he felt when his best reply was a repetition of something someone else said. Like father, like son, he thought whimsically.

"What books is your father holding?" Wyrd hissed.

"Why, he has volumes one through four of *Interstellar Maps of the Sky as Seen from Realm*." Argen paused. "Hey, I actually read the titles!" Argen placed his pile of books on the floor and took the stack from his father's arms. Sitting on top of the nearest pile, he began to leaf through one of the books. Within seconds he was so immersed in the book he was holding he almost didn't hear Wyrd speaking to him.

"Advantage number one," Wyrd told him. "Nyct is young, but he has powers he can share with you. The two of you will grow up together, and each will profit from the other's strengths. Now we go again," Wyrd said to Jarl.

Jarl never even had time to say goodbye. He found himself on the plateau above Fafnoddle and Ebony's cave.

Jarl looked around, but he didn't see Seren anywhere. It was a relief to know that Argen, at least, wasn't going to cause any problems for anyone. Now that he was able to read the books in the library, Librisald would have an energetic helper. Jarl hoped the old librarian could think of ways to keep Argen from trying to read all the books they had to catalog. Or perhaps Argen would sift through and find the books in Librisald's special areas of interest. Jarl could picture them together poring over musty volumes in some corner of the library.

The clouds which scudded ahead of the playful wind made shadows move over the ground. Then a pinpoint in the distance grew larger and Jarl could make out the form of a dragon. It was his old friend Fafnoddle. The huge dragon swooped down at a tremendous speed, however briefly, and landed, feather-soft, next to Jarl. Jarl greeted his friend with a smile and his usual queasy stomach. There was something about seeing a house-sized being literally dropping in on you that never failed to evoke a state of panic.

"Hello, Father," Seren said from his place on Fafnoddle's back.

"Were you responsible for Faf's diving demon routine?" Jarl asked.

"Not me. Fafnoddle wanted Fafnir to see how much he had to learn about flying." Seren's eyes shone as he remembered. "What a ride it was. Loops, in and out of the dark, and speed! Well, Fafnir hasn't showed up yet. He is still behind us—isn't he?"

"I set him quite a pattern to follow. He was getting a little big for his claws. It doesn't do any harm for a father to show his son a thing or two." Faf's eyes glowed green. "It will be some time before young First Egg thinks he is big enough to wear that name he chose for himself." Faf lowered his head so Seren could walk down his neck and jump to earth. The rumble that Jarl recognized as the dragon's chuckle sounded just like old Fafnir's. "Just blowing a little fertilizer off my scales." He hissed happily. "Beautiful day for a spin, isn't it? Care for a ride, Jarl?"

"No thanks. I just came to check on Seren." Fafnoddle didn't seem to be angry about Jarl's unscheduled gift of gold to his dragonette. Jarl decided he might as well not raise a fuss over the possible dangers of carrying Seren into what must have been quite a duel between the two dragons. Neither Seren nor young Fafnir appeared harmed by their experience, judging from the streaking form in the air that was now aimed right where they were standing. "How good is Young Fafnir at pinpoint landings?" Jarl asked in what he hoped sounded like a casual tone. While Jarl had been around dragons for years, he still had a healthy respect for their size, even small ones. He preferred not to be the landing pad for Fafnoddle's son.

"Quite good, father," Seren answered. "I help him practice."

Jarl tried to remain calm as he imagined those practice sessions. "And just how do you do that?"

"Oh, I ride up here on his back. Then I get down and stand someplace. He flies off and sees how fast he can go and still land right next to me."

Seren's smile sent shivers down Jarl's back. "Oh," Jarl managed weakly, seeing a mental picture of Seren in the hospital with casts on every limb.

"No need to fret, Jarl," Fafnoddle said. "I put a spell of safety on the boy, so even if my lead-winged son landed right on Seren, he'd bounce off safely."

"Thanks," Jarl said, wondering who the spell really protected.

"Both of them," Wyrd said in Jarl's mind.

Just at this moment, Fafnir sailed under his father's nose, hugging the ground, and landed right beside Seren.

"Not bad, Faf," Seren congratulated his friend.

The older dragon's head jerked to hear his nickname applied to his son.

"He did do well, didn't he?" Seren asked the two surprised fathers.

Fafnoddle rumbled and hissed an answer while Jarl nodded his agreement.

"Darn, I wish you wouldn't speak dragon. I never can seem to remember the words, no matter how hard I try. And Faf only laughs at my pronunciation."

"Perhaps I can remedy that," Wyrd said out loud so they could all hear him.

"You can?" Seren said, confident that Wyrd's powers could do anything.

Fafnoddle's plate-sized eyes focused on Jarl's bracelet. "You would give a man-child the power to speak to dragons in the language we brought from the stars?" He seemed slightly incredulous.

"Yesss. In years to come, the abilities I now make available to him may tip the scales and avert catastrophe," Wyrd answered mysteriously. Suddenly, a golden glow formed around the tiny form of the dragon. It grew, pulsed several times, almost as if it were breathing, then formed into a golden shape which flew to Seren and wrapped itself around his arm. As they watched, the shape became more definite. Finally, a perfect golden replica of Wyrd himself rested on Seren's wrist.

"Oh—" Seren began, looking carefully at the bracelet. "Thanks, Wyrd." He returned to the study of his bracelet.

Fafnoddle said a few short words which his son echoed. The strange syllables of dragon talk hissed on the air. Seren muttered an answer distractedly, then looked astounded. "Hey, did you hear that? I spoke perfect dragon, didn't I?" He looked at Fafnoddle for his answer.

"Indeed you did."

"What shall I call my bracelet?"

"Why don't you ask him?" Wyrd suggested. "You need not speak aloud."

CHAPTER SIX

Seren looked at his bracelet, which glinted in the sun. "What shall I call you?" he asked, following Wyrd's suggestion.

The tiny bracelet opened both green eyes and focused on Seren. "My name is Soladon," he answered. "And by what name shall I call you?"

"Seren. Seren Koenig."

"Very well, serenserenkoenig." The bracelet carefully repeated, syllable by syllable, what the boy had told him.

"Not serenserenkoenig. Just Seren. Koenig is my father's name."

"Seren?"

"That's it. Seren."

Seren looked at the dragons and his father. He seemed surprised to see them waiting for him to speak. Then he realized how swiftly the mental exchange had taken place. It was almost like carrying on a conversation with himself. He smiled down at his bracelet. "This is really neat."

"Soladon is my son. He will learn to unleash his powers as you learn how to command yours. You have a great affinity with the dragon races. For a human, you are surprisingly adaptable to the dragons. In time you will be able to aid your friends and others of their kind when trouble comes, many years hence. . . ." Wyrd's voice trailed off as if he were seeing the future. He said abruptly, "Now we go to find Lealor."

This time Jarl had prepared himself. When Wyrd said the first two words, Jarl raised his hand in goodbye, and so was able to bid farewell as he winked out of sight.

Perhaps it was just as well that he did not hear Soladon ask, "What shall we do now?" and hear young Fafnir's reply, "Oh, Seren and I have many things we want to try."

Fafnoddle shook his head and flew back to the cave where Ebony awaited him. His last view of the three showed them huddled together, obviously planning the day's activities.

Jarl and his bracelet appeared in a grove of trees. He waited a moment for the dizziness to abate, then looked around him carefully. He could tell from the health of the woods that it was under the protection of dryads. Only they could achieve the perfect balance between tree, grass, and flower that produced meadows of such surpassing beauty.

"I thought we were going to where Lealor was," Jarl said quietly to Wyrd.

"We are," Wyrd answered, allowing his amusement to show in a dragon grin.

"Hi, Daddy!"

Jarl looked around him, searching for his daughter.

Silvery laughter came from above, causing him to look up and catch a glimpse of the dryad who must live in the gigantic oak that dominated the clearing. He looked up twenty feet to the first limb, which stretched its protecting branches out over a portion of the meadow below. He stifled his gasp. Jarl didn't want to say anything to startle his daughter, who stood on the middle of the branch, at least ten feet from the trunk. She waved vigorously to him.

"Here I am," she announced. "Isn't it a beautiful day?" The precarious nature of her position didn't seem to be bothering her.

Jarl himself felt hollow inside. His overactive imagination conjured a picture of Lealor falling out of the tree. "You better come down from there, honey," he coaxed. "I need to talk to you and I'll get a crick in my neck if you stay up so high."

"You're not worried, are you, Daddy?" Lealor peered down on him and grinned before stepping off the branch into thin air.

Jarl took a few quick steps forward, but found himself pushed aside by the racing figure of a leprechaun, who screeched out, "Don't be afraid, darlin', Rory will catch you."

Jarl noticed for the first time how the leprechaun had grown. Since he was a magical being, he could probably be any size he chose. He had grown over two feet since Jarl first met him when he had brought Wyrd to Jarl's home. Rory ran close to the tree, then sat down abruptly as he struck some invisible barrier. Jarl heaved a sigh of relief. No wonder Wyrd had done nothing. The talisman had sensed the wards around the tree and knew Lealor wouldn't come to harm. Instead of falling to the ground, Lealor descended what must have been an invisible staircase until she reached the bottom of the tree. Her father could not help smiling as he listened to the irate Rory sputter. His face was as red as his hair and he shook his fist directly under Lealor's nose.

"Oh, Rory, don't be silly! Flowerface wouldn't let anything happen to me." Rory was still sputtering as she leaned over and gave him a kiss. "Now, darling Rory, don't be an old grouchy spoilsport. Next thing you know, someone will take you for a human."

"Indeed! And whose fault would it be if they did? Scarin' a poor innocent leprechaun half to death and then insultin' him by suggestin' he's actin' like a human. . . ."

Lealor threw her arms around him and gave him a big hug. "I'm sorry. I won't ever do it again if it really frightens you. I didn't think anything could frighten a leprechaun. At least, that's what you always told me."

"Well, it was just a manner of speaking, you understand. Nothing frightens Rory...." The leprechaun blustered on until Jarl, noting that his thick brogue had almost disappeared, broke in on his monologue.

"Fortunately, no one was in danger, Lealor. You need to remember that it's not kind to upset your friends."

"I'm sorry, Daddy. I knew Flowerface would take good care of me, and I forgot that you might not know it, too."

"Wyrd has a present for you, honey."

"Oh, good. I like presents."

A faint mist formed in the air, swirled in an almost invisible pattern, and then settled on Lealor's wrist. "Hello."

"Look, Daddy, Rory. It's a baby Wyrd."

"Yes. You are correct," Wyrd said, speaking telepathically to all three of them. Rory opened his mouth to say something, then shut it as he realized he was hearing Wyrd speak. "Your bracelet is my daughter, Myst. She will protect you and give you good counsel when you are about to do something foolish."

Lealor looked at the glassy iridescence of the dragon shape that clasped her arm. "You mean I can't ever take it off?"

"Not for many years, child," Wyrd told her.

"Thank you very much, but I don't want your bracelet, Wyrd. Take it back. It would be just like having Seren and Argen bossing me around all the time."

"Lealor!" Jarl warned.

"I don't care! It would be bad enough if it was just an ordinary bracelet, but if it's going to be telling me what to do all the time, I don't want it!"

"Very well, Lealor."

The girl's eyes widened as her bracelet mindspoke.

"I am sorry you don't like me. It is my destiny to keep you safe and about that I can do nothing. However, I will not speak to you again.

Lealor regretted her hasty outburst when she saw two small tears roll down Myst's nose, but she was too stubborn to try to make friends. "Okay. I guess you can stay on my arm, then," she said.

"I am sorry, Lealor. I thought my daughter would have a friend in you, but you have chosen otherwise. Myst, I sorrow for you. Protect, but do not speak. Do you hear the words of your father?"

The head of the bracelet rose a fraction so it could nod. Myst accepted the burden of silence.

"Now, just a minute. I'm sure Lealor will reconsider when she's given this matter some thought, Wyrd . . ."

"This is no longer a matter for humans. Keep silence before dragonlaw. Finished it iss." Wyrd closed his eyes as if in pain. "She shall rue this rash decision in time to come," Wyrd said solemnly. "We go."

Jarl's last sight of his daughter showed her being comforted by Rory. He only hoped he would be able to get Wyrd to relent after Lealor realized the magnitude of her error.

CHAPTER
SEVEN

Andronan smiled as Jarl materialized in front of the fire in his room. "Well?" he asked.

"Not well," Wyrd answered, then closed his eyes in obvious withdrawal.

Jarl looked at his sorrowing talisman. It was easy to see that Wyrd had withdrawn himself from the company of humans. In the past, when Wyrd retreated like this, it took a call from Jarl to get a response and return Wyrd to a consciousness of this world. Jarl allowed himself the luxury of a small sigh before seating himself in the second chair drawn up before the fire. It was a warm summer day outside, but within the university, there was often a sense of chill, almost as if the

builders had preferred a colder climate. Andronan sat before
the fire with his aged hands resting on his knees. Jarl supposed at his age he appreciated the warmth of the cheery
blaze.

"What went wrong, Jarl?" Andronan asked. "We can talk
now that Wyrd has so tactfully withdrawn his presence."

"I'm afraid it was more disgust than tact," Jarl admitted,
running his hand through his hair. "The boys now have bracelets that are Wyrd's children. They provide both protection
and friendship."

"Wyrd presented the boys with talismans like himself?"
Andronan's eyebrows raised.

Jarl realized that it was the first time he had ever seen the
old mage surprised. "Yes. And it looks like they will get along
just fine. Wyrd clearly considered the natures of the boys before giving them the bracelets. Seren has a talisman named
Soladon who started their relationship by giving him the
power to speak the dragon tongue perfectly. Seren was in sev-
enth heaven, chattering away to Fafnoddle and young Fafnir
with a perfect accent. Trying to speak the ancient language of
the dragons is something I never hoped to accomplish. I suppose Wyrd could have given me the power, but I always managed all right with everyday human speech."

Andronan asked, "And what power did Argen's bracelet
bestow on his partner?" Then he chuckled. "No," he said,
raising his hand. "Don't tell me. I'm sure I know. Argen can
now read all the books in the library—right?"

"You got it in one guess, Andronan. When I left him he
was sitting in the stacks reading some old tome. I suppose
you'll have to send someone to see he eats. Think of Librisald's delight when he discovers Argen's new ability. Between
the two of them, they may well have the stacks catalogued in
twenty or thirty years."

"What of Lealor? Did Wyrd not give her a talisman also?"
The look on Andronan's face said as plainly as words that he
could not believe the bracelet-giving didn't include Lealor.
Jarl knew Andronan loved the boys, but he had always had a
secret feeling that Lealor was the old mage's favorite. The
look on his face proved Jarl's intuition to be correct.

"Yes, but Lealor thought the talisman was only a way to

spy on her. She hates being told what to do. I suppose being the baby of the family isn't easy. I never thought before how many times Mirza and I correct her. Of course, you can't rear a child today on Earth without a good many cautions. Perhaps my mistake was allowing the boys to boss her around. That's what she told Wyrd. She didn't want a bracelet that would always be telling her what to do. She said it would be just like having her brothers bossing her all the time."

"Goodness! How did that strike Wyrd? I'm afraid there have not been many who contradicted anything he said. And for Lealor to actually refuse the bracelet—that is what she did, isn't it?"

"Yes, it is." Jarl looked into the fire, obviously remembering. He continued with his story after glancing at Andronan. His hands were clenched into fists. It was difficult for Jarl to believe the calm old mage could have emotion enough to actually feel antagonistic. Lealor was his great-granddaughter and even an ancient mage must feel some of the family ties that bound regular mortals.

"Was Wyrd angry?" Andronan asked quietly, leaning forward to hear Jarl's answer.

"Anger wasn't the emotion he felt. He seemed surprised and then—hurt, I guess, is the best word I can think of. After all, Wyrd has shown no emotion in all the years we have been together. I have no other experience with him to compare this one to. I tried to talk to Lealor, but while we both love her dearly, we know how stubborn she can be. When she gets one of those donkey streaks, talking to her is a waste of time. She damaged Wryd's pride in his offspring. He forbade Myst to talk to Lealor. Myst agreed. Her feelings were hurt, too, because she cried two tears. Lealor saw them and was ready to be more sensible, but it was too late. Wyrd would not listen. The best thing to do was let the whole mess die down a little. I hope eventually Lealor and Myst can become friends. If Wyrd stops being so hard to deal with, the whole thing will blow over—with time."

"It appears that Lealor is not the only stubborn being involved in this. So long as Wyrd did not invoke dragon-law—"

"But he did." Jarl watched Andronan shake his head sadly.

"In that case, there is nothing we can do. Dragonlaw is that ancient body of laws which binds dragons in all honor. For a dragon to change a command given under the law's binding would take a miracle. In all my studies of dragons, I have yet to hear or read of the law being broken. Just what did Wyrd tell Myst?"

"He told her to protect Lealor, but not speak to her."

"Did Myst agree?"

"Yes."

"It was a thoughtless question. Myst is Wyrd's daughter, and being newly created, she would agree like any obedient child. If she had only been older—"

"How can Wyrd have three children? Who is the mother of Soladon, Nyct, and Myst?"

"Dragons who are extremely powerful are capable of cloning replicas of themselves, complete with all the skills, but not the memories of the creating parent. The bracelets will have all the power of Wyrd."

"Kids shouldn't have that kind of power at their command. Who knows what they may decide to have their talismen do?" Jarl began to sweat, and he knew the small fire in the grate had nothing to do with his feeling.

"No, you don't understand. While the talismen have the power, they will only come into it gradually, as they need it. It will be years before they are a match for their father in power. They are like children. They will remember what they experience, they can probably return to Wyrd's horde—wherever it is—and read in his books to gain knowledge, but they won't be creating mountains of ice cream or burgers on command. Their main function is to protect the children, and it is only when they are doing this that they will be at full power." Andronan smiled when he saw the look of relief on Jarl's face. He knew one of Jarl's strengths was his ability to imagine contingencies, but sometimes an imagination could be as much of a curse as a blessing.

The two men sat in comfortable silence for a few moments. Then Jarl asked, "Do you suppose it's safe, checking on Lealor? I don't want to do or say anything further to upset Wyrd."

"Don't worry, Wyrd has withdrawn until you summon him to return," replied Andronan.

"Lealor should be safe with Cibby at her cottage in the woods even without her bracelet. I really need to find out what happened after Wyrd zapped me here," Jarl fretted out loud.

"That's easily done. We can use a little of my magic to check up on the girls."

Jarl hid a smile from his companion. Only an ancient mage would think of calling Cibby a girl. Jarl had met the witch on his first trip to Realm. She wasn't anything like the witches he had heard about in fiction. She seemed to be a one hundred percent huggable old granny type. There was nothing in her appearance or demeanor to suggest how powerful she was. She seldom stayed at the university with Andronan. She spent the greater part of her time in the woods, helping the animals. Her healing talent was truly formidable. Lealor had obviously inherited her love of animals, and she already had learned several of the simple spells to alleviate pain and heal wounds. Jarl was not sure if she spoke with the animals, or only understood them so well it appeared she could speak with them. When questioned, she answered, "Why, I just know. It's perfectly plain. Don't you know, Daddy?"

While Jarl was thinking, Andronan had opened a closet and brought out a crystal bowl, filled with what looked like pure mercury. "Now, let's take a look," Andronan said.

"What is that?" Jarl asked.

"This is a device we learned to build from some of the Old Ones' records Librisald finally deciphered. It works like a crystal ball, but the images are much clearer."

"What powers it?" Jarl asked after peering into the silvery depths of the liquid.

"I'm not absolutely certain, but the mind and determination of the viewer cause the liquid to reflect the scenes the viewer wishes to see."

"Then all we have to do is think about what we want to view?"

"That's correct. Just stand here beside me and let's both envision Cibby's cottage."

As Jarl and the mage watched, the silvery surface took on color and began to reflect a picture of Lealor and her Grandmother Cibby.

"Not bad," Jarl commented. "With sound, it would be almost like watching television at home."

"Oh, sound," Andronan said, absently passing his hand over the liquid with a few murmured words.

"Grandma, I was pretty bad today."

"Why do you say that, child?"

"Well, when Wyrd made Daddy disappear, Wyrd was mad and sad all at once, and my daddy didn't act pleased with me, either."

"Was it because you refused Wyrd's gift?"

"That's the worst thing I did. I made Myst cry. I could feel how sad she was inside, and she's still sad, but she won't talk to me. Rory said I'd just have to keep trying, that no female could stop talking for long, but he must be wrong. It's been all afternoon and Myst still hasn't said a word."

"Well, come sit on my lap, and we'll talk about it," her grandmother told her, as she sat in her rocking chair.

"What about the dishes? We didn't wash them yet," Lealor protested.

Her grandmother waved her hand impatiently at the dishes, which disappeared.

"Grandmother, you told me not to use magic when the job was something you could do without spells."

Her grandmother smiled at Lealor's righteous indignation. "Well, child, there are times when even the best of rules needs breaking. That's what it means to be an adult. Adults know when to ignore rules."

Lealor climbed onto the old woman's lap, thinking deeply. "You mean like when an animal's hurt, helping the animal comes first?"

"Ah, then you remember the day you didn't come when I called because you were helping that little bird get back in its nest."

"I could have helped it faster if I could have spelled it into the nest instead of having to climb up the tree."

"You remember when you explained, I wasn't angry?"

"I know you like me to obey—but you understood."

"That's another thing grown people hope they do."

"Understand children?"

"Correct, plus adults and dragons, too. Now, let's talk about what's bothering you."

"Well, I was playing in Flowerface's tree, and perfectly safe, you know, when Daddy and Wyrd appeared. Wyrd made Myst come on my arm and told me she would take care of me and tell me what to do. I told him I didn't want a bossy bracelet, and—"

"Did you actually say the words 'bossy bracelet' to Wyrd?" The old lady pushed her eyeglasses up on her nose to hide her smile.

"Not exactly. I said something like it would be just like having my brothers along, telling me what to do all the time, and I didn't want his gift."

"Oh, dear," her grandmother sighed.

"Well, then Wyrd told Myst not to talk to me for ever and ever, and she said she wouldn't."

"Perhaps Wyrd will change his mind—especially if you ask him politely and apologize."

"Somehow I know he'll never change his mind." Lealor let a big tear roll down her cheek. "Myst promised not to talk, too. Myst is so pretty. She'd never break a promise."

"Ah, Myst. Let me see."

Lealor obligingly held up her wrist.

"Hello, Myst," her grandmother said kindly.

Myst nodded her head in greeting.

"I don't suppose I could conjure you to speak, could I?"

Myst's eyes grew round, and her tiny head indicated not.

"Then I suppose Wyrd imposed dragonlaw on your promise and his command?"

The tiny bracelet nodded a vigorous yes.

"Why, Myst, you're talking to Grandmother," Lealor said with a smile.

"No, child, she's not. What she's doing is responding to what I say."

"Can you respond to what I say?" Lealor asked Myst, hope springing into her eyes.

Myst nodded solemnly.

"I need to tell you I'm awfully sorry for not wanting you at first. Wyrd made you sound all bossy and horrid."

"Wyrd didn't mean to do that," her grandmother said. "It's

just that dragons have different ways of looking at things, dear. Then, too, Wyrd was speaking human, which is not his native language."

"Like when I say something in Spanish to my friend Anita Morales and she laughs because I said it wrong?"

"Yes, that's it exactly. Now I think it's about time for you to be in bed—don't you?"

"Not really, Grandmother," Lealor said, and then spoiled the effect with a yawn.

Jarl looked away from the scene. He started to say something, but Andronan cut him off. "Wait," he cautioned Jarl.

Lealor hopped into bed and her grandmother leaned over and gave her a gentle kiss. "Sleep well, little one. Tomorrow you and Myst have many hours to discover one another."

"Do you think Myst will ever forgive me for being so mean?" Lealor's conscience was still bothering her.

"Why don't you ask her and find out?"

"Myst, I'm awful sorry. Will you forgive me and be my friend?"

The flickering firelight barely reached into the corner where Lealor's cot rested, but Myst's glowing eyes moved up and down.

" 'Night, Grandma," Lealor said, snuggling on her side with the wrist containing the bracelet on her pillow where she could see the slitted eyes of her new friend.

"Good night, dear." Lealor's grandmother watched her eyes flicker shut in sleep before touching her index finger lightly on Myst's head. Myst's eyes closed in satisfaction at her touch.

The old woman returned to her chair and sat quietly rocking before she said, "And what is it you two want, peeking into my cottage this time of night?"

CHAPTER EIGHT

Jarl looked at Andronan, who was shaking his head ruefully.

"I apologize, my dear, for seeming to spy on you."

"Oh, I was sure you had a good reason—such as a concern over how Lealor was faring."

"Yes, that's it exactly," Andronan said, clearly glad to escape so easily.

Jarl smiled. "What do you think about the bracelet mess Lealor has gotten herself into?"

Cibby rocked a few times in silence before she said, "It isn't a mess—exactly. In days to come, not having full communication with her bracelet will cost Lealor. Now that Myst will respond to questions, the situation is not half as awkward as it might have been."

"It's bad enough, I can tell you. Life hasn't been very pleasant on this end with Wyrd's feelings hurt," Jarl said.

"I don't know if that is really the case. Dragons are an awkward lot at the best of times," Andronan said, carefully pulling his sleeve away from the silvery material in the bowl.

"You don't remember anything like this ever happening when you wore Wyrd all those years ago, do you?" Cibby asked.

Jarl saw that she was patting her cat, Greymalkin, who had jumped on her lap. While Jarl knew that Andronan had been the previous wearer of Wyrd, he had not heard all the details.

"I've got a question, although it may not be the time to ask it."

"What, Jarl?" Cibby and Andronan said together. They chuckled gently at their mistake, for both had thought the question directed at them.

"Could either of you tell me why I am wearing Wyrd and Andronan is not? I mean, how exactly did Wyrd and Andronan separate? Is Wyrd so disturbed at my daughter that maybe he'll decide to disappear or something?"

Andronan shook his head. "No, Jarl, that is not how Wyrd works. Wyrd is bound to the mortal he chooses to serve until the mortal has done all he can to vanquish the enemy Wyrd is defending against."

Cibby smiled at Jarl, rocking gently. "My hero," she said roguishly, "vanquished his enemy in a fierce battle, and Wyrd returned to his velvet box until the need was great again."

"Now, Sibyl, my heroing was all done years ago."

"You're still my hero," she said firmly, rocking her chair so positively that Greymalkin fled from her lap.

For the first time, Jarl saw a definite resemblance between Mirza and her grandmother. Thinking of Mirza gave him a sharp ache in his chest. "Then I'm not likely to lose Wyrd in the middle of my search for Mirza?"

"No," Andronan told him. "Clearly, Wyrd believes you will still need his aid to combat the Shadowlord when he reappears."

"During your first encounter with the Shadowlord, his power grew greatly. You will find it even harder to vanquish him this time than previously." Cibby's eyes went strangely blank as she added, "And this time, you and Mirza will need the help of others—perhaps Wyrd's visualization of the future tells him his children and yours together will win the next victory."

"Cibby, was that a prophecy? Is Mirza in danger from the Shadowlord?" Andronan asked.

"I hope not, but I fear she is," Cibby admitted, rocking rapidly. She took her knitting from a bag attached to the arm of her chair, pulled her glasses down from the top of her head, and placed them firmly on her nose. A log popped in the fireplace and the knitting needles clicked sharply as Cibby's old fingers placed stitch after stitch.

"Try not to worry about it," Andronan comforted. "Remember, I once wore Wyrd and I know how powerful he is."

Jarl added, seeing that nothing Andronan said was going to make much difference to Cibby when she thought of her darling great-grandchildren in danger, "We know Lealor is in good hands with you watching her. I didn't want to go off Realm and leave her all upset if I could have calmed her. I know she will be all right now. Don't you agree?"

"Yes, she should be reassured now. I'll try to keep her interested and busy during the next few days while you disappear."

"Thank you. I'll be leaving in the morning for Achaea."

"Yes, you shouldn't delay. I have a little niggling feeling that this time Mirza needs your help."

"The gate to Achaea is unstable and it, at least, needs attention now if the Bright One within is to survive. I'll see that Jarl starts promptly in the morning. Good night, my dear."

"Bright Ones keep you safe, Jarl." Cibby blew a kiss. "Good night." The silver mirror in the dish rippled once and the vision of Cibby vanished. A cold wind emanated from the bowl as Andronan passed his hand over it.

"Put it back in the cupboard, will you, Jarl?" Andronan walked to his chair and sat wearily.

Jarl replaced the bowl carefully, shutting and locking the door when it was in its place. He crossed the room and sat down beside Andronan. "Say, there's no chance that the bowl would show me Mirza, is there?"

"Sorry. It will only work here on Realm. If you had the time to master the spells, you could learn how to make one and use it on Achaea by creating it there, but it would be a chancy business to try any magic there unless you were really desperate."

"Why?" Andronan had studied for so many centuries that Jarl always felt like a child when he had to ask him a question. Still, Jarl knew the only way to find out things is to ask when you don't know. Andronan always seemed eager to share the knowledge he had.

"Even as the wearer of Wyrd, you are still a mortal. The gods who live on Achaea are, after all, the gods of your an-

cient mythology on Earth. While I don't know them personally, the old tales depict them as pretty harsh to mortals who
tried to use magic that they felt was theirs."

"Yes, I can remember some pretty ghastly stories from the
myths. Any mortal who got too big for his toga ended up
punished severely."

"To the old gods of Greece, hubris was the only sin. Any
mortal who thought his powers matched those of the gods
found himself punished. I don't know if they would accept
your use of magic or not. It would be more tactful for you to
check and perhaps ask for permission before you tried any
spells."

"Believe me, I'll be really diplomatic while I'm there." A
puzzled look caught the old mage's attention.

"What is it, Jarl?" Andronan asked.

"Well, it just occurred to me. How is the Shadowlord disturbing the Achaean sun without the use of magic? Surely the
gods should be aware of what's happening."

"Perhaps the Shadowlord is using the Old Ones' science
instead of magic, and the gods have not paid any attention.
Then, his base may be so far away from Olympus that the
gods have overlooked his actions."

"You mean it's possible that the gods have had it all their
own way on Achaea for so long that it's impossible for them
to imagine any opposition?"

"Perhaps. Achaea is far away and the gods have had little
or no contact with the gates for centuries. I wish I could be
more helpful. The only answer is for you to visit the planet
and find out the answers for yourself."

Jarl watched Andronan smother a yawn. "You're tired, too.
If I'm to start early tomorrow, I'd better get some rest as
well."

"Yes, we must both be in good shape tomorrow morning."

"Are you coming with me?" Jarl asked, surprised that the
old mage would even consider such a trip.

"No, but I can control the power of the gate so that it will
not further disturb the Bright One in the Achaean sun. If we
destroy the sun, you and everyone on the planet would die.
Even seriously disturbing the Bright One might affect the

power of the gate. You and Mirza would be marooned on the world forever. There is a great risk in what you attempt."

Andronan's quiet words dropped into the stillness of the room. For a moment, Jarl wondered where the chill breeze was coming from. As he glanced around for the source of his discomfort, he saw the windows were closed.

CHAPTER NINE

Mirza had made many trips through the gate system, but none like this. Instead of an instantaneous arrival, she felt herself slowly being stretched thinner and thinner. She felt the memory of her shout, "Rogue gate!" drawn out into an indescribable echo—"—aaaaaaaa." Her physical body gradually changed to an energy form, and some new sense told her she was approaching her destination. She became aware of hundreds of tiny grey, threadlike forces that converged on a point where great energy was being formed. Then she realized what she was experiencing: the actual forces that someone had created to make a gate. One end of each grey thread came out of blackness, but all without exception curled around an energy form almost cocooned in the threads. It moved weakly, almost like an insect in a spider's web.

In the strange state between gates, Mirza could feel the bewilderment of the creature; it was very young. Mirza extended her hands and tried to pull the grey threads, but they were like wires, unbreakable. In her physical form Mirza had control of the molecules that formed her body. This made her able to shape-shift into any creature she wished. In this distorted state she was not sure what would happen if she attempted to change, but she knew she had to try. She willed herself into a giant crab with huge claws. Her claws quickly severed the grey threads. As each disappeared, she felt a tiny shock. The threads slowly quivered before turning to dust and disappearing. Only one thread resisted her claws. It was silver, and Mirza knew it was the thread of the gate itself. The silver thread gently spiraled around the area the other threads had covered. Mirza could feel herself coalescing, changing into a physical state, but she was sure she had saved the creature in the cocoon, now recognizable as a Bright One.

The tiny Bright One moved restlessly, like a child having a nightmare. Mirza found herself softly singing the words to a lullaby she had created for her own children: "Bye, bye, lulloo, my sweet Baloo, now rest, for none can harm you. Lullay, lullie, lulloo." In the strange state between the gates, the song did not seem to be sounds at all. Instead, a series of multicolored ribbons flashed into being. They twined around the silver thread and slid around and around the coils, gently fluttering in the eddies of energy around the infant Bright One. For a moment, Mirza felt a strangeness in her head. It was almost as if someone had rapidly thumbed through the pages of a book. Then, with a jerk, she felt herself being delivered to the surface of Achaea.

A glance around was enough to tell Mirza that she had made an unorthodox landing on the planet. For one thing, she was not at a gate point at all, nor was she upright. She rubbed herself as she prepared to rise from the ground. Then she slowly sat again, hoping she would not frighten the three creatures that came into the clearing where she rested, hidden by tall grass and flowers.

"Hurry up, Neso. We'll never find her if you keep dithering."

Mirza watched incredulously as a centaur pushed a sphinx into the little glade. A satyr capered behind them.

The sphinx half-unfurled her wings, reminded Mirza of her dragon friends. "Something's wrong. She didn't come through the gate."

"Well, I say if the Master can't deliver hostages for pickup where he sends us, then it's his fault, not ours!" The satyr leered at his two companions and blew a few notes on his pipes.

"Just tootle away like a fool, Sylvor. No one expects a satyr to show any sense. How you ever tore yourself from that group of fun lovers that fawn around Pan I'll never know. Why the Master chose you escapes me!" The centaur lifted his feet daintily in a little dance pattern.

"How you can dance, Kiron, when things are in such a muddle, is what I don't understand. My mother always told me that we sphinx needed to keep a cool head on our shoulders. As the most famous riddler on the whole of Achaea, I can understand why I am a chosen one. My lineage is impeccable. What are you, Kiron the Centaur, but an adventurer, out to have fun? And you, Sylvor, come from a long line of satyrs—and everybody knows what kind of dryad chasers you are. I notice that neither of you playboys is nearly so brave when the Master is around."

"It would be foolish to irritate him. When he finally completes his work on the island, we will have a world to rule. I will take all the centaurs with me, to a world where we will be supreme. No more of this looking over your shoulder all the time to make sure you haven't upset some goddess or other." The centaur reared, pawing the air with his front hoofs.

"I want to rule a world with many beautiful maidens, and not one dryad or daughter of any minor god or goddess. Just when you find a really lovely darling lost in the woods, she calls on daddy or mommy and you're in big trouble."

"Are you going to take any fellow satyrs along or do you plan to be the only one in your kingdom?" Kiron asked Sylvor.

"While it might be fun for a while, I'd eventually get tired of ruling alone. Besides, if I didn't take some of my friends along, who would I have to drink with? Nobody can drink like a satyr." Sylvor struck a pose and then played a small fanfare on his pipes.

Neso struck a tree with her paw and left a series of long gashes with her razor-sharp claws. Her small exhalation of breath sounded faintly like a hiss. "Being the most famed drunkard would be something *you* would be proud of. Now, my family—"

"Spare us, oh wisest of riddlers," Sylvor teased. "Kiron and I have heard many times about your ever-so-great-grandmother and her stand outside of Thebes on Earth."

"Only a sphinx would boast of getting killed because some ancestor or other was slain by a human hero. Believe me, it's a lot more fun to be alive, partying with your friends. Don't be so uptight. Satyrs and centaurs are about the only kinds of beings that really know how to have fun."

Neso crossed the meadow in four bounds. "Come on, you two, we've got to find her."

"Very well," Kiron answered, mincing his way along in Neso's path.

"Wait for me," Sylvor called, producing a brief tune on his pipes. He danced his way after them, playing and following a pattern of steps that reminded Mirza of the dance down the yellow brick road. The children and she had often watched a videotape of the old movie.

Sylvor's perambulations brought him next to Mirza. He stopped blowing on the pipes and asked with a leer, "And who might you be, lovely one?"

"I'm Mirza," she told him, accepting his hand. She expected him to help her to her feet, but instead, he leaned over and kissed her hand. She tried to pull away, but he kept a tight hold.

"By any chance are you related to any of the goddesses or gods here?"

"Here? Of course not. I just got here."

"You don't look like a dangerous and powerful sorceress," Sylvor said, dropping her hand at last.

Mirza rose to her feet as regally as she could. "That," she told him, "is not the issue at hand. I want to speak to your Master."

"Oh ho, not too proud to eavesdrop on the conversations of others," Sylvor said with an amused chuckle. "Well, follow me, and I will soon have you to a spot where you can converse with the Master."

"Sylvor," called Kiron, reentering the glade. "Oh, no, you

fool. Now is definitely not the time to be frolicking about with this," Kiron paused to look closely at Mirza, "delectable wench."

"Wench, indeed," Mirza said crossly. "I want to see your Master. Take me to him now."

"Your wish is his command," Kiron said, unable to resist playing with words.

"Let us gambol on that, my dear," Sylvor said, resuming his piping.

With Sylvor leading the way and Kiron following behind her, Mirza left the glade. In only a few minutes' walk they caught up with Neso, who was somewhat chagrined to have missed seeing their quarry. She stalked ahead, following a path that ran down to the water's edge. A small boat, tied to a rock, floated gently on the surface of the water. As soon as they entered, it skimmed rapidly across the water, leaving land far behind, proving it was a magical craft.

"And might I ask where we are going?" Mirza's long red hair spun out behind her like a banner. While she rather enjoyed the ride, she was curious.

Neither Kiron nor Sylvor answered her. Their clutch on the sides of the boat made her think they might be seasick. Neso, however, obviously enjoyed the ride. She lifted her wings enough to catch the cool breeze before answering. "Look at the great rulers, frightened of a little trip to Atlan."

"Atlan?" Mirza repeated.

"The Island of Wizards," Neso told her. "The Master is the mightiest Wizard of them all. He will open gates to many worlds, and because we help him, our reward will be a world of our own to rule as we wish."

"And if these places already have rulers of their own, or the beings there have no wish for you to be their ruler—"

"The Master will have great armies to do his bidding."

Mirza didn't like the sound of what she heard. If one of the gods was responsible for the rogue gate, it was going to be tricky indeed to save the Bright One. While Mirza had special training and the ability to shape-shift her own body and other items under the right conditions, tackling a full-fledged god was more than a mortal with any brains looked forward to trying. She wished she had remained at the gate. With what she knew now, she would have stepped back through to get Jarl. Having him near and the power of Wyrd to call on would have been comforting. She glanced over her shoulder at the centaur and the satyr. Her hair blew in her face and she pushed it back so it could flow with the wind. Both of them looked miserable. Neither was very well designed for boat riding. Ahead of her, Neso held her face to the wind.

"We'll soon be there," the sphinx shouted, and the wind obligingly threw the words to the three behind her.

Mirza watched carefully. She saw shore birds flying ahead of the boat. Then she could smell the land itself. Gradually the island came into view. A tall mountain dominated the north end. To the south, great marble buildings sprawled, forming a city. Small cottages and occasional estates climbed the sides of the mountain. One long piece of land jutted out to sea. A large building housed an odd tower on the very end of the spit of land. As the strange craft in which Mirza and her captors rode drew closer, Mirza could see the tower was some type of celestial observatory. Somehow it loomed over the rest of the building of which it was a part. In spite of the size of the city, the mountain and the observatory were the real focal points of power on the island. Mirza felt an odd ripple, like pages being rapidly turned in her head. She wondered how long the aftereffects of the strange gate trip would produce the weird sensation. She could only hope nothing had been permanently scrambled in her mind by her experience.

The water became shallower with each passing minute. Just as Mirza began to worry that the great speed the boat still displayed was going to dash them against the cliffs, the craft slowed. Then, with no steering from Neso that Mirza could detect, it headed of its own volition toward a deep fissure in the great granite cliff ahead of them.

Mirza looked carefully around as the boat entered the giant crack. The steep sides looked impassable. If she needed to escape the Master—whoever he was—she would have to fly, birdlike, or turn herself into a fish as she cast herself into the water. She saw men running along the sides of the cliff above. Ahead, the water opened out into a harbor which was obviously not natural, for a series of tiers stood tall, blasted from the rock. While there were many steps, the top of the cliff was now accessible.

Neso jumped lightly from the boat when it rested beside the dock. Mirza accepted the hand of one of the men who was there to moor the craft. She had no time to watch Sylvor and Kiron disembark because Neso was urging her to hurry up the stairs. Mirza did not often regret her impetuosity, but this was one time she wished she had told someone back on Realm what she was doing. She had barely made it through the gate. How long would it take the Master to repeat his work if she did not dissuade him? Would the gate work correctly now that the grey threads were removed? It had not deposited her at the regular gatepoint. For the first time, she realized that it might not be possible to reach Achaea through the gate at all. If that were true, she was quite literally "on her own," for Jarl might not be able to reach her, even using the power of Wyrd.

Neso, walking behind her, kept urging Mirza forward, up the steps, until they reached a great open space before a door in the building. The size of the doorway dwarfed Mirza, which did not add to her feeling of security. Because she was able to shape-shift, she understood that size wasn't everything. She did hope the Master wasn't going to be as large as the doorways she was seeing while Neso hustled her down one long corridor after another. Why did trouble always seem to come in such large packages?

The guards standing before each of the doors were ordinary humans, Mirza was sure. Except for them, the building reminded her of the university at Realmgate. Only three people passed them as they traversed the corridors, and two of those carried papers, while the third read a scroll as he walked slowly by, not even noticing Mirza and Neso.

"Open!" Neso commanded a guard at one of the great doors.

The guard followed her orders quickly without saying a word. Mirza could see that Neso expected obedience—at least from the guards in the buildings.

Neso did not give Mirza a chance to say anything to the guard. She pushed Mirza into the room and said, "Wait here."

The heavy wooden door closed soundlessly behind the sphinx, leaving Mirza in a large room. Surprisingly, considering the heat of the sun outside, the room was cool. Mirza supposed it was because the walls were made of thick marble. The room was dim, with the only light entering from a small, barred window set in an outside wall.

Curious, Mirza walked over and looked out. The view spread out below the cliff, revealing the city at the south end of the island in detail. The clear air and bright light made it possible to see for a great distance. Mirza looked at the plan of the city: the four quarters, the canal system, the great buildings. She exhaled softly. "Not Atlan. This is Atlantis as it might be on Earth if the island had not sunk below the waves more than ten thousand years ago."

CHAPTER TEN

She walked around the room, carefully noting everything. She knew she could escape from the window because the bars were set so far apart. If she changed into a hawk, she could easily fly away. The furniture was sparse: a chair, a couch, a table. In one corner a small fountain of water fell into a marble basin. When the basin was full, the water overflowed into a pipe set into the floor. The water made a soothing sound as it splashed into the basin. It was the only audible sound in the room. She looked at the murals on the walls. One showed a mountain scene; the second, a seascape; the third, a forest;

and the last, an underwater scene. The room was pleasant—
for a prison.

Mirza reclined on the couch. No sense in being miserable
and pacing back and forth, she thought. She might as well
save her energy for her meeting with the Master. Which god
would it be? Apollo was reputedly interested in truth, but
would he want armies to enforce his rule? Ares would love to
mastermind human and inhuman armies. He was something of
a coward, and Mirza doubted he had the brains to plan an
invasion scheme. Could Athena, the goddess, have decided to
use her wisdom to make a gate? Why would gods want another gate? They already had one that worked fine—until
someone meddled with it. Mirza closed her eyes and tried to
think.

The great door opened silently, but Mirza was aware that
someone had entered her room. She opened her eyes and saw
one of the guards standing in the doorway. She tilted her head
and raised her eyebrows in inquiry.

"You are going to face the Master now," the guard told her.

She got up, brushed off her robes, and preceded him
through the door. She turned to the right at his command and
continued down the corridor until he indicated she should
enter another corridor which led ever deeper into the center of
the building. Finally he stopped her at a door where he
knocked sharply. The door opened into a room filled with
scrolls, strangely shaped glass containers, and models of
things Mirza didn't recognize.

Mirza entered the room and the door closed behind her.
Then through a doorway that led to another room, a cowled
figure entered.

Before the figure had said a word, Mirza muttered, "I
should have known."

"We meet again, Mirza Koenig," the Shadowlord said.

"Not exactly by my choice," Mirza answered, holding her
head high. "We of Realm thought that you were so badly
frightened by our last meeting that we would have years of
peace before there was need to face you again."

"Not frightened, foolish woman. Injured! Now I have
healed and grown more powerful than ever. You and your

husband—even aided by that conscience-driven worm, Wyrd, will not be able to stop me this time."

"I wouldn't call a dragon with the power which Wyrd can command a worm, if I were you. Dragons can be touchy. If he finds out about your opinion, it may anger him."

"You foolish gatekeepers do not even know what Wyrd really is!" The Shadowlord half rose from the chair in which he sat.

"And you do, I suppose?" Mirza taunted. Perhaps now she could get the answers to some of the questions Jarl and she had puzzled over in the past.

"The reason I know about Wyrd is that I have collected within this building the greatest number of scrolls, books, and stone tablets anywhere in the universe."

"Then I was right. This is some kind of university or school."

"Yes." The cowled head nodded briefly, as if it pained the great wizard to grant her being correct about anything.

Mirza wished the Shadowlord would throw back his cowl. She could see nothing of his face except an occasional golden flash, which she gathered must come from his eyes. She wanted to hear the story of Wyrd, but she also wanted to see the face of her adversary. He almost radiated power. She could sense it. At least he was not lying when he told her his power had increased. Somehow, she wished he had been exaggerating about that.

"I bet that you didn't gather all of the material that's here," Mirza baited, trying to get as much information as she could.

"Not personally, no. I was able to add to this library significant information about the gate system. The Old Ones were not gods. They were wise because they were so ancient, not because they had better minds than we do."

"They certainly had a better system of ethics. They didn't harm any Bright Ones when they formed the gates."

"Ethics! That is a word for the weak who do not dare to do anything they wish. Look where ethics has got the Dragonlord Wyrd."

"Yes—you were going to tell me about him."

"Long before you were even a gleam in your misbegotten

father's eye, Wyrd was as ancient as the Old Ones them-selves."

Mirza swallowed. All the Keepers had thought of Wyrd as an animated power source. They had vastly underestimated him, if what the Shadowlord said was true. "That seems pretty farfetched. Why, Wyrd is only a few inches long."

A dusty chuckle emanated from the Shadowlord. "In your dimension that is his size. However, there is a great deal more to Wyrd than meets the eye. He allows only a small part of himself to enter this universe. He didn't want to destroy your frail egos. Just enough matter exists in this universe to focus his power. He made the rules himself, thousands of years ago."

"Why would any being that powerful allow himself to be-come the servant of an ordinary human?"

"Quite simple. He is atoning for destroying a Bright One."

His quiet words hit Mirza like a bomb. On the one hand, she didn't think Wyrd would do such a thing, but on the other, the Shadowlord's flat recital had the ring of truth. He had nothing to gain by lying about Wyrd. Indeed, he had admitted Wyrd was more powerful than anyone thought.

"Do not look as if I have told an untruth. Wyrd was the highest dragonmage in his dimension. The gates left by the Old Ones fascinated him, once he discovered this dimension. He wrote that the gates were the only things in our universe that had any worth."

"If he felt that way, then why did he consent to become a bracelet and help the beings here?"

"His race considered the Bright Ones to be a life form equal to theirs. When they discovered his gate studies had caused an infant Bright One to die through his negligence—which I admit was caused by ignorance, not intent—they banned him from their midst until he could redeem himself by saving a Bright One from destruction."

"Then why is he still sticking around? He saved the Bright One in the Realmsun by helping us drive you away before you could finish forcing your version of a universal gate."

"That is the joke of the universe. In all those thousands of years aiding the heroes of the lesser races, he came to believe that they, too, were worthy. He could now return to his dimension in full honor—but he refuses to go."

Mirza was having trouble accepting all the information about Wyrd. Why, she had always thought of him as a cute little bracelet, an artifact of the Old Ones, left behind to aid their younger races. She was glad she wasn't wearing the bracelet. When she was younger, she wanted the bracelet to use her as the hero to protect Realm from evil.

"That's interesting, but it isn't the reason I'm here."

"Spare me your lectures. This time, my gate will be even more powerful than those of the Old Ones. Not only will my gate be universal to every world, but it will also be able to choose the time I want. I will have the greatest army of heroes and warriors selected from every time and world that exists!"

Mirza wouldn't give her enemy the satisfaction of knowing what an impression his latest news had created on her. Instead, she flew to the attack. "And, I suppose, if you destroy the Bright One in Achaeasun, it is of no account?"

"Don't you who live on that backwater world of Realm have a saying about having to break an egg to make an egg pasty?"

"Backwater?" Mirza's red hair almost crackled with her wrath. "Realm and its inhabitants were good enough to send you fleeing when we defeated all the foreign beings and evils that you could call to help you."

"Admitted. I was not fully prepared. Now I am. There I had no allies. Here I do. There are some very good minds here on the island."

"That's another thing. How have you kept from having trouble with the gods of Achaea? They don't like mortals usurping their powers."

"I deliberately chose a place where the gods would not interfere. Atlan has long had an agreement with the gods. So long as they only use their powers on the island, the gods allow it."

"Eventually they are going to find out you are tampering with their sun, and when they do, I have a feeling you will be sorry—very sorry!"

"Before they find out what I am doing, it will be too late. I have planned long and well. This time my gate will be universal and multitemporal."

"In that case, you have no need of me. I'll just go back to Realm—"

"Your tampering with my gate has caused a further imbalance in the sun. The Bright One seems to be resisting our attempts to reset the gate. However, I will allow you to join us. Your gateknowledge, added to my own, should allow us to complete the project with little damage to Achaeasun and its pulsing Bright One."

"What you are really telling me is that there is no way for me to get home using the regular gate." Mirza hoped her dismay at the prospect of staying on Achaea did not show.

"There is a way off Achaea—but you won't be using it. I remember how unreasonable you were the last time we discussed joining forces. So before we talk further, I'll have to make a few preparations." He waved his hand and Neso appeared in the room. "You and Kiron and Sylvor are to go collect those three . . . items I thought I might need. Send Mirza to her new home. She'll not escape my jailer, Medusa."

Neso's face paled. "Won't she be in danger?"

"Now, would I send a prospective ally into danger?" The black-cowled figure tsked. "Don't worry yourself over her. A powerful spell by one of the Old Ones protects her. It is not worth my time to try and break it. Mirza will be joining us of her own free will when you have finished bringing me her children." He gestured a second time with his hand and Neso disappeared.

Mirza gasped. "A spell prohibits you from returning to Realm!"

"Now, my dear, there is no rule that says visitors from Achaea may not come to Realm. And if they each bring a souvenir with them when they return, who is to stop them? The minigates they will use are so small we power them from here on the island. When they leave Realm they'll siphon power from your gate to return. And then we'll talk. I look forward to your future cooperation."

The last sound Mirza heard was a rasping laugh. The Shadowlord's negligent wave sent her into darkness.

CHAPTER
ELEVEN

Sylvor capered under the canopy of trees in the Realmforest. It was hard for him to believe that he actually stood on another world. It wasn't his style to worry or do close examination of the trees; therefore, the slight differences in the forest made no impression on him. He knew he would meet his quarry soon. The star that he wore around his neck to activate the gate grew warm, just as his Master had promised. The child was near. Sylvor played a captivating melody on his pipes. His tune worked as if he were the Pied Piper of Hamelin. Seren appeared almost magically.

"Hello. Who are you? I've never met you before." Seren said to Sylvor with a friendly smile. He recognized him as a satyr, a being he had never seen on Realm until this moment. Many afternoons spent in front of the television with his father and his brother had familiarized him with most types of monsters and unusual beings from fantasy. His mother said she knew more fabulous beings than any on what she called "those tasteless children's programs." When he met more of the beings on Realm, Seren agreed with her.

"My name is Sylvor." The Master had not told him how big this child was. He was almost as large as Sylvor himself. There was no way Sylvor could force Seren to go with him, but the satyr thought he could trick him.

"I'm glad to meet you," Seren said politely. Then his enthu-

siasm took over. "Just wait until Faf sees you. I bet he's never
met a satyr either. I can't wait to see the look on his face."

"And who is this Faf?" Sylvor didn't think the minigate
would transport three people at the same time. The essence of
the whole operation was to get the child on Achaea before
anyone who had the power to stop him from going appeared.

"Oh, he's a dragon. He's one of my best friends. Soladon is
my other friend."

"You mean the bracelet you wear on your wrist is Faf?"

"No. That's—"

Soladon tightened on Seren's wrist. "Do not tell this strange
satyr who I am."

Seren thought his bracelet was being overly suspicious, but
he didn't argue.

"What?" Sylvor asked.

"Oh, nothing." Seren tried to change the conversation. "I'm
going to the ruins of Fellkeep to meet my dragon friend, Faf.
Would you like to go along?" While it would be good to tell
Faf about the satyr, it would be even more spectacular if Seren
could actually produce Sylvor to show him. It wasn't very
often that Seren saw anything before Faf did, because Faf
could fly. Even when Seren rode on Faf's back, he usually
was so busy holding on he didn't see much unless Faf pointed
it out to him. Fafnoddle, the dragon's father, had a much
smoother ride. Seren had not thought about it much before,
but riding Faf was a lot like bike riding on someone's handle-
bars. He was probably a pretty heavy load for the young
dragon. Maybe that was why they only flew on short trips.
Seren meant to ask his friend about his new discovery. He
didn't want to be too much of a burden. On the other hand,
without Faf's power of flight there were a lot of places they
couldn't get to. And that meant missing new experiences,
giving up some of the adventures they might have. Seren
didn't think Faf would want that any more than he did.

"Fellkeep? Is that a local landmark?"

"You mean you haven't heard of Fellkeep?" Seren was astounded.

"Not that I remember."

"You must really be from the deepwoods if you don't know about Fellkeep."

"Realm is wide. Is it really so strange that I would not know of this Fellkeep?" Sylvor realized he had made an error, and he was groping for a way to keep the boy from noticing it.

If Sylvor had thought to look, he would have seen that Soladon's eyes had become green chips of ice. Soladon listened and watched carefully. Perhaps this was a creature that would menace Seren. The small talisman gathered his power, ready to strike if he became aware of the slightest danger. It was not only that Wyrd had created him and set him the task of guarding Seren. He really liked the boy and his hulking dragon friends, especially the young one. Existence on this level with these life forms was interesting, very interesting. At night, when Seren slept, Soladon made use of the time to study the dragon lore in Wyrd's huge library. The talisman didn't notice anything strange about going someplace else with his mind when only a small portion of it had to watch the sleeping boy. For all he knew, Seren himself was studying human lore during the sleep periods.

Seren, excited about his new friend, paid no attention to the significance of Sylvor's ignorance. For once, he would get to tell someone about his parents' exploits. "Fellkeep is where the Shadowlord lived. It's where my parents defeated him in a final battle for the safety of Realm!" Seren paused in his breathless recital to see if he had properly impressed Sylvor.

"Oh, that Fellkeep!" Sylvor nodded wisely.

Seren continued. "Come on, and I'll tell you as we walk."

The satyr nodded and took a place beside Seren on the path. This was fine. His minigate had deposited him near the ruins of a great castle fortress. The place must be Fellkeep.

"In the old days, the Shadowlord used Realm as a gathering place for his armies. He set up a rogue gate. That's one not authorized by the Old Ones. It stressed Realmsun, which was just about to explode when my parents took a hand. Faf's mother and father carried my parents to Fellkeep just in time for them to use magic. Wyrd, my father's—"

"Keep silence about the power of the dragon bracelets," Soladon warned mentally.

"There's nothing wrong with Sylvor. Why shouldn't he

know about your father's part in saving Realm?" Seren's thought flashed.

"Now the satyr believes I am nothing, a mere ornament on your wrist. It is best so. Someday the ignorance of your enemies may be to our advantage."

"We don't have any proof he means me harm." Rapid as this exchange of mental conversation was, Seren could sense he was losing the argument.

"Do you expect those who mean you harm to announce their villainy upon meeting you? Humor me. Let us wait to tell Sylvor of my real identity until there is more of a reason."

"Well, okay," Seren agreed, still certain his friend pushed the guardian business to its farthest limit.

"Wyrd, your father's what?" Sylvor asked.

"I was trying to think of a word to describe Wyrd. His name means fate in some old language. Wyrd is a powerful magic user. Somehow he's able to augment the magic powers of my father. Without him and the wyverns who live in the marsh, the humans on Realm would not have won the war."

"Why do you meet Faf at Fellkeep?"

"Oh, Faf and I like to have adventures and find out things. His mother had some terrific adventures when she was younger. My mother had fun, too, but now both of them are always worrying about Faf and me. If it wasn't for Gram Cibby, I wouldn't know half of the neat things my mother did when she was young. Faf's grandfather told us about the wonderful adventures the dragons in his family had. Faf's grandfather is the only one who encourages us to explore. He likes to hear what we find out about. We fly there every so often to report. He knows a lot of interesting things. Some of our best adventures started with interesting bits of old stuff he told us about. Fellkeep is one of the places we think our parents would worry about. So, we meet there and then we don't have any grown-up asking, 'And where are you two off to today?'"

"Aha! It keeps you from lying!" Sylvor leered his understanding.

For the first time in their brief acquaintance, Seren got a glimpse of the satyr's real nature. He found the passing expression disturbing, but he told himself it was his imagination. That's what comes of listening to Soladon, he thought.

"We wouldn't lie to our parents, Sylvor. We wouldn't do anything they expressly told us not to do, either. We don't want to worry them. Sometimes we've been in pretty narrow squeaks, but we managed to get out of them." Seren's eyes shone with the memory of how they had outwitted several of the odd denizens of Realm.

"Somewhere around here is Leafshine's oak. That's one of the things Faf and I want to do someday, find Leafshine and let her tell us about the aerial battle that Faf's father fought with the mechanical birds the Shadowlord created. My father never wants to talk about it, but we found out about it from Faf's grandfather."

"How much farther is it?"

"Not far now. We have to skirt the marsh before we reach Fellkeep."

"Is there no path through the swampy ground?" Sylvor asked, piping a brief tune.

"Well, yes, there is, but we'd have plenty of trouble using it."

"Isn't it much shorter to go through the swamp?"

"Sure, it's shorter, but we're males," Seren said, as if that explained everything.

"What does our sex have to do with passing through the marsh path?" Sylvor asked between short bursts of music on his pipes.

"The wyverns live there, you see," Seren explained. "They are strange beings. The lady wyverns run everything."

The path abruptly came to an end at the edge of some murky water. Seren turned to the left and continued through the trees. The damp ground bore witness to their passing. Sylvor's hoofprints and Seren's footprints showed plainly where they had been and pointed their direction of travel. "How long will we have to go through this mud?" Sylvor asked. He was not in favor of leaving so clear a record of his passing. The minigate that would leave no trace of his visit to Realm was safely located on dry ground.

"We're very close to Fellkeep now. Any minute the ground will start rising and there will be much more rock." Seren turned around and grinned at Sylvor before continuing his monologue. "The wyvern ladies are super magic users. They're very attractive, too. My father rescued one of them. Wyverns are not usually very friendly to men, but Fafnoddle's mother was the wyvern queen's friend. It turned out that the wyvern my dad rescued was a wyvern princess, so they helped cure Faf's father of the wounds he got fighting the bird-things. While he rested, the wyvern princess guided my father into Fellkeep, where he rescued my mother. My father said the wyvern princess was very brave and awfully intelligent. The magic they used impressed my father, but he wouldn't give any details. He said maybe the wyverns didn't want other people to know how they worked their magic. I'd sure like to meet one of those wyverns, but they seldom stray far from this marsh."

Sylvor hoped the boy was right. One of the last things he wanted to meet right now was any wyvern. Especially, he didn't want to meet any being who was a friend of the boy's father. Wyverns sounded like a group of creatures he could well do without.

Through a break in the trees, Seren and Sylvor got their first sight of Fellkeep. Sylvor hopped gratefully onto a large, flat rock. He could tell they were very close to the minigate. He was almost certain it rested behind a large rock to the right. Now, how could he best get the boy to cooperate?

Seren solved the satyr's problem for him.

"Faf's not here." Seren's face fell. The satyr probably had things to do and wouldn't want to wait around until Faf arrived. "If you don't have anything important to do right now, we could look around while we wait for my friend," he said, delighting Sylvor.

"That sounds like a good idea to me," the satyr agreed. Luck was with him. In a few minutes, he would have the boy positioned, and then he could activate the minigate and finish his task.

Seren hopped from rock to rock like a mountain goat. Sylvor was unused to young humans and expected him to fall momentarily. It was all he could do to keep from calling out a warning. The satyr had enough sense to know his only hope of manipulating the boy lay in his being a friend, not another parental figure. The satyr hurried to the place behind the rock where he thought the minigate waited. He was right. He turned and shouted for Seren.

"Seren! Come see what I found!" The star on the chain around the satyr's neck pulsed redly. The proximity to the gate activated it.

"Where are you, Sylvor?" Seren looked around for his friend.

"Over here behind the big squarish rock," the satyr answered.

Seren examined the many blocks of stone which littered the area. "Call again," he urged. "There must be a million of these squarish rocks," he muttered to himself.

"Here!"

This time Seren was able to pinpoint which rock Sylvor meant. He clambered down from his rock and worked his way in Sylvor's general direction.

"Stop, young manling," a quiet voice said.

Seren turned and saw a green humanoid step from behind a boulder. "You're a wyvern!" he said.

"That is correct."

"Something's wrong, Wyverns don't speak with human males."

"That also is correct, young manling. However, in this case, something is owed."

"You don't owe me any money," Seren said, bewildered. How could a strange wyvern owe him anything?"

"Money is one of the curses your race bears. No wyvern has such a debt."

"Why stop me?" asked Seren.

"The wyverns owe a debt to Jarl Koenig. My own honor repays. I offer safety in place of danger."

"Just what do you mean by that?" Seren understood that wyverns were weird creatures, but this one didn't even make sense. "What danger?"

"The danger that comes from traveling by an unauthorized gate."

"There's no gate here now. My father and mother destroyed it when the Shadowlord fled Realm."

"Think you that we watch not the area around our home?

We learned not to ignore the activities of humans in our area. If we had watched the strange one you call the Shadowlord, he who was our great enemy, we would have stopped his evil long before it grew past simple containment."

"Then I'll bet you know my father?".

"Yes."

"Are you Seabreeze?"

A nod was his answer. Seabreeze pulled a sharp dagger from her belt and motioned Seren to stand where he was. Sylvor came from behind the rock and motioned Seren to come to him. He did not see the wyvern who had stepped into the shadow formed by the narrow crevice between two stones.

"What's keeping you? Don't you want to see what I've found?"

"Sure I do but—" Seren took one step forward, then halted.

Seabreeze stepped from the crack and stood between the two.

"This is my father's friend Sea—"

Soladon hissed, "Shhhh!" in Seren's mind.

"We do not give our truename to our enemies, Young One," the wyvern said.

Seren looked at the satyr and the wyvern. He didn't know what to believe. His bracelet and the wyvern both warned him, but nothing about Sylvor seemed dangerous.

"You doubt me, Young One?" the wyvern asked.

"Not exactly, but—"

"Speak, Hoofed One. Tell Jarl Koenig's son what lies behind the rock and why you desire his presence so urgently."

"I just want to show him something," Sylvor almost whined his answer. He could tell Seren was beginning to doubt him.

"See the star around his neck, manling? It pulses with the energy that will activate another gate that leads to great evil."

"Hey, Sylvor, she's right. Your star is shining. It wasn't dimming and brightening like that when I first met you."

"Very well. Yes, there is a gate, and you will come to me now." And with these words, he began playing a strange little tune on his pipes.

Seren tried to resist, but the very notes pulled him forward.

"Stop, or you are doomed!" Seabreeze commanded.

"I'm trying!"

"Look at your bracelet!"

Seren tore his eyes away from Sylvor and looked at his bracelet, even as he advanced ever closer to the satyr. Soladon's eyes seemed to grow larger and larger, then, with a wrench, everything disappeared in a golden haze. He heard the wyvern speak farewell in his mind and everything faded to black.

CHAPTER TWELVE

Jarl arose before the sun on the morning he planned to go to Achaea. He wore boots, his ever-durable jeans, a shirt, and his cowboy hat. No Texan was ever more ready for adventure than he was that morning.

He passed through the silent hall of the university to the great refectory. A short stop at the window brought Calor, the head cook, with a plate of steaming pancakes.

Calor gave him a wide smile, showing the gap in his front teeth, for the cook liked fighting almost as much as he did cooking. "Sun rises early, doesn't it, Jarl," he boomed, his voice filling the empty refectory.

"Indeed, my friend," Jarl answered, "but not early enough to catch you unawares." Jarl gestured to the heaping plate.

The cook beamed and handed Jarl a glass of freshly squeezed coralberry juice. "Coffee will be ready in a minute," the cook promised. "So sit down and begin to eat or cold pancakes will be your fare this morning."

"Nobody makes these like you do, Calor. I don't know

where you got the recipe," Jarl told his friend, sitting at the nearest table to the food window.

"It was your own good wife, the Lady Mirza, who brought the recipe to me. She told me how fond you were of these strange cakes baked in a skillet. The children always eat better breakfasts when I make pancakes. Well I remember the first time I served them good oaten porridge. You'd have thought I planned to poison them. Seren and the little miss still won't eat porridge, but if I put plenty of coralberry jam on the table, Argen will."

"I remember the fuss when he started the fad. Now almost everybody mixes coralberry jam with their porridge."

"I find I prefer it that way myself—" Calor stopped abruptly, his wide eyes looking comical in his broad face.

A leprechaun had materialized on the end of Jarl's table. "Bewitched it is I am," he sputtered. "Sent hither and yon, Bright Ones know where, at the flick of a finger!" He thumped a small knapsack on the table. "Well, this errand's done." He said this more cheerfully, as he looked longingly at the pile of pancakes on Jarl's plate.

"Good morning, Rory," Jarl told his friend.

"Top o' the morning to you," the leprechaun answered.

"And how are you today?"

"Well, but I might be better if I had a little something to stick to my ribs." He eyed Jarl's plate which was rapidly being emptied.

"Calor." Jarl raised his voice slightly. "Have you a few more pancakes going begging in the kitchen?"

"Coming up, Jarl." Calor came to the window and shoved a small mountain of pancakes through.

Rory made a magical pass with his hands, and the plate sailed over to rest in front of him. He wasted no time in digging in.

Calor came to the window with a pot of coffee and two cups. Jarl hid his smile with a large hand. Calor's lower jaw dropped open, and he stared at Rory. The leprechaun paid no attention to the cook. He kept shoveling pancakes into his mouth as if he had had no food for months.

Jarl couldn't resist a chance to tease his friends. "Didn't

you get a chance to have any breakfast this morning?" he asked, winking at Calor.

"Of course I did! Didn't Cibby just send me with a provender bag for your trip?"

"What did you eat out of the bag?" Jarl asked with real interest.

"At Cibby's I had eggs, bacon and fresh bread. I found myself with a real thirst. I knew you wouldn't mind if I conjured up a small potation to wet my whistle as my granny used to say." Rory reached into his back pocket and pulled out a small flask. He tipped it up and allowed a stream of amber liquid to cascade into his throat.

"And what would that be?" Calor asked, not knowing Rory as well as Jarl did.

"A taste of old Ireland." Rory smacked his lips and took another drink.

"You're drinking alcohol for breakfast?" a scandalized Calor asked.

"I'd not drink just any old thing with so delicious a meal. Nothing but the finest Irish whiskey. It gives a zip to pancakes that coralberry jam never did!" Rory rubbed his stomach, which stuck out in an alarming fashion. It reminded Jarl of the way a small pup looked after finishing a bowl of food. "I'll have to be off, Jarl. Give my regards to Mirza when you find her. Look!" he commanded.

Both Jarl and Calor glanced over at the door where Rory pointed. Andronan entered, chuckling.

"You two let Rory get away with his pot of gold again, didn't you?"

"If that leprechaun has any gold, it's spent at the first tavern he materializes next to," Calor said, picking up the empty plates Jarl set on the window.

"He likes to keep his hand in, he told me once," Jarl said. "So I always pretend I'm fooled when he points. It pleases him to slip away behind my back."

"What can I get you for breakfast, Andronan?" Calor asked.

"Nothing, thank you." Andronan raised his hand in negation. "And don't lecture me, Calor. I will come and eat something after Jarl has gone. I promise."

Calor stood, arms akimbo. "I won't lecture you, then, but one of these days the wind from some spell will blow you over if you don't eat regular meals."

"You stay after him about eating, Calor. Mirza and I trust you to keep him from starving himself."

At the sound of Mirza's name, Andronan's face lost its look of amusement. "Mirza," he said softly. "Yes, Jarl, now is the time of your departure."

Jarl pushed in his chair, took up the provender bag, and told Calor goodbye. Then he followed Andronan through the door and down the hall to the Courtyard of the Gate.

Vigilan stood and stretched when Jarl and Andronan entered the courtyard. His shift was over and someone would be replacing him shortly. He bowed respectfully to Andronan and nodded to Jarl. "Good day to you both," he said.

"And to you," Andronan replied. "I know how very tired you are, but would you stay and help anchor the gate for Jarl's trip?"

"Of course. I would be honored." Vigilan's thin face flushed with pleasure.

Jarl moved to stand within the star that formed the gate. Andronan motioned him back.

"Why?" Jarl asked.

"We do not know the condition of the receiving gate on Achaea. First we must test the gate. I don't know what would happen if you transported yourself into the gate matrix without having a reception point that would receive you."

"Then you believe there is a damaged gate at its terminus on Achaea?"

"All may be well, but sensible precautions should be taken before trusting a gate blindly when we know there has been trouble on the other end."

"So how do we test the gate?" Jarl asked impatiently.

"First we need someone at each point of the star. We three must have two others to stand watch."

"Are we too late to see Jarl off?" the welcome voice of Guardy asked. With him was Argen.

"Dad's still here, Guardy," Argen said. "Hi, Dad."

"And what brings you out to the gate so early? Usually you'd be sleeping until noon."

"That's not what I do when I'm here. At home things are usually pretty boring, so there's no hurry to get up on a Saturday. Here Librisald and I have lots to do and I get up early. Besides, Calor won't make pancakes after ten. He says it interferes with lunch preparations."

"Are my other two children going to grace my leave-taking with their presence?" Jarl asked mock solemnly.

Argen, who did not have much of a sense of humor, took his father's words at face value. "Lealor is with Gram Cibby, and Seren and Faf are off together somewhere. I'll be the only one here this morning."

"Argen, do you think you could hold one of the points of the star?" Andronan asked quietly.

"Me?" Argen's voice rose in a squeak of excitement.

"Are you sure this is safe for him to do, Andronan?"

"It's just to give balance to it. There should be no danger to him. Mirza was just about his age when she started working with the gate."

"Okay, then," Jarl said, hoping the old mage knew what he was talking about. Jarl was glad his children wore the bracelets. To him they made an extra margin of safety.

Nyct opened sleepy silver eyes and spoke mentally to Jarl. "Do not worry. While I am on guard, nothing truly evil can come to the child."

"Does Argen hear you speaking to me?" Jarl asked curiously.

"No. The reassurance was for your mind only."

"I just wondered. If Argen heard you call him a child, he'd probably be angry."

"I shall remember and call him—" Here Nyct obviously searched for a word.

"Try calling him youth or young man if you must," Jarl suggested.

"Thank you. I master your language slowly although I can read all the languages in the library," Nyct said, puzzled by the gap in his ability.

"Don't worry about it. Spoken language and written languages differ greatly. Your father, Wyrd, is probably a master at written communication, but he doesn't speak all the languages he reads. If you share his abilities, learning to speak the languages of the worlds will be something you must learn to do, in addition to Wyrd's talents."

During this time, Andronan had placed everyone but Jarl around the star. He motioned to Jarl to take his place which he did quickly.

The sun gilded the Courtyard of the Gate with mellow sunshine. The four robed figures stood like statues. Argen wore the robes of a novice Keeper while he was on Realm. Only Jarl wore pants. Somehow, in spite of the fact that this was the first time Argen had stood in a star, he looked more at home than Jarl did.

"You are all familiar with Achaea?" Andronan asked.

"Yes," they answered.

"Raise your arms, palms downward, and concentrate on that world."

They did so, and Jarl was astounded to see hazy gaps form in the lines of the star. He knew the star mosaic was solid. Suddenly, it was only a shell with so many gaps that Jarl would not have known it was a star if he hadn't seen it before.

"Drop your hands now!" Andronan commanded.

They did. Jarl looked at the faces around him. Guardy shook his head and muttered to himself. Vigilan's face was white with strain. Argen looked puzzled. One look at Andronan's face brought Jarl to his side. He helped the tottery old mage to a bench against the wall.

"What is it? What happened?" Jarl asked.

The others drew around. "The gate—the gate—the gate to Achaea. It's gone!"

"Then how is Dad going to rescue Mother and bring her home?" While the question was childlike, Argen's face had taken on the maturity he was not due to deserve for many years.

Guardy said, "Go get the healer. Have him bring a restorative."

"Yes, sir," Vigilan said, hurrying off on his errand, relieved to be able to do something.

Andronan sat quietly, taking deep breaths. He seemed normal, except for his talc-white features. Jarl sat down beside him and took one hand while Argen sat on the other side and leaned against his great-grandfather. Guardy stood before them, shaking his head. No one said anything for some time.

Jarl asked, "Is there no way we can reach Achaea?"

The healer bustled into the courtyard and went directly to Andronan. "So, my old friend," he said, "you are ill?"

"The gate to Achaea is inoperative," Jarl told him while he poured a small amount of golden powder into a vial and offered it to Andronan. The old mage took it silently. Color gradually returned to his face.

"Are you all right now?" the healer asked. "You must rest."

Andronan rose with the aid of Guardy and the healer. He left the courtyard without saying anything to Jarl and Argen.

"Now what do we do?" Argen asked, sure his father would have some plan of action.

Jarl put his arm around his son's shoulders before saying, "Son, I don't know." Jarl and Argen both jumped when they heard the loud "pop" which echoed in the courtyard.

"Uncle Jarl, Uncle Jarl!" young Faf panted. "My father will be here any minute. Don't let him turn me into a feather duster."

"What in the world—" Jarl began just before a second loud popping noise came from the courtyard. Argen drew his knees up on the bench to make more room and Jarl moved his legs until they hung over the side of the bench. The Court of the Gate filled with dragons. Faf was trying to get as close to Jarl as he could and Fafnoddle, his father, filled the rest of the area. In fact, it was such a tight squeeze that Fafnoddle's tail wrapped around a pillar and draped over the second floor balcony that ran around the courtyard.

Smoke poured from Fafnoddle's nostrils. He lifted his head so his friends didn't suffocate and tried to control his temper.

"Uncle Jarl, save me!" Faf screeched, almost crushing Jarl in an attempt to get as close as possible.

"Only on Realm," Jarl thought wearily to himself. "Over my head in dragons. How in the world am I to protect Faf from his father—especially since he's a full-grown dragon? And what is Fafnoddle so angry about?"

"First Egg, you are within a scale of being turned into a coralberry tartlet!" the irate Fafnoddle hissed.

"I'm not First Egg any more. That's a baby name. I'm Fafnir, like my grandfather! I'm not a baby any more."

"Don't you dare stamp you foot, Faf. It will crack the tile in the yard," Jarl warned, trying unsuccessfully to push Faf away so he could get a breath.

"Jarl, why are you calling this child by an adult name?"

"Well, he told me he had grown up. Just look at the size of him! You certainly can't go around calling anything that large an egg," Jarl explained.

"Oh, scales!" Fafnoddle shook his head. "I'm afraid it's all a misunderstanding. My son has to study the *Dragon Chronicles* and learn a great deal of dragon lore before any dragon will consider him even half-grown."

"I'm sorry if I contributed to the misunderstanding—"

"But, Father," the little dragon broke in, "I have a piece of gold for my hoard, too."

"What did I teach you about breaking into adult conversations? You apparently haven't learned about basic courtesy. Why can't you keep silent like Argen, here." Fafnoddle flicked his tongue in the boy's direction. "He probably knows more dragon lore than you do, too!" Here Fafnoddle raised his head to expel a cloud of smoke in his indignation.

"I'm afraid he does have a piece of gold, Fafnoddle," Jarl said. "If it makes any difference," Jarl drew a deep breath and added, "I gave it to him. It came from Earth."

"Well, I'm glad to hear he hasn't taken up lying, along with his disobedience. However, he is still mistaken. It is true he can select an adult name and that he must have gold to start his own hoard. If he had studied a little more diligently, he would have found out there is a test and ceremony he must pass through to make everything official. One piece of gold is a piddling amount to begin a hoard with, my son," Fafnoddle said, partially mollified by Jarl's explanation.

"Thank you, Father. Then I can use my grown-up name— Faf?"

"Well, perhaps not around your mother. What she will do if she ever hears of your behavior tarnishes my scales just to think of," Fafnoddle concluded.

"And it's permitted to add to my hoard?"

"Yes, I suppose so. A dragon can't have too much gold. I

suppose you and Seren will be adventuring all over Realm looking for hidden caches of gold," Fafnoddle grumbled. "Well, it may just keep you two out of more serious mischief. Remember, now—no stealing. This gold has to be unclaimed!"

Jarl didn't have to be in mental contact with Fafnoddle to know what he was thinking. All he needed was to have irate denizens of Realm showing up on his cavestep complaining about their missing gold.

"One other thing. You have to spend at least two hours a day studying. Dragon's honor." Fafnoddle solemnly scratched a large "X" on a chest scale with a claw.

"Oh, father—" the little dragon began.

"Oh, father me not!" Fafnoddle roared in a truly magnificent bellow. "Home! Now!" he commanded.

A "pop" and the courtyard was missing one small dragon.

"If I had known what a bother a family was, I might have stayed a bachelor," Fafnoddle said. "If it isn't one thing Ebony wants fixed around the cave, it's another. And First Egg would be Last Egg if I had my way. Only Ebony wants a big family. I do nothing except get the boy out of one scrape after another. When I really need to concentrate, I come here to the university to think. Andronan lets me use that big pool at the back of the grounds to soak my tail when I study." Fafnoddle looked at his friend. "Jarl, here my family has been fretting you and something's wrong. I can tell."

"You could say that," Argen put in. "The gatelink between here and Achaea is now broken. Dad doesn't know how to get Mother home."

The huge saurian raised his eyelids, turning them dinner-plate size. He asked Jarl mentally, "Is this true?"

Jarl nodded.

"Well, then Wyrd will have to take a hand," the dragon said.

"I'm afraid not," Jarl answered. "He seems to be sulking. When Lealor refused his bracelet, he really got—" Jarl paused, looking for an appropriate word.

"Ticked," Argen said helpfully.

"Perhaps not exactly," Nyct said to Argen mentally, "but

very disturbed. He is considering the Cosmic All and may stay like that for days."

"Whatever Wyrd feels, he is not communicating with me at present," Jarl said. "I need to get to Achaea, and the gate can't take me."

"I have been doing a little experimenting with the dragon ability to travel dimensionally. If you are sure of where you want to go, I'll attempt to take you there."

"Yes, I'll gladly accept your offer. Argen, tell Andronan that we have gone to Achaea. Tell him not to worry."

"Sure, Father," Argen said with a smile. He didn't let it fade from his face until he was hurrying down the hall to Andronan's room. Sometimes Argen thought he knew where his brother Seren got his tendency to follow through his hare-brained schemes without calm deliberation. Argen would have felt better about the trip if his father had taken time to put a safety spell on himself and the dragon. What if Achaeasun had exploded? Argen didn't have the slightest idea what happened to travelers who arrived at the place where a world had just disintegrated. Somehow, he didn't think his father had even considered that scenario. Maybe that's why Seren was so brave. He didn't have the brains to think about all the things that could go wrong.

Back in the courtyard Faf popped in. "Greeks had gold, didn't they?" he asked.

"Home!" his father's voice roared as again a small dragon form popped out.

CHAPTER THIRTEEN

Argen scuffed leaves with his feet. How could Andronan send him out to play? He had held a point of a star that morning, and this afternoon Andronan had sent him away like a child.

He couldn't even work in the library until the next day. Librisald had been adamant, too. All the adults had just ganged up on him, saying it was for his own good. He took the thick book out of his inner pocket. Thank the Bright Ones he had something to read. He looked around for a convenient log to sit on and became lost in the history of Realm.

Argen raised his head at the sound of hoofbeats. Who would be riding here in the woods, off the path?"

"Hello, young man," said Kiron when he noticed Argen seated on the log.

"Hello." Argen looked at him carefully. "You're a centaur, aren't you?"

"How well read you must be to recognize me." The boy's friendliness delighted Kiron. It would be easy to transport him to Achaea.

"My name's Argen. What's yours?" Argen asked, plucking a sprig of greenery and sticking it in his book to mark his place.

"I'm Kiron."

"What are you doing here?"

"My master sent me on an errand into this part of Realm. You know it well, don't you?"

"Pretty well, I guess. My brother Seren is the one who knows all about Realm. I like to read, but he's an adventurer."

"You mean you never have adventures?" Kiron sounded astounded.

"None to speak of. My brother doesn't sit still long enough to read anything. He likes to run and climb and fly around on Faf's back. I get a little airsick when I ride Faf. Besides, Faf is Seren's special friend. My special friend is Librisald."

"Is this Librisald a dragon, then?" Kiron asked.

"Only if he catches someone not taking care of the books in his library." Argen smiled at his joke. "Actually, Librisald is the old librarian at the university."

"Well, if he's an old scholar, he wouldn't make a very good person to have an adventure with. We centaurs, on the other hand, can climb, run, jump—" The centaur cocked his head to the side. "I've just had a marvelous idea. Why don't you come along with me to seek the cave I need to find?"

"I don't know if I have the time. They'll worry about me if I'm not back for dinner." Argen stood and thought.

"No wonder you never get to have any adventures. You spend so much time thinking, you never venture anywhere."

Argen frowned. Next he looked up into the centaur's face. "You know, you're right. I'll go and help you look."

"Fine!" replied the relieved centaur. "Our quest would go much faster if you would ride on my back. You have ridden horses, haven't you?"

Not for anything would Argen admit his experience consisted of pony rides around the ring at the local fair at home. He swallowed, and ignored the question. "How will I get on your back?"

"If I kneel down by the log over there, you can mount easily." Kiron suited his actions to the word and Argen climbed on.

Kiron walked carefully through the woods. He had no intention of breaking a leg in some burrow or other. His cautious movements also allowed Argen to get the feel of riding a tall mount. Kiron could tell the boy was a novice rider from the death grip the boy's legs kept on his body. The boy worked harder to stay on than Kiron did to keep moving.

"Say, Kiron, what exactly did your master send you to bring to him?"

"My master said I was to find a cave containing some old books he left there for safekeeping."

"Seren and Faf were talking about some caves north of Realmgate. They explored a couple, but they said there were too many to waste time looking in all of them."

"Oh, that's no problem. When I get close to the cave, this star I wear around my neck will start to shine. That's how I'll know I'm in the right place."

Nyct spoke in Argen's mind. "I do not like the star. Something tells me it is evil."

"I'm sorry, Nyct. I thought you were asleep. I'd better introduce you to Kiron," Argen mindspoke to his bracelet.

"No, it is better not. I will introduce myself when the time is right."

Kiron finally reached a road. "Hang on to my waist. Now I will really give you a ride." And with these words, Kiron began to trot with Argen struggling to stay upright, fighting the strange rhythm which put his bottom in position to slap into Kiron's back with every step. "Here is an easier pace, Argen, but it's faster." And Kiron began to gallop.

The wind blew in Argen's face. He thanked the Bright Ones that he had tucked the book securely inside his robe. He wasn't sure what Librisald would do to him if he damaged or lost it, and he didn't want to find out.

Kiron galloped tirelessly while Argen held on as if it were a matter of life or death.

"See that path to the left?" Argen called.

"Yes," the centaur answered.

"That path cuts around Realmgate and leads directly to the hills." Argen didn't want people to see him hanging on for dear life. Besides, someone was sure to stop him because it was almost time to eat. He deserved to have an adventure.

"Very well. Whatever you command," Kiron said, aware that it was a joke he couldn't share with the boy. It suited his purpose also to avoid the city. His master had sent him to Realm through a minigate, and he knew taking Argen with him would depend on his swiftness and his secrecy.

Kiron could feel the star warming against his chest. They were approaching the minigate.

"Kiron, after we find the books, will you have time to meet my brother and Faf?"

"Perhaps. Who knows? We may meet sooner than you think," the centaur answered, certain he would meet the boy's twin brother when they were imprisoned on Achaea.

"I'd sure like to show him he's not the only one who can meet new people and have adventures." He remembered that sometimes Faf and Seren had been in danger on their adventures. He asked cautiously, "Er, Kiron, there won't be any monsters or anything guarding these books, will there?"

Kiron could tell what his answer should be from the tension in his rider's body. "No. Of course not."

Argen relaxed. "At any rate, I've done something my brother's never done."

"What is that?"

"I've ridden a centaur. Why, Seren's never even met one."

"He's never met me," Kiron said. "In fact, if you're looking for records, I've never allowed a human to ride on my back before. Riding a centaur is a great honor. Several of us have been famed teachers, but we don't go giving rides to just anybody, you know."

"Would you do me a favor?"

"Depends on what it is."

"My little sister Lealor is a real nut about—" Here Argen paused. He knew better than to say animal to the centaur. "—rare creatures. If she sees you, I know she'd love to have a ride." Argen plunged on before Kiron could say no. "It wouldn't have to be a very long one. Just a walk up and down the road, you know. She's kind of little, but she's a real fast learner and I know she wouldn't be afraid."

"If I meet your little sister and it is possible, I'll give her a ride," Kiron promised.

The ground had been gradually ascending, and now the path became a rough track. It dawned on Argen that it must be hard for Kiron to keep carrying him up into the hills.

"Hey, I bet you're tired. Why don't you let me down and I'll climb for a bit?"

The centaur thought for a moment. They hadn't seen a soul

all afternoon. The boy could never outrun him. Back on
Achaea the centaurs played tag in the rocky mountains. If the
boy tried to run away, he would grab him and take him to the
gate. They must be very close because the star was almost too
warm to be comfortable. It wasn't very likely that anyone
would be able to stop him from abducting Argen now. He just
hoped Neso and Sylvor were doing half so well as he was.

"How thoughtful of you," Kiron said, stopping so Argen
could dismount.

"There are two caves just ahead," Argen said.

The centaur approached, but neither affected his star. "Neither is the right cave," he told the disappointed boy.

They continued their search.

The sun was an orange ball low in the sky before they
finally found an opening that caused the star to flicker.

Argen had been getting a bit worried. Soon night would
come, and how was he to get home? Andronan might ask for
him and would be concerned if he was not at the university.
Everyone expected Faf and Seren to be out late. Argen didn't
think it was fair, but very few things on Realm were large
enough or dangerous enough to bother a half-grown dragon.
With Faf to protect him, Seren had more freedom than Argen.
He, however, knew that everyone expected him to be safe in
the library in the evening.

"I'm sure glad we've found the right spot. I'd better be
starting for home pretty soon," Argen said.

Kiron threw up his head. "Why, you wouldn't want to leave
now, would you? You haven't seen the books that are in the
cave. I am to bring two books with me—I'm sure my master
wouldn't mind if you read the rest."

Books to read? And books that were not in the library?
Perhaps even some new ones that someone could copy and
add to the collection? Argen made his choice. Nothing would
stop him from seeing those books, even if he had to climb all
night.

"I'd really like that," Argen said. The centaur stood at the
mouth of the cave, urging Argen to climb up and enter.

"Stop, Jarl Koenig's son," Nyct said in Argen's mind.

Argen could tell what Nyct had to say was important because he called him Jarl Koenig's son. That sounded like some kind of official dragon pronouncement. "Stop what?" he asked, pausing a few feet from Kiron.

"Do not approach the centaur. He means to do evil to you."

"What makes you think that?" Argen puffed a little before taking another step upward.

"It is not what I think, but what I know."

"Argen," Kiron said, "are you coming or not? Do you want me to help you up?" Kiron held out his hand. It was inches away from Argen's if he held his out.

"Argen!" Nyct hissed imperatively.

The boy had never heard his dragon sound so—so dragonly.

"Do not take Kiron's hand. Look into my eyes. Look now!"

Kiron stepped down to come close enough to take the boy's hand. He was only seconds away from success. He saw the boy glance down at the bracelet he wore. The strange eyes of the creature seemed almost alive. And then Argen vanished.

————

CHAPTER FOURTEEN

Argen blinked his eyes. He was in Cibby's cabin. And Seren stood there in front of him, looking bewildered.

"Nyct, what happened?" Argen was still recovering from his dizzy spell and spoke aloud.

"I'll tell you what almost happened," Seren broke in. "You almost got yourself transported off Realm by an agent of the Shadowlord."

"Oh, coralberries! You have to be out of your mind. I just

met this centaur named Kiron today. We were having an adventure. He had to retrieve some books from a cave north of Realmgate and I was helping him."

"You certainly were!"

"Yes, I was! And why not? Do you think only you and Faf deserve to have adventures? I had Nyct with me. I wasn't in any danger. You've got to stop acting like I'm a baby. I'm only five minutes younger than you are, anyway. That doesn't give you the right to boss me around and treat me as if—"

Seren pushed his brother into Cibby's rocking chair. "Just listen a minute, that's all I ask."

"That's all I've been doing since I got here." Argen rocked angrily back and forth while Seren looked at him silently.

Seren knew his brother was stubborn. There was no use trying to reason with him until he calmed down. So Argen rocked and Seren waited.

"Come to think of it, how did I get here?"

Seren relaxed. Everything would be all right. Argen was thinking again. He wasn't so bad—for a brother—and he was really smart when he wasn't being dragonheaded. The only creature Seren knew that was harder to reason with was Faf. After one of their disagreements, Faf's father told Seren to be patient with his son. In spite of his size, Faf was really a very young dragon. Seren said "yes sir" respectfully. You didn't argue with anything that weighed over a ton and breathed fire. Still, Seren noted that Faf's granddragon, old Fafnir, acted a lot like young Faf. After that, Seren went to great lengths to make sure nothing got wedged in Faf's mind that required changing later. He'd have to remember to treat his brother the same way. They were getting too old to settle everything as they had when they were younger—in a fight.

Soladon spoke. "Brother, have I your leave to tell Argen what we found out?"

"Yes," Nyct answered.

Both Argen and Seren heard the exchange. It was a mark of the difference in their characters that Argen thought the courtesy was nice and Seren thought it was rather overdone.

"I will mindspeak, for my voice is weak in this form."

It occurred to Seren to wonder what other form Soladon

possessed, but the thought vanished when the dragon bracelet continued.

"The wyverns used their scrystone to understand the situation we have here. Someone wants to abduct you two humans and transport you to another world. The wyverns say they are certain this person is the one your parents call the Shadowlord. Magic spells barred the Shadowlord from ever returning to Realm, but the spell casters did not think to bar his agents from this world. Therefore, Kiron and Sylvor entered Realm. Because these two creatures are like those in the mythology of Earth's Greece, the wyverns think the destination planned for you two is Achaea, the world from which the ancient gods came to civilize the Greeks of Earth."

"Wait a minute, Soladon." Argen leaned forward in the rocking chair. "If someone tried to kidnap us, maybe they are also trying to capture Lealor."

"I never thought of that!" Seren said, jumping up from the bench and striding to the door.

"Hold it," Argen advised. "Let's use our heads before we rush off in six directions."

"That is wise," Soladon commended.

"Do you two know anything more than what you have told Seren and me?" Argen naturally took command.

"There should be no reason to worry. The wyverns are great mistresses of magic. They have placed a spell that will keep all three of you Koenig sibs on Realm unless you wish to go to another world," Nyct said.

"Oh, then I guess I worried over nothing." Seren returned to his seat on the bench.

"Perhaps not, brother," Argen said. "Is there any way to get in touch with Lealor's bracelet? You know what an animal lover she is. If we were attracted to a satyr and a centaur, maybe some strange beast will entice her. I was willing to go with Kiron until Nyct zapped me here." Argen shot a private thought to his bracelet. "Thanks, Nyct."

"Appreciation acknowledged," Nyct replied to Argen alone.

"Our sister has been forbidden to speak. I do not think she will respond unless there is dire danger to her small charge."

"Isn't there anything you can do?" Seren stood again.

"We will search for her thoughts, but there are many who think in Realmforest. I will alert the wyverns as well. Being female they may have a greater affinity for her thoughts than we do."

Seren agreed with the sentiment, but Argen, really thinking now, noticed that although they were four males, they were hoping that a group of females could help them with their problem.

Lealor was deep in the twilit forest. She carried a whole fistful of moley in her hand. She sat very still under a tree. She hoped that the unicorn she tracked for most of the afternoon would finally decide to trust her and come to make friends. The beautiful white beast took dainty and hesitant steps toward Lealor at last. Lealor was glad. Her arm felt ready to drop off. She knew that if she moved it a fraction, the unicorn would probably run away. She was certain that once the unicorn ate the moley she could persuade it to give her a ride.

The unicorn advanced. Only a few feet separated it from the girl. Its delicate nostrils quivered, catching the moley scent. The wild unicorns loved moley above all other plants. Lealor had tried before without success to tame a unicorn. She almost always carried some dried moley in her pocket, but this time she was having wonderful luck with the fresh green leaves. She also had a half pocketful of moley seeds. When she saw a promising patch of ground, she planted a few seeds. Her dryad friends gave her the idea. They promised to tell the unicorns who was responsible. Lealor loved unicorns best of all the creatures on Realm.

The pure white coat of the unicorn stood out in the dimming twilight. Lealor hoped Cibby wouldn't worry. Cibby knew Lealor could understand the animals and was safe in the Realmforest. Also, Lealor had the protection of Myst, the dragon bracelet given by Wyrd.

The unicorn looked at Lealor out of its wise eyes. Lealor watched the beautiful animal. She could tell it was going to eat out of her hand. Another two steps would bring the magical beast close enough to eat. Lealor held herself stone-still.

Suddenly the unicorn raised its head and shied away. It

looked to the left, whirled, and trotted away into the uncertain light of the early evening.

To say Lealor was vexed would be an understatement. She jammed the moley into her pocket. Then she blew her long bangs out of her eyes. She wiped her moley-stained hand on her apron, knowing a small spell would remove the marks later. Now whatever caused the unicorn to go away was going to be sorry! It was probably one of the boys sent to look for her.

Brothers were a constant bother and older brothers were the worst. They thought they knew everything. Someday she planned to turn them into toads. Not permanently, of course. She knew her parents wouldn't like that. She had already turned a small pebble into a butterfly, but she couldn't turn it back. She felt embarrassed that she had to get Cibby to help. The older witch had given her a good lecture on not working magic until she was sure she had mastered the entire spell, both change and return. Lealor knew Cibby wouldn't tell on her. How her brothers would laugh if they knew about some of her mistakes. Witchcraft was like anything else. You had to practice. She didn't want anyone but Cibby to know all the things she could do. She was afraid her father would forbid her to practice—and then how could she ever become a witch like Cibby?

Lealor's ears were not as keen as the unicorn's, but now she heard something approaching. She looked into the trees and saw a sphinx silvered by the moonlight. Lealor was not a bit frightened. The sphinx delighted her. She knew there were many unicorns on Realm, but she had never heard of a live sphinx. Neither of her brothers had seen one, either. Of that she was sure, because they would have told her all about it if they had.

Neso spoke softly so as not to frighten her quarry. "Hello."

Lealor looked at Neso, who padded closer, wings furled to look as small as possible. "I'm Lealor. What's your name?"

"My name is Neso. I am a sphinx."

"Yes, I know that. I've seen pictures of wonderful creatures like you in storybooks. I didn't know there were any of your kind here on Realm. Do you live in the desert?"

"Not exactly. I do live far away from here, though," Neso

told the girl. She crouched down next to her. "What are you doing here in the forest at night? Don't your parents worry about you?"

"I should be going home now," Lealor admitted. "I'm staying with my great-grandmother. She has a cottage over there." Lealor waved a hand in the general direction of Cibby's home.

"I'm on a quest," Neso told her. "Somewhere very close to here lies the magical casket that Snow White slept in. I have a magic talisman to help me find it. Wouldn't you like to help me?"

"It's funny that I haven't discovered it already. I've gone in these woods many times," Lealor said, frowning.

Myst tightened on her arm to warn her, but Lealor didn't pay any attention. Since Myst didn't speak, Lealor often forgot all about her dragon bracelet.

"Oh," Neso said, thinking fast, "you couldn't find it unless you had my magic talisman. See?" And Neso allowed a claw to flick the star that she wore around her neck on a chain.

"How does it work? My—" Lealor broke off. Myst was so tight her wrist hurt. She guessed the little dragon didn't want her to mention their relationship. After all, not being able to speak was pretty terrible. No wonder people said that a being that could not talk was dumb.

Neso almost purred her satisfaction. Imagine! The child was asking the very question Neso wanted to answer. It was going to be easy to trick the child into the magic box her master had fashioned to look like the glass-lidded casket in the fairy tale. Neso, of course, had not known the tale, but her master assured her that little children on Realm all knew the story.

"If you would help me find it, I would let you try it if you were brave enough."

"I'm very brave," Lealor said matter-of-factly. "My brother Seren rides dragons and Argen, my other brother, knows everything in the library at Realmgate. I'm friends with all the animals in Realmforest."

Neso looked around her warily. If the child had so many friends, perhaps it might be well to lead her to the minigate immediately. "Will you help me?" she asked.

Neso impressed Lealor. She wanted to aid the sphinx. "Yes, I'll help. I just hope it won't take very long."

The catlike creature turned and paced off in the direction of the minigate. Within a few minutes her direction finder, the star, began to glow. "See," she told Lealor, who hurried to keep up with her, "we are getting very close."

Lealor was so intrigued by Neso, she paid no attention to Myst, who was feeling very agitated indeed. She wouldn't even look at her bracelet, so Myst could not transport her to safety. The glow of the star mesmerized her.

"Aha!" Neso said triumphantly. "Here it is!"

The disguised minigate rested in a forest glade bathed in soft moonlight.

Lealor approached the glass-topped casket with awe. "Are you sure this was Snow White's?"

"Why would I lie? Doesn't it look just like the one in your storybook?" Her master has assured her it did.

"Yes, it does. Will you open it? Please?"

"I'd be glad to," Neso said. She opened the casket and boosted Lealor, who was too short to climb in the high box by herself.

Lealor stretched out on the satin bed within. "My, I feel just like Snow White. Do you suppose if I stayed here long enough a prince would come for me, too?"

Myst's senses were so alert to danger she actually hissed aloud. It was this sound that drew Soladon and Nyct's attention to their sister's predicament. They saw the danger instantly.

"Make her look at you!" Soladon advised.

Myst gave a frustrated hiss. Didn't they realize she had tried that already?

"Use your eyes to transport her to Cibby's cottage!" Nyct commanded.

It was too late. With a lightning move of her paw, Neso snapped the lid of the box closed. The star at her throat exploded with light. Neso, box, and Lealor vanished, leaving only silver moonlight in the abandoned glade.

CHAPTER
FIFTEEN

Jarl looked around him in surprise. Fafnoddle and he stood on a great plain. The Courtyard of the Gate had vanished. A bright yellow sun bit the dried grasses that struggled to survive in the dusty soil.

"Good heavens, Faf, that was fast! I didn't feel anything."

"I should hope not. I've been studying for some time. I have improved since those first few desperate trips we took together."

"Will you be able to stay with me or will you have to return?" Jarl rather enjoyed having Faf with him again. This world looked tame enough, but Jarl had experience with magical places before and he knew that innocent surroundings might well hide dire dangers. With Wyrd still communing with his Cosmic All or whatever, Jarl liked the idea of a fierce, magical friend's company—just in case. Wyrd's present behavior reminded Jarl of his children when they were sulking, which was rare.

"I'll stay around for a while, at least," Faf said. "They should be able to manage without me at home. First Egg will be studying, and Ebony is perfectly capable of taking care of our cave and the egg." He delicately scratched his back with the end of his tail. "You know, this is like old times! It's been far too long since we've had an adventure together, old friend."

Jarl nodded his agreement even while he smiled at the

thought of being called "old friend" by a dragon who was over a thousand Earth years of age himself.

"Which way shall we go?" Faf asked.

"I have no preference, but those mountains in the distance look promising," Jarl answered, settling his pack on his shoulders.

"Shall we walk, or would you like to fly?"

"Why don't you do a short reconnaissance flight to help us get our bearings? I'll start north. You'll be able to find me easily enough. This grass is only about six inches tall."

"Very well," Faf thought in Jarl's general direction, as he unfurled his wings and let the breeze raise him.

Jarl watched his saurian sidekick float upward as if he weighed nothing at all. It was a wonder what magic could do. Jarl had felt the solidity of his friend. There was no way a nonmagical creature that large could ever get airborne, yet Faf flew as easily as any bird Jarl had seen. One thing Jarl had learned from his magical encounters—if it works, don't try to figure out which laws of physics are being broken. That was a sure way to get mental indigestion.

He remembered trying to understand how his wife shape-shifted. She had to have control of the molecules of her body somehow. There were billions or zillions, for all he knew. When he asked her how she shifted, she said, "It's easy. All I have to do is think what I want to look like and my body takes that shape. Anyone should be able to do it." When he told her she had to be able to explain her ability better than that, she answered, "Tell me exactly how you lift your arm." Jarl thought a moment, then said, "Let's just forget the whole thing, okay?" That was the last time he had tried to really understand magic. Sometimes he could will impossible things to happen, and if they did, well and good. He comforted himself with the thought that a person didn't have to understand a car's engine to drive, either.

Fafnoddle made a lazy circle above him, then landed directly in front of him. Jarl looked into the dragon's dinner-plate-sized eye, for Faf lowered his head to talk to his human companion. "Well, there's a slit place ahead in those mountains that looks as if it goes clear through to the other side of this world. I'm a little large to fit it, but you could enter it easily. This whole place reeks of magic, by the way."

Pop!

"What was that?" Jarl asked, whirling.

"First Egg!" The look on Fafnoddle's face was one Jarl had never seen before. The dragon's bottom jaw dropped until it hit the ground with a thud. Jarl mentally noted that a dragon's jaw was like a snake's. That explained why some dragons were reputed to eat whole elephants in one gulp.

"As I asked before, Greeks used to have lots of gold, didn't they?"

"What has that got to do with your appearance here?" Fafnoddle said in parental stern mode. Jarl understood his feelings. He could almost here Fafnoddle reciting to himself, "Stay calm."

"Well, there I was, studying my scales off for hours—"

"Hours!" Fafnoddle roared. "Thirty minutes haven't passed yet!"

Jarl could tell his friend was steaming—literally. He moved to the side to be out of possible parboiling range. In moments of stress there was always a chance Fafnoddle might forget that Jarl was a human and didn't have any fire-resistant scales to protect his tender hide. Jarl, however, had reckoned without considering he was the little dragon's godfather, and as such, considered a protector by Young Faf. Somehow he had managed to insinuate Jarl between him and his irate father. Jarl wondered if Wyrd would protect him from incineration, because Fafnoddle was almost bursting with rage.

At the last possible moment, when Jarl contemplated finding out first hand how charbroiled steak felt, Fafnoddle raised his head and emitted a truly impressive sheet of red hot flame.

Jarl thought he heard Young Faf breathe an awed "Wow!" but he couldn't be certain.

"I'm going to warm some scales around here if you don't go home this instant!"

The little dragon's "Yes sir," was followed by the popping sound that Jarl was beginning to associate with Young Faf's precipitate arrivals and departures. He was almost certain he heard a thought as well— "Adults get to have all the fun."

Fafnoddle let off a few more brief flares into the air.

"Didn't want to start a fire in all this grass," he commented. "Look, Jarl, much as I'd like to stay, I'd better go home and keep an eye on First Egg. He'll probably have a mountain of gold stored before he's learned enough of the dragon history and law required for recognition as an adult. It's getting so it's not safe to take your eyes off him. Now that he's learned basic travel he'll be even worse. I despair of keeping him at his books." Faf gave Jarl an apologetic look.

"I understand, Faf. Remember, I'm a father, too."

"Yes, and you have *three* children." Faf gave a delicate shudder. "Sorry. Good luck." Faf disappeared silently.

Yes, Faf certainly had been practicing. As huge as he was, not even the smallest sound occurred to mark his transition to Realm.

When Jarl heard the slight pop from behind him, he didn't even turn around. Oh, no! he thought to himself.

"Say, Uncle Jarl, you don't need a little help finding Auntie Mirza, do you?" Young Faf stuck his neck over Jarl's shoulder, which brought "uncle" and "nephew" nose to nose. Jarl noticed that Faf had taken time to grab a few kippers for a snack. Jarl abominated kippers second hand. Partially digested fish smelled almost obscene.

Trying not to inhale, Jarl mouthed, "Your father just went home to help you study."

"Oops! Guess you'll have to do without my help." And Young Faf disappeared almost as soundlessly as his father.

Jarl stood alone on the vast plain. Achaea resembled the Greece that Jarl had visited once on Earth. The bright blue sky and clear air made distant objects like the mountains seem closer. Jarl remembered that no place in Greece was more than fifty miles from the sea. He decided he would look when he got higher in the mountains. He believed it was the same here. He began his lonely walk toward the northern mountains.

He made good time, and by nightfall was in the foothills. He made a fire, ate, and slept. So far Wyrd showed no signs of life; however, Jarl felt relatively secure. The night passed uneventfully. The next morning, he continued his climb. It wasn't until noon that he discovered the slit in the mountains that Fafnoddle had seen the previous day.

It didn't look very promising, but the landscape appeared deserted, so Jarl felt he had no choice. It was almost as if he was compelled to continue. Something about the slit made him feel uneasy, but he had Wyrd, so he decided to enter. After all, if he made a mistake, he could simply turn around and walk out.

The path into the slit seemed worn to the point of feeling smooth, as if many footsteps had passed that way before Jarl. The walls of the place were rough, as if riven from the rock. On Earth, Jarl would have thought the rock formation resulted from an earthquake, but on Achaea, he supposed the natives would say the thunderbolt of Zeus, Ruler of the Gods, had caused the giant crack.

The bright sun no longer shone on his shoulders. He welcomed the cool feel of the shade in the cleft. He took several steps into the natural passage before deciding he did not want to continue. He turned to retrace his steps, and he found the sunny opening filled with the largest dog he had ever seen. Usually Jarl liked dogs, but this one set the hair on the back of his neck straight up. The huge beast had three heads.

"There, there, fellow," Jarl said in his most disarming fashion. "Move aside like a good boy."

The dog looked at Jarl with all six eyes and stood, rocklike, blocking the opening.

All of a sudden the sunlight that Jarl had been so glad to get out of seemed very attractive. He approached the dog. While the animal made no threatening movements toward him, it didn't move out of his way, either. Jarl patted one of the heads and tried leading the dog to the side, but he couldn't budge the gigantic canine.

"How about a little scratch behind the ears, mortal," the dog said.

Jarl looked at the beast in surprise. "You speak?" He scratched the indicated place.

"Why not?" the dog said. "You won't be leaving here any time soon, so who's to hear about it?"

"I don't think he knows who we are," the second head said, nudging Jarl with his nose so Jarl would scratch him behind the ears as well.

"Perhaps we should introduce ourself," the third head said.

Jarl reached over to scratch the animal's third head. It couldn't hurt to try to keep on the beast's good side. Perhaps if he were friendly, he could get it to move aside.

"We're not here to make friends with the dead, you know," the first head said.

"You're not going to tell Hades we talked to you—are you?" The second head made a soundless snarl. The sharp white teeth impressed Jarl mightily.

"Of course not. Do I look like the kind of person to do that?" Jarl told the head he was scratching.

"He can't tell Hades about us. He doesn't know our name," the first head said.

"Ignorant one," the third head turned to look at the first, "we are famed throughout the land. All mortals know Cerberus, the Guardian of the Gates of the Land of the Dead."

Jarl agreed with the third head. If he had seen the dog before entering the slit, he would have realized he had arrived at the Land of the Dead. Cerberus had been a monster in several movies, but none of the copies came close to the real thing. Jarl swallowed.

"Ah, pleasant as this scratching is, we can see you must be thirsty. Travel down this path only a short way and you will come to an icy brook of clear water. Someone created it to satisfy the thirst of mortals." The first head smiled wolfishly. The sight of all those teeth did little to reassure Jarl.

"Indeed, waste of water," the second head added.

"We tell you this because you are the first mortal to scratch our ears in such a long time," the third head told Jarl.

"I'm not nearly as thirsty as I am anxious to get out of here. How about letting me pass back into the light?" Jarl asked.

All three heads growled. "Not allowed. Pass on."

Jarl had no way to compel Cerberus to allow him to return to the Land of the Living. He remembered enough mythology to know getting out would take permission from the King of the Dead himself.

Jarl noted that as he stepped deeper into the Kingdom of the Dead the path became ever broader. Smooth, seamless, it wound ever deeper. By the time Jarl came to the brook, he really was thirsty. He knelt, prepared to slake his thirst. Wyrd tightened on his arm. Jarl looked around him. Where was the threat? He saw nothing and bent for the second time to drink, lowering his cupped hands into the icy water.

This time Wyrd hissed, "No!"

"I'm thirsty," Jarl complained. "Why not drink?"

"No wonder Rory calls you a lackwit mortal fool in his anger," Wyrd told Jarl mentally. "Do you not know of the waters of Lethe?"

"Lethe?" Jarl repeated, cursing himself as he did it. He really tried to break the habit of repeating a word when he didn't understand.

"Those who drink these waters forget everything. The piteous dead of Achaea do not spend eternity remembering their lives."

Jarl lost all desire for a drink. He let the water trickle through his fingers and wiped his hands on his pants, jumped over the stream and continued to follow the path.

Now it began to wind about, and Jarl felt lost. It was almost a relief to come to the river. On the far side he could see a boat poled by a shrouded figure.

"Who's that?" he asked Wyrd.

"Charon, the Ferryman of the Dead. This is the River Styx. Charon will take you over."

Jarl hailed the boatman, who turned to look at him. A shiver ran down Jarl's back. Charon was a skeleton. Jarl watched the thin figure manipulate the pole as he brought his craft around. Once pointed at the bank where Jarl waited, the boat moved smoothly through the water without any movement on Charon's part.

"Ho, mortal, where are your pennies?"

"My pennies?" Jarl was at a loss. Pennies? He practically never carried any. What could you buy for pennies in this day and age?

Charon extended his skeletal hand, palm up. "Your fare, mortal."

Then Jarl remembered. The dead had two pennies placed over their eyes. It was to pay for the ride into the actual Land of the Dead. Jarl fished in his pocket. He found the first penny easily, but he had no other. He dropped it into Charon's hand.

"And where is the other?"

"I don't have another," Jarl told the ferryman. "I'm sorry."

"This is most irregular. I don't make a practice of hauling people around for half fare, you know. It is hard enough to make a living in such a dead-end job." Charon heh-hehed at his macabre witticism.

"What do you suggest I do now?"

"You could wait until someone comes along with an extra penny," Charon suggested, not very helpfully.

"That would take too long. Could you take a dime or a quarter? They're worth more than a penny."

"This first copper you gave me is debased metal. I'm already being generous. No penny, no boat ride."

Jarl watched as the current began to pull the boat farther from the bank where he stood. He found himself trapped between Charon and Cerberus. How was he going to produce another penny? Then he remembered the magic provender bag Cibby had sent. It was still in his pack. The spell she put on it made it produce food at the request of the owner. Would it produce a penny? Jarl knew it was dangerous to use magic on Achaea, but he hoped magicking a little food and a penny would be forgiven.

"Well, here goes," he said to himself, as he reached inside. The bag seemed empty. In frustration, Jarl tipped it upside down and shook it. He thought *penny* as hard as he could. The bag obligingly dropped a thin copper piece onto the rocky bank.

"Charon, I have the other penny."

The boat returned to the shore. Charon held out his hand which still held the first coin Jarl had given him. When the second penny joined the first, Charon nodded his acceptance and Jarl entered the boat. On reaching the other side, Jarl stepped from the craft and looked at the boatman. "Where do I go now?" he asked.

Charon waved a bony hand in an all-inclusive sweep up and down the bank.

"I need to find the King of the Dead next," Jarl explained.

"No need to hurry," Charon's dry voice whispered. "You have eternity, you know."

Jarl stared at Charon as an awesome thought occurred to him. What if the boatman was right, and Hades, King of the Dead, would not release him?

CHAPTER
SIXTEEN

Jarl turned abruptly and began walking along the path that had been behind him. As he passed, he noticed that the dim blue light in the long corridors had no source. It simply existed. He felt soft whispers like the rustling of leaves as he passed. There were others traveling the same path, but they seemed as insubstantial as the almost understandable voices that existed just out of Jarl's range of hearing. Even when Jarl looked directly at one of the shades, it remained shadowy and indistinct. Jarl wondered if some quality of the blue light made his eyes useless for distinct vision. As he considered the problem, he realized that he was the only living person in the corridor. The shadowy people led half-lives, and only by drinking the waters of Lethe could he join them in whatever kind of existence was possible here in Hades' dread kingdom. He shivered. No wonder they were called the piteous dead.

The indistinct, whispery voices grew in number until he realized he must be approaching a place of some importance. When he turned the next corner, he saw the vast Hall of the Dead where Hades and his queen, Persephone, held audience.

The dim blue light which permeated the corridors grew somewhat brighter here. The grey and blue exasperated Jarl.

When he looked at the two thrones centered against the far wall, he saw a beautiful woman seated alone. Her pale hand beckoned him closer.

"Who are you, mortal, who dares to invade the Kingdom of the Dead without permission of its royal master?"

"I am Jarl Koenig. I seek my wife, Mirza."

"Mirza? There is no shade present here who bears that strange name."

"Actually, Your Highness, I came for information. I thought that perhaps here, in your kingdom, I might find it."

"If this Mirza is not here, how would you expect me to know where she is? I have not been with my mother for some months. She is free as I am not. Oh, to return to the Land of the Living!"

Jarl heartily agreed with that sentiment. "Perhaps your husband might be able to send me to a place where I could find out."

"I doubt that. The last time he tried to help a mortal it turned out badly. Orpheus played so beautifully, too."

"I need the information as soon as possible. My wife is being held captive."

"How exciting! A hero on a quest for his wife. So many interesting things happen on the surface. Here it's just boring, boring. boring." An almost imperceptible pout marred the perfection of her features.

"Don't you get to spend some time on the surface?" Jarl asked.

"Well, yes. You see, I was abducted by my dread Lord Hades when I was just a young girl." Her eyes widened as she remembered. "I was terrified. When Hermes came to tell Hades he had to release me, Hades offered me a pomegranate seed. Like a fool, I ate it. Hades said I had to spend half the year with him because I ate here in his kingdom."

"Your mother must miss you when you are not on the surface."

"Yes, she mourns for me. The humans call her time of mourning winter. She was so clever to think of a way to free me. And then I ate that seed and spoiled it. She spoke quite sharply to me about it. I can still recall what she said to me after all these centuries." A sad smile passed over Persephone's face.

"I'm sorry that you are so unhappy here, but—"

"Please don't think that! I've grown quite fond of Hades. He'd do anything for me. It's not every girl who gets chosen by a god, you know. When I get tired of bathing, and trying on my new dresses and combing my hair, Hades allows me to pick somebody and he causes them to remember about when they were alive. I've heard many interesting stories."

"Isn't that kind of cruel? I mean, to make people remember their lives—" Jarl shivered. Personally, he thought it was a gruesome idea.

"After they've told their tales, Hades makes them forget. He's really very thoughtful. If I ask to have someone remember a second time, they don't even know they've talked to me before."

Jarl thought Persephone was still very young, as goddesses go. The centuries seemed to sit lightly on her. While she looked beautiful, she was obviously not an intellectual. He wondered if Hades considered this before he kidnapped her. To live eternally—even for only six months a year—with someone without Mirza's quick wit and keen intellect would have been hell, no matter what the Achaeans called it, in Jarl's estimation. Where was Hades, anyway?

"How long will it be before your husband returns here to this chamber?" Jarl asked Persephone, who was looking in a small polished hand mirror that she had attached by a ribbon to her waist.

"He won't return here," she began, then stopped speaking to gather her hair to one side and gaze into her mirror again.

"He's not coming here for some time?" Jarl questioned, aghast. How was he to contact the god if he did not return to his kingdom for years? Jarl had forgotten that to an immortal, time meant nothing. After all, gods had forever to get things done.

"What a silly question," Persephone said. "To get him to return all I need to do is call him."

"Will you please call him now?" Jarl was fast tiring of Persephone's company. Maybe that was why Hades made himself scarce, he mused.

"Do I look all right?" Persephone peered anxiously into her mirror. "I always try to look my best, you know. Mother said even if I had to live down here, it was important not to let myself go. In just a few more months, it will be spring and I can return to the surface."

"Yes," Jarl assured her. "Could you call him now?"

"Oh, very well. I don't see what all the hurry is for. After all, you'll be here forever."

Jarl fervently hoped Persephone was wrong. He listened as her sweet voice called for her husband. Within seconds a chill wind blew through the hall. Hades had arrived. He strode to the front of the room and sat upon his throne. He did not seem to notice Jarl.

"Did you call, my dear?" Hades asked, smiling at his wife.

Jarl went unnoticed as Persephone gazed deep into her husband's eyes. Jarl couldn't really blame her. The marble perfection of the god's skin and his handsome features compelled attention. His curly dark hair and beard reminded Jarl of the handsome Greek young man he had seen on his trip to their country. Perhaps there was more of an immortal admixture in the Greek population than anyone admitted. Hades' short chiton bared his knees, which were perfectly formed. Any artist would have loved having him for a model. The Lord of the Dead possessed the same imposing looks as the old ruined statues of the gods of Greece on Earth.

Persephone finally remembered to speak. "Yes, I summoned you. We have here an unusual case. A mortal has come to visit."

Hades' penetrating eyes fastened on Jarl. "A mortal, hmmm?"

Jarl nodded. He seemed to have lost his voice somewhere.

Hades returned Jarl's nod and smiled, which relieved Jarl greatly. Hades was one person he didn't want to annoy.

"Well, mortal, do you have a name?"

The rich tones of Hades' voice soothed Jarl. "Yes, sire. I do. My name is Jarl Koenig."

"Isn't that an odd name, dear?" Persephone interjected, as if Jarl had no feelings at all. Perhaps she forgot that ordinary people would feel insulted. It would make no difference to the remembering dead. Jarl thought that hearing of the lives of the dead must be like television was back home. Many people said things to the set that they wouldn't repeat to the actor's or umpire's face. He'd done it himself.

"It is not an odd name on Earth, his world of birth," Hades explained patiently.

"Yes, I do come from Earth. I am seeking news of my wife, Mirza."

"Did she get her funny name from Earth, too?" Persephone asked like a little child.

"Originally it was the name of a star visible from Earth," Hades told her.

Hades' answer surprised Jarl. He had not known that fact himself. Evidently the gods were as knowledgeable as they were reported to be.

"Now, tell us your tale, for it will amuse my wife," Hades commanded.

Jarl did not like being in a position where Hades could order him around so cavalierly, but he appreciated that in his position he had little choice. For one thing, if he was ever to leave the Kingdom of the Dead, it would be with Hades' approval.

"I have come from Realm, the home of the Keepers." Hades nodded, gratifying Jarl. Clearly the god knew of the gate system. "My wife was investigating a rogue gate that someone is creating here on Achaea."

"Are you certain, mortal?"

"Yes. You might not have noticed here beneath the earth, but Achaeasun is not behaving normally."

"What difference does that make to us? I don't get to go to the surface for months yet."

Hades seemed to be thinking. He ignored his wife's statement. He muttered, "The Bright One."

"The Bright One does not seem permanently harmed. When my wife arrived, she did something to hinder the rogue gate."

"What god dares tamper with the gate? Notify Father Zeus at once!"

"Sorry, but I believe the person creating the gate is not a god."

"Punish the *hubris* of this mortal immediately." The words of Hades chilled Jarl. Mirza had certainly placed herself in the middle of a class-one mess this time. Would the gods of Achaea think that mortals who tried to stop the tampering were also guilty of overweening pride? If Jarl recalled correctly, hubris, which was just a fancy name for what Cibby called "getting too big for your britches," was the only thing mortals could do to really bring the gods down on them with a vengeance.

Persephone noticed the change in Hades' mood, too. She fanned herself with her mirror and paid no attention to the disarray it caused her hair.

Jarl didn't really want to call any attention to himself, but he needed to get out of the Kingdom of the Dead. Hades might just hare off to Olympus or wherever the gods on Achaea stayed, and then he would find himself locked up for the duration.

"My wife and I saved the Bright One in Realmsun," Jarl said with an almost unnoticeable quiver on the last word.

"Mortals did such alone?"

"Not alone," Jarl was glad to say. He didn't like the look on Hades' face.

"I aided," Wyrd said, just as Jarl prepared to turn into a shade himself.

Hades peered at the dragon bracelet. "Is that you, old friend?"

The chilly atmosphere warmed perceptibly. Jarl could tell because the sweat running down his back felt less like ice water.

"Yes. This mortal is under my direction. It is his task to stop the transgressor." Wyrd's thoughts filled everyone's minds.

"In what way can I aid you?"

"The mortal must be reunited with his wife. Can you assist him in this?"

Hades replied, "Such a trifle! Is that all you ask? Done—" and the King of the dead began to wave his hand.

"Oh, dear, and he was just coming to the interesting part," Persephone said. "You'll send him off, and I never will find out what happens."

"Perhaps I was making it too easy for him," Hades said, dropping his hand while he thought. "I know. I will give you a sword and shield. Whoever heard of a hero without weapons? And Wyrd, you must promise to let him do everything—until the actual confrontation, that is—by himself."

"Agreed," Wyrd intoned in his dragonlaw voice.

"I want to help, too," Persephone said. "I'll send his wife a box of my famous beauty salve. She'll probably have frown lines from her captivity." Persephone waved her hand and a box appeared. She offered it to Jarl.

Jarl stepped forward awkwardly to take her gift. He held a sword in one hand and a shield in the other. Which one dared he drop to take the box? Either choice could bring down retribution. Would Hades think he preferred the box to the weapon he dropped? On the other hand, what if he didn't take the box? Would Hades feel offended, believing his wife slighted by a mere mortal? "Wyrd!" Jarl thought adamantly. A soft snore was his only answer. The dragon really meant it when he said he would not help Jarl. Jarl felt frustrated. What business had a mortal mixed in with the touchy gods of Achaea? His hesitation amused Persephone.

"Here, mortal," she said, rising graciously to place the box in his shirt pocket and button the flap. "What odd clothes you do wear." She shook her head. "Do not feel bad, though. You look ever so much more normal than you did when you arrived. The sword and shield are very becoming."

"Are you quite finished?" Hades asked abruptly.

"Don't be jealous of an ordinary mortal," Persephone laughed, a silvery tinkle on the icy air.

Jarl's blood pressure dropped and he felt like hypothermia had set in. Was Hades the jealous type? Surely not, Jarl hoped.

"Oh, my dear," Persephone chuckled, "if you could only see the look on your face. This has been a most diverting experience. Now it's over," she said, her merriment disappearing.

Noting her sad look, Hades said, "Would you like to be able to watch what happens to Jarl and his wife?"

Persephone clapped her hands. "Oh, could I?"

"Surely. Mortal, kiss her mirror."

Jarl felt relief that the command wasn't anything worse. As he kissed her mirror, he saw that it now reflected a miniature of the audience hall.

"You may watch until he has freed his wife," Hades promised.

Hades' wife had been right. The god was thoughtful. Jarl gave thanks that his actions would not continue to be royal amusement during his entire time on Achaea.

"Ask your questions of the Graiae, who, with only one eye, see all," Hades advised with a wave of his hand.

Jarl found himself back on the plain, bearing the heavy sword and the awkward shield. The fact that both seemed made of pure gold made him doubt their practicality. He considered dropping the weapons until he remembered that Persephone watched. "Ye gods," he thought to himself before continuing in the direction he faced. He hoped it was a clue to the whereabouts of the Graiae—whoever he, she, it, or they might be.

CHAPTER SEVENTEEN

Mirza paced before her window, frustrated by the powerful isolation spell her old enemy had placed on her room. The Shadowlord was waiting for something, she was sure. Did he really mean it when he said he was sending those creatures to kidnap her children? She and Jarl had many friends on Realm whose magical power could protect them if the Shadowlord tried any outright type of kidnapping, but deviousness and stealth were the Shadowlord's middle names. If he did manage to have his creatures infiltrate Realm, they would operate from the shadows, barely noticed by any who would protect the children. Mirza allowed Seren, Argen, and Lealor the freedom of Realm because those who lived there knew they were protected. The most evil creatures that conspired with the Shadowlord had died in the battle at Realmgate. Any who survived did so on sufferance and were unlikely to call attention to themselves by an act against the children.

Mirza reluctantly admitted that the Shadowlord would try to steal the children, but he would be facing two main obstacles. For one thing, Mirza knew her children were intelligent. Even considering her possible motherly prejudice, they were well above average not only in intelligence, but in resourcefulness. Mirza and Jarl still had many discussions about the degree of freedom the children had. Mirza carefully monitored the first excursions of the young Koenigs. Had they not proved worthy of the trust they desired, no amount of pleading would have secured them their freedom.

Mirza had carefully watched Lealor. While the youngest, she had the most magical potential of the three. Not until it was clear that she would neither hurt, nor suffer hurt, was the young witch given freedom from supervision. Then, too, the strong bond between Cibby and the girl was another safety factor. Mirza stopped pacing and shook her head ruefully, remembering. Lealor would go to Cibby with her problems and questions before she would ask her mother. The second obstacle faced by the Shadowlord was the actual transportation of his allies and their prisoners—if they should capture the children. Mirza paced and pondered.

The room grew noticeably dimmer. From force of habit Mirza glanced out the window to see how dark the clouds were. Then with a shudder, she continued pacing. Achaeasun itself dimmed and brightened. Mirza feared greatly for the development of the Bright One inside. No one now living had seen an infant Bright One, but there were descriptions left behind by the Old Ones, the original creators of the gate system. Mirza was almost certain the cocooned shape within the power nexus was Achaeasun's infant Bright One.

She wondered just how much of a setback she had managed when she had cut those strange strings. She hoped what she had done was a major defeat for the Shadowlord. For at least a brief time, the Bright One was unbound. Was it old enough, wise enough, to take steps to keep itself safe? Mirza doubted it greatly. Somehow she had sensed contentment when she had sung the multicolored lullaby to the infant. The baby needed more than an infantile appreciation for a lullaby to protect itself from the magical machinations used against it.

Her fists clenched. She strode to the window and pounded on the stone sill. Her magical senses stretched to the fullest, she searched for some chink, some tiny flaw that would give her an entryway to freedom. Once out of the Shadowlord's prison, she would shapeshift to a hawk's form and fly to the gate. Willing to try anything, even to risk her life using the unstable gate, her motherly instinct took over. She didn't even care if she offended the gods of Achaea by shape-shifting. She wanted to alert the Keepers to the danger to the Bright One. She wanted to ask them to join her on Achaea. Together they would attack and defeat the Shadowlord. The ache in her hands alerted her that she was still pounding the stone sill rhythmically. Common sense said her dream was impossible. If the gate was weird enough to give her an unusual passage, who knew what might happen if many people tried to pass?

Dejected, she sat on the bench, positioned so she could look out the window. She wanted Jarl. He had always been beside her in the past, but she knew that this time, his presence might not be possible. Her eyes focused on the shape flying outside the window. In the past, the black dragon Ebony had been another being she could trust. If only it were Ebony, but it was not. It was the sphinx, Neso. The sheer beauty of the flying creature comforted Mirza briefly. Although she could not shape-shift while in the Shadowlord's power, she could remember the feeling of the wind beneath her wings and the joy of riding an updraft.

She heard the door open. It was not time for a meal. What would the Shadowlord want now? She was growing tired of his daily harangues. Didn't the man know the meaning of the word no? She used it so often, she sometimes felt as if it were the only word in her vocabulary. With a weary sigh, she turned to face the door.

One of the guards stood in the doorway. "You are to come immediately."

Brilliant, Mirza thought. All the emotion of a grade Z movie. She rose, however, and prepared to follow him. Perhaps today she could pry some answers out of her wily opponent.

Mirza entered the Shadowlord's vast audience hall unannounced. Mirza's womanly intuition, which had nothing to do with magic, told her the Shadowlord was in a towering rage. Neso the sphinx stood before him.

"You have failed me, Neso," the Shadowlord said. His voice sent ice cubes skittering through Mirza's veins.

"But, Master, I brought you the box—"

"Oh, yes, you brought me the box, but somehow you allowed it to malfunction. I cannot open it to get at the contents!"

"But, Master—" Neso's wings quivered. "My part was to fetch the box with the child within. It is no fault of mine if you cannot open it."

A child within a box? Could it be one of her children? Mirza wondered. If so, which one? If the Shadowlord could not open the box, there must be some magical spell protecting its contents. For this, Mirza was glad.

The Shadowlord glided across the floor. It looked as if he had no feet, Mirza noticed. What a foolish observation to be making at a time like this, she chided herself mentally.

He glided across the floor several more times, reminding Mirza of the way she paced in the room that was her prison.

Finally he spoke. "You are right, sphinx. You have completed a part of the task I set you. Therefore, you may choose. You may go to the room in which Medusa waits and see her in all her beauty—"

Neso gasped. "I would turn to stone! It is the doom Athena pronounced on her centuries ago!"

"—or," the wizard continued as if Neso had not spoken,

"you may allow me to choose an alternate punishment that will allow you to live."

Neso's bunched muscles relaxed. "Anything except turning into stone, Master."

"You are content with your choice?"

"Yes, Master." Neso's voice was barely audible.

"Indeed." The Shadowlord's voice held a satisfaction that frightened Mirza. She was glad the spell the Lady had given her protected her from the magical evil she sensed in the room.

The Shadowlord nodded to two of the guards who stood at the door. "Take this creature to the labs and tell those who work there to remove her wings for study." He added, "Painfully!"

Neso's catlike eyes glowed. Her muscles tensed to spring, but a negligent wave of the Shadowlord's hand changed her demeanor to docility. She seemed to go willingly with her guards after that.

Mirza hoped her shudder was not noticeable. The powers of the Shadowlord had grown indeed.

"Guards," he commanded. "Send in Kiron and Sylvor."

Mirza watched curiously to see what manner of men or creatures these two might be. She had already figured out that they were probably the ones sent to kidnap her other children.

"Kiron," the guard announced as a centaur entered the room.

Mirza recognized him immediately. He was one of her original captors. In her concern over her family she had forgotten all about meeting the centaur and the satyr when she had met Neso. She made a mental note to keep alert and try to remember everything that happened. Any scrap of information might prove useful if she ever got a chance to battle the Shadowlord.

Kiron sidled and pranced nervously, but said nothing.

"Sylvor," the guard announced as the satyr entered. The satyr seemed more self-possessed. He waved his syrinx at Mirza, but he did not speak.

"Well?" the Shadowlord said.

Sylvor spoke first. "We came, Master, as you wished."

"As I wished?" The silky tones of the wizard's voice alerted Mirza and she stood as still as if she had been the one to see Medusa and turn to stone.

"You have both failed. Your quarry escaped you. I shall be merciful—this time. I have an errand for you. You are to go to the room at the end of the corridor, enter, and tell the woman who awaits my orders she is to come to me here."

The relief of Kiron and Sylvor was palpable. They nodded and turned to leave. Kiron and his companion both flashed smiles at Mirza because they thought them hidden from the view of the Shadowlord. They exited the room promptly, obviously relieved to have escaped punishment and eager to do their master's bidding.

Mirza felt sorry for them. They were small ciphers compared to the prime number who remained in the room with her.

"Oh, Great One," one of the guards spoke.

"Speak, captain." The geniality of the wizard thickened Mirza's blood. She did not understand exactly what was happening, but she felt it was terribly important.

"May I and my guards retire until your guest leaves?"

Mirza could feel the fear of the men.

"So, you do not like Medusa? You fear her power?"

"Yes, Great One," the captain replied, not caring if he appeared cowardly.

"Then begone!"

The guards turned on their captain's command and marched double time from the room.

Then Mirza understood. Sylvor and Kiron had gone to order Medusa to come. When they spoke to her, they would look at her and turn to stone. Such was the Shadowlord's mercy.

He had always been powerful, and his powers had definitely increased. However, Mirza found his newest trait, that of conscious cruelty, to be even more daunting. Her powers and Jarl's had grown also, but their adversary was more formidable now. In their first meeting, he had seemed detached in some way, but now his active malice was truly frightening.

Mirza stood alone in the chamber with her enemy.

"And are you not afraid of Medusa also?" he asked in a mocking tone.

"No," Mirza answered, looking straight at the Shadowlord.

"One can admire your spirit, even as one seeks to tame it," he replied.

Mirza was about to sink her pride and inquire about the box, when Medusa entered the room.

"Greetings, Great One," Medusa said. "Am I called to turn this red-haired woman to stone?"

"No, Vain One, a spell protects her—at least at present."

"If you remove it, I shall be glad to show her my unusual beauty face to face," Medusa said, careful not to look directly at Mirza.

"To remove the spell would take a great deal of magical power and more important, time. I have uses for her before turning her to stone. She is a most foolish female, but I have hopes of convincing her to join me yet."

"Why should you need her? You have my powers at your command," Medusa said.

"Your vanity is showing," the Shadowlord told her. "Her powers are far different from yours. Allow me to introduce you. Mirza, meet Medusa."

"Without her, ye shall never shine. True power be yours through witch's line," Medusa murmured.

"I beg your pardon," Mirza said, "I don't understand."

"Nor do I," Medusa answered. "It's a shred of an old prophecy that came to mind for no reason."

"Foolishness! Success does not wait on prophecy," the Shadowlord said angrily.

"Perhaps I misunderstood. I thought that foolishness of which I spoke was the reason you are so patiently awaiting this one's change of mind when you could have me as your willing ally."

Mirza looked at the strange being who stood before her. She had the body of a beautiful woman. The material of her robe was rich and intricately patterned. Her head, however, was horribly adorned with a number of writhing snakes of various kinds. Their constant hissing was nerve-wracking. Mirza wondered how the poor creature stood it. Did the poisonous kinds never bite her? Mirza wondered. While she felt only pity for the hideous parody of womanhood that stood before her, Mirza sensed that Medusa felt a kind of jealousy. How vain the creature was! She had evidently decided to cope with her affliction by accepting it and being proud of her difference from normal women. Mirza smiled. Hadn't Medusa used the term *unusual beauty* to refer to her looks? That was coping, with a vengeance. Even the Shadowlord took care to cater to her vanity in his conversation.

That thought brought another to Mirza. When she first had faced the Shadowlord, there had been no humanity in him at all. Now he had somehow acquired a sense of power, an enjoyment of cruelty for its own sake, and the ability to understand the creatures about him. She reminded herself to be very careful what she said and did around the wizard. If he sensed the slightest weakness in her, he would use it to the fullest extent. It was not a comforting thought.

"She seems to be a harmless mortal type," Medusa said. Her hair hissed an agreement.

Mirza listened, astonished as Medusa said, "Be still, my darlings. Mother is busy now."

The tenderness in Medusa's voice was heartbreaking. Medusa would never have children. What man or creature could have an interest in someone whose face, no matter how pretty, remained framed forever with a wide selection of slithering serpents?

"Beware!" the Shadowlord said in stern tones. "Do not underestimate this flame-tressed witch. She will use every wile she knows to lull your suspicions so she can escape. Do not trust her—ever."

He really makes me sound like a dangerous force, rather than a person, Mirza thought. On the other hand, she admitted to herself, he had reason to fear. She had been part of a group of magic users who had trounced the Shadowlord thoroughly when he had tried to use Realm, her home world, as a base for his illicit gate. That gate was part of the plan of the Shadowlord to move the evil armies from one alternate earth to another. Somehow he had gained the knowledge to attempt a gate that not only transferred people spatially, but temporally. Mirza fought to keep her hands from clenching as she thought

about all the damage the Shadowlord might do if he were free
of time as well as space.

"I shall watch her carefully, Great One."

Mirza noted that those the Shadowlord considered to be
creatures addressed him as Master, while humans addressed
him as Great One. Had the wizard developed prejudices, as
well? Both terms indicated a subservience that Mirza de-
plored. He had learned pride, too. Mirza only hoped it went
before his fall.

"That is well. I will do what I can, however, to see that she
gives you little trouble." At this point, he waved his hand and
a curtain across the corner of the room opened, displaying a
glass casket. Within lay Lealor in a semblance of sleep.

In spite of her resolution to do nothing to alert the Shadowlord to her feelings, Mirza gasped and took a swift step forward.

"Would you care to have a closer look?" His hand made a
sweeping gesture that urged her forward.

Medusa stepped forward too and looked within the box.
Mirza was happy the casket was tightly shut. She hoped Lealor wouldn't wake up and see Medusa. Mirza had no idea
what form of spell held her daughter, but she had no wish to
see her frightened or turned to stone.

"The young one looks like her," Medusa said in a disgusted
tone of voice. She moved back of her own volition.

As she retreated, Mirza advanced. She looked down at
her sleeping child. Her color was good. Her chest rose and
fell normally. She was breathing. Mirza put her hands on the
transparent top. Something—someone, she mentally corrected herself, within the box was powering the spell which
held it shut. It did not seem like human magic. Where on
Realm had Lealor learned such a spell? Mirza gazed carefully
at her daughter. Then she noticed the almost invisible crystal-
line bracelet on Lealor's arm.

Unknowingly, Mirza must have given some sign of what
she saw because the Shadowlord said, "Ah, is there something there that a mother might sense that I, master mage that
I am, cannot?"

"I doubt it," Mirza said dryly. The Shadowlord became

more human by the minute. Perhaps, Mirza thought, his newly acquired humanity might be the agency through which defeat was possible. She felt that she had learned much about her adversary. She hoped he had not learned as much about her.

Her gaze returned to the tiny dragonoid form. She mindspoke to the bracelet. "Who are you?"

Never had Myst felt more like breaking dragonlaw. She bit her tiny tongue to keep from replying. Her eyes flew open. She allowed her tongue to flick out and in once to show Mirza she was alive and sentient. Myst could only hope that Mirza would continue trying to communicate with her. If only Mirza would ask a yes or no question that Myst could answer with a nod or a shake of her small head!

Somehow, Mirza seemed to understand Myst's desire. Her next words proved it. "Are you connected with Wyrd?"

A tiny nod, almost imperceptible, was her answer.

"Are you holding this box under a shut-spell?"

A second nod.

"Is my daughter all right?"

A third nod.

Mirza wanted time to stand and ask many more questions, but the Shadowlord moved beside her. She realized it was dangerous to try to keep communicating, even on a tight mental band, with her enemy near. She stepped back and looked at the Shadowlord.

When her hands moved from the box, they trembled, so Mirza deliberately held them still at her sides by an effort of will.

The Shadowlord must have noticed, for there was satisfaction in his voice as he said, "Ah, all that folderol about a mother's love is true."

Not for the first time, Mirza thought that perhaps the Shadowlord was literally inhuman as well as inhumane. Mirza gazed at him, silent. Why, by all the Bright Ones, did he wear his cowl so his face was always in shadow? No wonder he was the Lord of Shadows! In a confrontation such as this, being able to read an enemy's face was invaluable. Mirza felt quite vulnerable, and though in the past she had scorned veils, she wished quite desperately that she wore one now.

"Please note the small air holes at the foot," he said in a voice that reminded Mirza of the one he used when talking to Neso.

Mirza looked. It was true.

"In a few days, I shall pour the contents of this vial into those holes. I'm not sure how long I shall wait, but a few days at least."

A noxious green liquid that Mirza recognized with a shock of horror filled the vial. It was the same green liquid that had threatened to turn her into a monster on Realm when she had refused to join the Shadowlord and had not yet received the protection of the Lady.

"I see that you remember. After I pour this liquid in those holes, it will begin at Lealor's feet and move to her head. The same conditions will prevail as when you were enchanted. If the green growth reaches the child's head, the transformation will be irreversible. If I should hear of an escape attempt—" The Shadowlord was silent. He could see that Mirza understood.

"I will not attempt escape," she said reluctantly. His planning ability had grown as well. For how long had his spies gathered data on her family? He knew her daughter's name and Bright Ones only knew what else. Why had they believed it would take many years for the Shadowlord to regain enough of his power to challenge them again? In a few short years he had not only regained his powers but increased them. Their inability to believe in his fast recovery was likely to cost them dearly, Mirza thought. She almost despaired.

"Good. I see you understand. Remember, in a few days more I will call you for another audience. You would like to see me pour the elixir—wouldn't you?"

Mirza could sense his fiendish joy. Truly the Shadowlord was now a greater threat than ever to the peace of the worlds and the safety of the gates. Mirza's only hope lay in the thought that Jarl had to be searching for her.

With an almost casual wave of his hand, he sent the two women to Medusa's cave, almost half a world away.

CHAPTER
EIGHTEEN

The huge dragon spread its wings over a cowering Seren. This was no Realmish dragon! Its teeth filled its cavernous mouth, a forest of ivory daggers, each one serrated to rend and destroy. The sulfurous stench in the air proved the fire-breathing capability of the dragon, as did Seren's smoking clothes.

Seren raised his weaponless hands to ward off the next breath of the evil saurian. "Please," he begged. "I have done nothing to you." He gestured to the dragon's horde, a mixture of gold and human bones. "I have not even touched one treasure that is yours. I came to see the mightiest dragon on this world. I mean you no harm."

The dragon's eyes glittered his hatred of everything human. It ignored the frightened boy's words. Its snakelike head reared high, then swooped down on the helpless human, mouth opened to take one bite and rid the universe of another hereditary enemy.

Seren faced his doom bravely. He stood with his hands at his side, a grave look on his face.

"Motherrr," a shrill voice screamed. Argen, chained high on the wall, called out in agony from the dungeon. His arms seemed too frail to hold the weight of his body. The moldy walls could just be discerned in the feeble light of the one candle that guttered, close to its end, on the rickety table across the cell. The sickly smell of long imprisonment and despair radiated through the air.

With a hollow boom, the great door to the huge torture chamber opened to admit the evil wizard who had imprisoned Argen. "Now will you tell me of the ancient book you found in the library? It contains the most powerful spells of the Old Ones' greatest wizard, Alchemor."

"Alchemor was evil. It was largely through his spells that the Old Ones almost destroyed all the lower life forms on Realm, including the human race. No one must ever have the opportunity to learn those spells. The book guarded by the most powerful magic enchantments known on Realm wasn't even catalogued. If I told you where to find it, you could not read it," Argen whispered through dry lips.

"I will be the judge of that," the angry wizard thundered, making Argen cringe.

"May I please have a drink of water?" Argen asked. He had thirsted for two days. If he had any thought other than the pain in his arms, it was of the constant thirst he endured.

"Water?" The wizard smiled. "You shall have more water than even a thirsty prisoner can drink. This is your last chance. Will you speak?"

"Never!" Argen said proudly. Although there was small chance that the wizard could open the book to learn the spells and live, yet Argen would not take it. He tried vainly to moisten his lips with his dry tongue. Finding no moisture, he closed them firmly and looked as resolute as he could.

"Guards!" the wizard called.

Two monstrous creatures entered the room and awaited the bidding of their master.

"Throw this prisoner into the moat!"

"The moat, master?" the larger of the two creatures rasped.

"Do you not have ears?"

"Yes, Great One, but there be hungry water swimmers in the moat. This small boy will be but a snack for them."

"Indeed," the wizard said with a smile. "Then he will have no further need of our hospitality, will he?"

The two creatures grinned at their master's macabre joke

before advancing to take Argen from the wall. The wizard left
the room. The candle guttered futilely, then went out . . .

"Oh, it's so dark here," Lealor said. "I don't like the dark.
Mommy? Are you there, Mommy? I want to go home."
A huge roar echoed in the chamber where Lealor stood.
"Oh, mommy, I don't know what it is, but it's big and hungry.
Mommmmmy!" The child's voice shrieked her terror.

Mirza sat upright in her bed, wide awake. She couldn't
think what to do. She needed freedom to help her children.
She stood, trying to shake the sleep haze from her brain.
Where was she? The rough stone walls of the cave she slept in
flickered in the light from the small fire in the center of the
chamber. She lay down again on the crude cot which was her
bed. While the Shadowlord spared no expense on his lodgings
and work areas, the places prepared for the imprisonment of
his enemies were lacking in all but the most rudimentary
comforts.
Mirza closed her eyes and remembered the three dreams
which had awakened her. Her magic told her they were only
dreams and not reality. She wished she could have a few minutes to talk to her Grandmother Cibby, who had true sight.
Mirza's own power in that area was slight, coming unbidden
and leaving only tantalizing fragments of information which
might be true or not. Cibby's own power to foresee came
unbidden, but what she saw was true. Mirza, however, had
one power her grandmother did not. Sometimes Mirza was
able to clear her mind of all thoughts and "see" what was
happening to those she loved. During all the days of her imprisonment she had never lost hope that Jarl would come for
her at last. So sure was her faith in her husband that she had
never tried to use her powers to find out what he was doing.
Using magic on Achaea was dangerous unless one had the
permission of the gods. At this point Mirza was willing to
take the risk of offending the powerful beings who ruled this
world. She closed her eyes and relaxed her body. She had the
strange feeling that someone watched over her, and yet it was
no being she could actually recognize. She set the intriguing

puzzle to one side and widened her search for Jarl. If he was on this world, she would know it.

Jarl walked on a treeless plain. His backpack looked familiar. Many times Mirza had seen him like this on camping trips. She could not recognize the place, but she knew he was searching for her. She mindcalled, but Jarl showed no signs of hearing her. Nevertheless, she smiled as she saw First Egg pop into sight. The young dragon and Jarl talked animatedly. Mirza wished she could hear the exchange, for she had carried on conversations with the spritely dragon herself. Finally Jarl nodded, and First Egg sprang at him, clutched his belt in his claws, and shot into the air, after which both disappeared abruptly. Clearly the young saurian had mastered basic travel. Mirza was certain First Egg's parents had no idea he was popping in and out from hither to yon. Mirza hoped he wouldn't stunt his growth by overusing his powers. Remembering the dragon's precipitate ascent and disappearance, she could only hope Jarl's belt was up to the trip. She sat on the edge of the cot before lying down again. Her lips curved in a smile as she remembered the look on Jarl's face when the dragon had taken off.

The little dragon set Jarl down gently, considering the way he had so abruptly picked him up and flown off with him.

"Sorry, Unc—I mean, Jarl. I can't spend much time here. My father and mother are taking turns checking on me. I've got an alarm rigged that lets me know when they are coming. So far, it's worked because they only peek every forty-five minutes or so. That gives me enough time to pop in and see what's happening here."

"Wouldn't it be an even better idea to study those *Dragon Chronicles* and learn the material? I can manage without you. If your parents ever find out you're popping in and out like this, I dread to think what they might do. Have you considered that not only do you face the danger of traveling from Realm to Achaea, you also may have to brave your father's wrath? I've never seen him as mad as he was the last time I caught you here."

"Uncle Jarl—oops, sorry. It's a hard habit to break, you know," the dragon apologized. "What would you do without me? It might have taken you days to find the Gorgonian Plain without me to help."

"That's true. But there are some things you don't know."

"What, for instance—the location of a small treasure in gold?" Faf asked, cocking his head inquisitively.

Jarl admitted to himself that the little pipsqueak was cute— if a half ton or so of anything could pass as cute. "Fact one: Hades' wife, Persephone, is watching all I do through a kind of magic mirror."

Jarl watched in horror as Faf preened a little and waved insouciantly. "Hello, there," Faf said in his most polite voice. "Isn't this exciting?"

Jarl half choked and decided his best bet was to ignore the whole thing. "Fact two: Wyrd has promised not to help me. Perhaps Hades will be angry if you do."

"I bet Persephone will think I'm interesting. You don't get a chance to see a Realmish dragon every day, you know."

Jarl decided to try one more time before he gave up. "Maybe so. Dropping in as you do could get you into trouble. Don't you think you should stay at home?"

"What! And miss all the action?" With a rather endearing wink of one huge eye, the little saurian disappeared.

Jarl caught his final thought. "Gotta fly!"

Jarl stood a city block from a singular mountain. He could see the cavelike opening in its face. "Gotta fly; indeed," he murmured to himself as he started walking toward the mountain.

CHAPTER NINETEEN

Seren and Argen stared at one another. Their sister had vanished. Through the rapport they had with their talismens, the boys had experienced their sister's disappearance simultaneously with Soladon and Nyct. Finally Seren managed a weak, "Now what?"

"Don't look at me for answers. Lealor has done some weird things in her time, but allowing herself to be trapped in that box—"

"Yeah," Seren said, clearly still awed by what he had witnessed. "How could anybody be so dumb?"

Soladon hissed his distress. "To think that our sister failed in her care of her charge!"

Nyct's mental voice spoke to all three. "Now is not the time for bewailing what is done. Gone is a scale fallen. Only time will replace the loss."

"What have falling scales got to do with anything?" Seren said, plunking himself down on the bench near the table.

"Nyct only means that we shouldn't be crying over spilled milk," Argen explained.

"Where do you hear all that strange stuff, anyway?" Seren asked with an exasperated look on his face. "That's what comes of spending all your time with those greybeards at the university. You sound like some weirdo. Don't ever talk like that in front of our friends or they'll think you're a freak," he warned.

"There's more to life than television and videos," Argen rejoined heatedly.

"Let us put our heads together and plot what we must do to free our sister and yours. If they are speedily returned to Realm, perhaps our father never need know," Soladon said, tightening on Seren's wrist to assure his attention.

Argen paused to wonder where the dragons learned to speak English. Sometimes they sounded strange, but their meaning always came through. He said aloud, "Well, one thing's for sure."

"That's a relief. You sound like you've got our problem all solved." Seren smiled at his brother.

"Don't relax too soon. What I mean is, we've got to handle this by ourselves."

"Would it not be wiser to inform Andronan or Cibby and let them aid Lealor and Myst?" Nyct said.

"No!" both boys said, in agreement for once.

"Then what would you have us do to aid you?" Soladon asked.

"You mean you haven't got any ideas?" Seren's raised eyebrows showed his astonishment.

Argen, who had probably worked more closely with his new friend and protector, had a more realistic view of what might be possible with the aid of the dragon bracelets. "Seren, they're not supposed to do our thinking for us. They'll be glad to help, but we need to offer them a plan and then find out what they can do to help us."

"That is correct," Nyct said, obviously proud of his charge.

"Right on," Soladon said, trying to use the slanguage he heard Seren use with Faf.

Nyct shut his eyes and reprimanded his brother privately.

Soladon gazed at his brother with amber eyes and then stuck out his tongue so quickly that neither Seren nor Argen noticed.

"Our first job is to find out where Lealor and Myst are now."

"Sensible," Soladon told his charge.

"I bet they're on Achaea. That seems to be where all the

action is. If the wyverns are right and the Shadowlord is at the bottom of this mess, Lealor and Myst are sitting right on top of the pile."

"How can we make sure, Argen?" Seren asked.

"Well, if Nyct will zap me into the Room of the Book, I can check the changes added about Achaea during the last few hours."

"Done!" Nyct said as Argen and he disappeared.

"Soladon, now that we're alone, can you explain to me how you dragons get from here to there so quickly?"

"It's quite simple. Space doesn't really exist for us as it does for humans. Therefore, we need only envision where we want to be and we are there."

"Somehow that doesn't make sense to me."

"Do not worry. There is much in the life of humans that makes little sense to them. Is it not enough that we are capable of 'zapping' you when it is necessary? Must you understand everything? Can you not just accept?"

"I'd still like to know just how it's done. After all, I'm the zapee, so to speak."

Soladon emitted a dry chuckle. "Indeed you are."

Argen and Nyct reappeared as swiftly as they had vanished. Argen said, "Achaea it is. Lealor and Myst are there, all right."

"It will please you to know that Lealor is safe, but imprisoned in the magic casket. Myst has been able to seal it so that the Shadowlord may not harm Lealor."

"Good. She has done well, then," Soladon said. "Keeping the girl safe may well shield our sister from the wrath of our father should he find out about this."

"Even I can figure out our next step," Seren said. "How are we going to get to Achaea?"

"Using the gate is out," Argen told his brother. "The Book of Worlds says Achaeasun is destabilizing."

"And what exactly does that mean?"

"That something continues to disturb the Bright One within the sun," Soladon hissed, clearly somewhat disturbed himself at the news.

"If the rogue gate is not quickly brought under control or

allowed to disintegrate, Achaeasun may nova, destroying the Bright One," Nyct clarified.

"Crisping our parents and sister to a cinder," Seren added, showing his comprehension of what the bracelets had told him.

Argen shuddered. Sometimes his brother's choice of words lacked finesse. "We must act now." Argen knew his parents had special powers, but his reading of heroic histories told him that even with magical aids, sometimes evil triumphed over good. Seren didn't really believe anything bad could happen to his parents. Argen understood the situation better and realized that his parents were facing a much more serious situation on Achaea than they had on Realm. For one thing, there was no way to determine the level of disturbance which would cause a sun to nova. For another, the power of the Shadowlord must have increased to allow his allies to steal Lealor, protected as she was by Myst. Argen almost wished he didn't understand what could happen. Knowledge could make an uncomfortable companion.

"Agreed," said Nyct.

Soladon's tiny head nodded.

"Okay, fellows," Seren said to Soladon and Nyct. "We're ready to go. Zap us there." He waited in complete confidence.

"Our powers limit us to Realm," Nyct said sadly.

"That is not quite true," Soladon said. "We have the absolute power to protect you anywhere, but our father did not give us the immense amounts of power necessary to transfer humans from one world to another."

"If our bracelets can't zap us there, can Faf take us?"

"I'm not sure. I haven't seen him for a while. His parents expect him to study a lot. You know how much he wants to become an adult! Well, mastery of the dragonlaw and *Dragon Chronicles* is part of the grown-up deal. He's had his nose buried in a book every time I wanted to see him. I get the idea that I'm not any too welcome in his home cave right now," Seren said.

"You can't mean Faf wants to study! From what I've seen of him, he probably needs to work hard. Still, I can't see him turning down a chance to adventure for a bunch of old laws and the complete history of dragonkind from year one on."

"Faf's not the problem. It's his mother, Ebony. She can be pretty chilling without saying a word. When I ask if Faf can come out and play, she's terribly polite. I can almost feel her eyes boring into my back if I try to walk into the side chamber where the library is. I mean, a couple of tons of annoyed mother can be pretty hard to take, you know."

"Well, this is an emergency. At least we've got to try. If Ebony won't let us go, we may have to tell her about Lealor."

"Mortal lackwit!" Seren said in his best leprechaun imitation. "There's got to be a way."

"Perhaps you two should talk to Fafnoddle," Soladon suggested.

"Fafnoddle? Whatever for?" Seren asked.

"Fafnoddle took your father to Achaea. Could he not also take you two?" Nyct said, unwilling to allow his brother to take full credit for an idea he, too, had harbored.

"No!" both boys said simultaneously, in perfect agreement for once.

"I understand that it is your job to protect us and maybe Fafnoddle would be safer transportation than his son, but you don't know what grown-ups are like," Argen told them.

"They just take over everything," Seren said. "Why, I bet in no time at all, we would be told to go play with our marbles or something while a bunch of grown-ups took over." The face Seren made showed his opinion of the dragon bracelets' idea more clearly than his words. "We could get in trouble for not taking care of Lealor."

"And besides, Mother and Father are both busy already. Even your father, Wyrd, might be pretty upset if we distracted him over this," Argen said.

A look of surprise passed over Nyct's face. "I had not considered fully the results of our suggestion."

"Nor had I." Soladon flicked his tail. "Perhaps we should save telling our father until there is no other way of managing," Soladon hissed.

"Now you're showing sense!" Seren told his talisman. "We

haven't even challenged anyone yet. We'll save any parent-type help for a last resort."

The two dragons nodded. At least they had tried to make their charges see sense.

"Let's go to Faf's and try before we give up," Argen said.

CHAPTER TWENTY

No sooner had Seren nodded his agreement than both boys found themselves standing at the foot of the mountain where the von Fafnirs lived.

"Thanks, fellows," Seren told the bracelets.

"Yes, thanks," Argen added, wishing his stomach didn't react so badly to being zapped from one place to another without any warning. He wanted to seem like his father, capable of doing anything. He didn't realize from whom he had inherited his queasiness.

"Faf!" Seren called.

Ebony's huge head snaked from the cave. "Who calls my son?" she asked.

"Ah, hello," Seren said, managing to sound apologetic. "I'm sorry if we came at an inconvenient time—"

Ebony's huge eye glittered greenly as she lowered her head closer to the boys.

"—but we were hoping to play with Faf for a while," Argen finished his brother's sentence, a thing he hadn't done for years.

Seren shot his brother a look that said plainly as words that he didn't appreciate the verbal rescue.

Argen tried to hide his exasperation. Seren often rushed into a situation without thinking. He then hoped the right words would come to him in time to avert disaster. It would serve him right if Argen left him to extricate himself from the mother dragon without any help. Then Argen remembered how important it was for them to contact Faf and he said, "It's just—" he floundered momentarily himself, before continuing, "—well, to tell the truth, we're lonely. With mother off Realm we just wanted someone to be with, I guess," Argen said, trying to look like a deserted child. If dragons had maternal instincts, Argen planned to take full advantage of them.

Seren nodded, a smile of relief on his face.

"Oh, you lonely boys, I hadn't thought of that. Come in, come in," Ebony offered expansively, grabbing Argen by his belt and hoisting him up to the ledge where she stood.

Argen tried to look happy while he told his stomach to settle, or else. How could Seren be so friendly with dragons, of all things? Even when they did you a favor, meaning only kindness, it turned into a disaster.

"Thank you," Seren said with a small bow to Ebony, who placed him gently beside his brother.

"It is well to see your mother reared you to be polite," Ebony said. "You are a credit to her." She cast a disapproving glance at Argen as if she was making a comparison in which Seren came out much better than did Argen.

"You'll have to excuse Argen," Seren offered. "He hasn't been lucky enough to be around dragons much and he's kind of shy. Dragonkind are pretty magnificent to ordinary humans, you know."

"Botheration!" Ebony said, clearly not as taken in by the flattery as Seren hoped. "You just want me to offer you a few steakfruit, don't you?" The dragon chuckled. "Go on with you. You know where Faf studies. Go and get him. He can go out for the rest of the afternoon. He's been studying hard for hours," his proud mother said.

Seren lost no time in entering the cave. Argen, looking at the imposing bulk of his companion on the ledge, smiled what he hoped was a polite smile and entered the cave rapidly. He wasn't exactly afraid of dragons, but he doubted he'd ever get used to them towering over him with mouths full of daggers that seemed ready to rend and tear any moment. And Seren chose dragons over any other creatures on Realm. Argen hurried after his brother. Sometimes he thought Seren was a bit of a fool.

"Have some steakfruit," Ebony bellowed after them. "Help yourselves."

Argen felt the warm exhalation on his back. He shivered in spite of the warmth. Catch him making a buddy of a dragon. No sir. All he asked of life was a room full of interesting books to read. This adventure stuff was already palling on him.

Seren reached into one of the trays that held greenery. The walls were lined with row upon row of hydroponic plant holders. Seren tossed a glossy fruit at his brother. "Catch," he said with a smile.

Argen hadn't been in the home cave of the dragons for years. He remembered coming when he was younger, but now he was awed by Fafnoddle's gargantuan horticultural effort. At any other time, he would have enjoyed talking to Fafnoddle about his indoor garden. Now, however, knowing the real purpose of their visit, he just wanted to convince Faf to come with them and leave. What, he wondered, could an irate dragon do to a human who tried to coax her young into a dangerous undertaking? Argen firmly suppressed another shiver. He sincerely hoped that he, for one, would never find out.

Seren had already entered the huge corridor that led to another cave. Argen hurried after him. The hallway seemed long to Argen, but when he compared the relative sizes of the dragons and humans, he realized that for a dragon, it was only a few short steps.

Faf and Seren were already talking when he entered the room. Argen looked around him in awe. This part of the cave was as large as one of the huge rooms in the University library. There were hundreds of books piled on shelves, stacked on a table, and resting on a ledge that ran around the room.

"Come on, Argen," Seren urged. "Faf will fly us to the

plateau that's above the cave. We don't want to stand around here all day, do we?" The last two words were said with special emphasis, as if to remind Argen of the real purpose of their visit.

"Oh, yes. That's right. We have only a few hours before dark, and who knows how long—" he broke off because Ebony entered the room. "—it will take us to finish our game," he said, somewhat lamely.

"You children just run along. First Egg needs plenty of fresh air so his scales don't tarnish. A growing dragon has to take care of his health," she explained to the boys.

"Oh, Mother," Faf complained.

"We'll see he has a chance to get plenty of fresh air," Seren promised, almost pushing Argen into the hallway.

"Thank you for the fruit," Argen said.

"You're very welcome. We have a great deal of it to harvest right now. We're always glad to share with our friends," Ebony said with a wide smile that sent shivers down Argen's back.

"Hurry up. We don't want to waste any of this lovely afternoon," Faf said for his mother's benefit.

The three hurried out of the cave. Once on the ledge, Seren let out a large laugh. "Bright Ones in a basket," he hooted. "All you needed was a teacup in your hand to sound like some of the ladies my mother has over to the house to play bridge."

Faf let out a small puff of smoke, and while Argen coughed and hacked, he said, "You did want to get out of the cave—didn't you?"

"Okay. You're right. It always pays to keep your mother happy. If a little fancy politeness will do the trick, I guess it's in a good cause."

Argen had waved enough of the smoke away to take a breath of uncontaminated air. Smoke always nauseated him.

"Upsa daisy," Faf said, grabbing Argen in one claw and Seren in the other. Argen very nearly disgraced himself as they rose rather unsteadily into the air. He blessed the fact that he had saved his steakfruit to eat later, rather than gobbling it down as Seren had.

"Hey, Faf," Seren complained, "you should be more careful."

Argen longed for the feel of the ground beneath his feet even as he mentally applauded his brother's attitude. The awkwardness of their ride and the indignity of being hauled up by his belt should be avenged, Argen felt. And Seren liked flying with dragons! He simply had to be crazy, that was all.

"Why?" Faf asked, carefully dropping them both at the same time with a small thump. He flapped his wings once more, landing beside them.

"You might hurt yourself trying to lift both of us at once. We're pretty heavy," Seren said, making a fist and socking his friend on a mammoth front leg in a friendly gesture.

"Dragons are a hardy lot. You don't have to worry. If two of you had been too much to handle, I'd have dropped Argen."

Argen's eyes flew open. "What?" he gasped.

"Well, you've got a magic bracelet, just like Seren. It would have saved you," Faf explained with panache.

"Gee, thanks," Argen muttered, glad the dragon couldn't read his mind just then. The words he was thinking would have earned him a stern lecture from his parents if they had heard him. He knew some terms his parents definitely would disapprove of. It was one of the benefits that came from wide reading.

Seren explained what had happened to Lealor and their reason for needing Faf's help. "So," he concluded his story, "would you be willing to risk helping us? If you can't travel like your parents, we'll just have to ask their help."

"Not be able to travel like my parents? Naturally I can. Ever since my parents discovered their ability all adult dragons on Realm can travel the way they can."

"Yes," Argen said, feeling he owed Faf a semi-setdown, "but are you adult enough to travel to Achaea? You'll have to take the location from my mind. I'm the one who knows all about the place. I know you and Seren are a team, but can you work with my visualization?"

"I'll just take you both on my back, and we can go," Faf said, taking the matter so casually that even Seren looked at him, estimating his chances of success.

Argen saw the look on his brother's face. He felt relieved to know that his brother did have some sense, after all. Argen had feared that Seren would want to rush into this adventure without proper safeguards.

"Climb on my back," Faf said, stretching himself out on the ground.

Seren wasted no time in mounting his friend. "Come on, slowpoke," he teased. "The air up here is great. You're gonna love dragonriding."

Obediently, Argen started to climb aboard the dragon.

"Not back by my tail," Faf commanded. "In front of Seren. You're the navigator," he said with a twist of his head and a smile.

Argen thought the bravest thing he ever did was dismount almost in Faf's mouth and clamber up in front of his brother. He fully expected to have nightmares about this flight.

Faf's takeoff was not reassuring. He lurched into the air with full power, said, "Here we go, ready or not," and disappeared from Realm.

The coldness cut through Argen's robes and he thought he heard his brother warn him to hold on. Blackness turned into bright sunlight so rapidly that he didn't even have time to worry about falling off.

"Hey, Faf," Seren called. "Where are we?"

"Where do you expect?" Faf said silkily.

Argen shivered. Sometimes Faf did seem like an adult dragon.

"We've got to get to Achaea," Seren explained.

Faf rippled his scales, depositing both boys on the dry ground. "Achaea," he said proudly.

"But—" Argen began, stopping to swallow firmly. "You didn't get any images from my mind. I didn't even have time to think about Achaea."

"Oh, that," Faf said, with a wink to Seren. "I just thought I'd give it a try on my own," he told Argen, who had turned pea green.

At this bit of news, Argen did deposit the contents of his stomach on the grass.

"I'm sorry, Faf," Seren apologized. "He's supposed to be housebroken and relatively civilized."

Faf giggled. "Frightened humans are so funny. It really doesn't take much to scare your brother, does it?"

"Much to scare me?" Argen turned to face his detractors. "Just because I have the brains to understand how dangerous this form of dragon traveling is, you two idiots make fun of me! Let me tell you, if Faf had made an error, history would find us scattered over twenty different planes of reality. No one with the tiniest atom of sense would consider traveling as we did unless the need were exceptionally great. I consider rescuing my sister to be worth risking my neck for, but you two set out as if this was an afternoon picnic! Faf, 'fess up. How many times have you made the trip to Achaea before?"

"Oh, scales! I thought I'd surprise you both. How did you ever find out my secret?" Faf pounded his tail on the ground to show his chagrin.

"The transition was so quick and so smooth. The very fact that you were so sure that this was Achaea told me you'd been here before," Argen said.

"Maybe I'd better start spending some time in the library myself," Seren admitted. "I really didn't think about the danger of making the trip. Besides, the talismen we wear would protect us."

"No," two sililant voices spoke in three minds. One voice continued speaking to the three. "On a world, especially Realm, we have power. In that space between one world and the next, only the gates offer any certainty of safe harbor."

Argen and Seren looked at each other in horror. They realized how much they had come to depend on the protection which Wyrd had provided for them both.

"Well, that's not our problem now," Faf told them. "On Achaea, even Wyrd limits his powers. The gods who live here are extremely proud of being the only major magic wielders."

"That is true," Soladon said.

"Yess," Nyct agreed, the hiss in his voice showing his concern.

"Now what are we going to do?" Faf asked Seren.

Seren glanced at his brother.

"Don't look at me. You're the adventurer in the family. You tell me," Argen told him.

CHAPTER
TWENTY-ONE

Argen, Seren, and Faf looked at one another. They stood on a vast plain on Achaea, but not one of them had given any thought to what they would do when they got there.

"Oh, boy. We may have really messed things up," Seren admitted.

The sunlight dimmed and returned.

Argen glanced skyward. "Yes," he said. He hated to have to agree with his brother, but this time Seren was right. Mess was a rather tame word to use to describe the predicament they were in.

"Hey, fellows, I don't mean to cause any trouble or anything, but I can't stay here too long. Any moment my mother is liable to start looking for me. If she can't find me on Realm, you may be looking at a grounded dragon."

"How can she ground you, Faf?" Seren was intrigued by the idea.

"Oh, mother dragons can bespell their offspring so that they must stay in the home cave." Faf shuddered. "It gives me the horrors thinking of it. If my sister hatches and I'm cooped up like some Realmish fowl, I'll go crazy."

"What's so bad about your sister hatching?" Seren wondered aloud.

"Well, dragon mothers sing to their new hatchlings as they dry."

"So what's so bad about that?"

"Have you ever heard my mother sing?"

"Well, to be honest, no. I wouldn't have thought her voice was that bad, though. She sounds fine when she talks."

"Oh, it isn't how she sings. It's what she sings— the *Dragon Chronicles*."

"Deadly," Seren said.

"Hour after hour, hour—"

"Look, you two, time is passing. We've got to think this thing through," Argen broke into their conversation.

"Okay. So think, brother, think."

"Why me? Whenever the going gets tough—" Argen began.

"—the tough get thinking!" Seren finished brilliantly.

For the first time, Argen understood why it irked Seren so when he finished his sentences for him. He made a private vow never to do it again, then continued trying to reason with his two fellow adventurers.

"Are you both agreed that we can't handle this alone?"

"You mean that we need help?" Seren said.

"Assistance?" Faf added.

"Help, aid, assistance—whatever you call it, we can't manage here without some kind of magic." Argen looked at them, obviously expecting them to see the wisdom in what he said.

"Magic, huh?" Seren said.

Argen privately thought his brother could be thick-headed sometimes, but he didn't say anything about it. All they needed now was one of those brotherly arguments that went on for hours.

"Magic?" Faf said, as if he had never heard of the word before.

"M-a-g-i-c," Argen spelled in exasperation. He wondered how high an ax would bounce off their thick skulls.

"Mortals can't use magic here. They get in big trouble with those guys on Mount Whatchamacallit," Faf said.

"Brilliant, Faf," Argen said under his breath. "Right," he said aloud. "So who do you think we need to get to help us?"

"The gods themselves!" Faf and Seren echoed each other.

"Yes. There is a temple on Achaea. It's called the Temple

of the Oracle. The gods sometimes answer the petitions of mortals who visit there. It's our best bet."

"How far is it?" Seren asked.

"I'm not sure, but it's near Mount Olympus," Argen told him.

"I think I know where it is," Faf offered tentatively.

"Then you have been making unauthorized trips to Achaea!" Argen said.

"Well, yes. I followed my father and yours the first time. It's such an interesting place, and the gods gave the Greeks all that gold . . . I just kept coming."

"Why aren't you in big trouble with the gods, then?" Seren asked.

"I don't know. I haven't found any gold yet. I never gave it any thought." Faf frowned in puzzlement.

"I know. Flying is a natural dragonly ability. Even those trips through the dark are natural. That's why. Just let a mortal whisk through the air on his own and see what happens. I've read some really horrendous stories about mortals who were punished for being what Grandmother Cibby calls 'uppity.' The Greeks call that kind of overweening pride *hubris*. And boy, do they punish mortals who show any. Arachne, Tantalus, Ix—"

"Okay. Cut the mythology lesson, Argen. Let's get going," Seren said, climbing on Faf's back.

Argen carefully considered the possibilities. On the one hand, he could stay here. Faf and Seren might foul things up and then the sun would nova. That was one option. Then, on the other hand, he might climb on Faf's back for another ride. He was on the horns of a dilemma. Or, to be more in keeping with his location, he was between Scylla and Charybdis, the devil and the deep blue sea.

The sunlight dimmed. Argen clambered aboard Al Fafnir Airlines.

Seren handed his brother his not-too-clean handkerchief. "Try to hold on to everything until we get there, okay?"

Argen took the proffered hanky.

"Is everybody ready back there?" Faf inquired in bright tones. He reminded Argen of the stewardesses on real airlines.

"Of course," Seren called to his friend.

"I guess soooo," Argen managed as they winked out of sight.

Faf did a shrug that deposited both Argen and Seren on the ground. "Sorry, but I gotta fly," Faf explained as he popped out of sight.

"Some friend he is," Argen commented.

"Let's be fair. If our mother was on our tail like Ebony is on his, wouldn't you make sure you didn't get caught doing anything she would disapprove of?" Seren defended his friend.

"Yeah," Argen grudgingly admitted, "but can you see either one of us being so rock-headed that our folks had to make us study?"

"Not you, maybe, but Mother has had talks with me." Seren peered around them. "Let's start walking on this path Faf set us near. It goes up into those mountains." Seren started out, not waiting to see if Argen followed.

"Okay. Okay." Argen puffed his way behind his brother. He'd had more exercise in the last two or three days than in the previous two months. He longed to return to the safety of the library. Even riding on Faf beat all this walking uphill. Earlier, Argen had been tempted to tell his brother that these were only foothills, but now that they had climbed awhile, mountains did seem a better word. He swore to himself that if they came out of this adventure with a whole skin, he'd never envy his brother again. Argen much preferred his adventures between the covers of the books in the library. He liked reading about daring feats—heck, someday he might even write about them. He was most definitely cured of any wish to partake in the excitement firsthand. He noticed that he wasn't puffing so much any more. He hurried to catch up with Seren, who forged ahead as if he wore seven-league boots.

The next bend in the path gave them a full view of the Temple of the Oracle. "Wow!" Seren mouthed silently. Argen's small gasp of awe showed his state of impression, too.

"Oh! So there you are. I was about to stop and wait for you to catch up."

"So I noticed," said Argen dryly.

"Well, here we are. Now what do we do?" Seren asked, expecting his brother's hours of reading to pay off now that they had arrived at the Temple.

"I think the next thing to do is to stand on the porch and wait for someone to come speak to us."

"You think? You mean you don't know for sure?"

"How could you expect me to? I've never been a suppliant before."

"Suppliant? What's that mean? Be careful what you say about me."

"A suppliant asks the gods for help."

"Same as a beggar, isn't it?"

Argen winced. Trust Seren to put things in their proper light. No fancy face-saving words for him. "I suppose so."

"And I know so. Fafnir says calling a digging tool a digging tool simplifies things."

I bet he does, Argen thought. Then he asked, "I wonder where Faf heard that expression. It's a pretty old one."

"Not Faf. Old Fafnir, Fafnoddle's father."

Argen nodded. He should have been able to figure that out on his own. While Seren's young friend was a bit of a kook, his English was some of the best Argen had heard spoken by a dragon. Quite idiomatic. His association with Seren probably accounted for it. Now old Fafnir wouldn't see any difference between a digging tool and a spade. In fact, if he were corrected, he'd probably flame someone's eyebrows off.

"Come on, Argen," Seren interrupted, just as if ascending the stairs to the porch had been his idea in the first place.

"I'm coming."

While Seren peered inside the huge open door, Argen turned around to enjoy the scenery. It was magnificent.

"Do you suppose we should just go in?" Seren asked.

"I don't think so." Argen shook his head. "The open door allows a breeze to blow through the temple. How would you feel if someone walked in our kitchen when Mother was airing it?"

Seren shifted his weight from side to side. Patience was not his strong suit. Argen stood quietly, glad for a chance to rest and think about what he was going to say when someone did come.

The boys did not wait long. An old man dressed in a white robe appeared and spoke to them in a language neither understood.

"Uh oh," Seren said. "Now what do we do?"

"Do not worry. We will help you," Soladon promised. And as suddenly as that, the boys understood the old man's words.

"Who stands before the Temple of the Oracle?"

"We do," Seren said.

Argen cast his eyes upward briefly and replied, "Argen and Seren Koenig, suppliants to the gods."

The old man peered at them. "Suppliants to the gods? Young boys such as yourselves?"

"Yes, sir. We have lost our sister and need to find her. She's very young," Argen explained.

"Ah," the old man said. "Now I begin to understand. And were you two not asked to watch over her and take care of her?"

"No, sir," Seren replied. "We just thought we should take care of her since our parents . . ." His voice died down. How was he to explain travel between the worlds? And would the old man believe them anyway? While Seren sweated for an answer, Argen filled the breech.

". . . would expect it of us, I'm sure." Argen gave a small sigh of relief.

"Perhaps you two would like a small meal before you visit the oracle," the man said.

"Yes," Seren answered. He felt as if he hadn't eaten in days. He was sure he could eat more than Faf at that moment.

"If you please." Argen nodded his answer.

"Then follow me." The man walked through the huge door and turned left down a narrow corridor. At its end was a kitchen containing a huge table. "Sit, and I will see what I can find for you to eat."

Argen and Seren watched the man get milk, break, and cheese. They were so hungry everything tasted delicious.

"My name is Palemon," the old man said as he sat.

"We're very happy to meet you, sir," Argen said.

Seren nodded. His mouth was full.

"Now, tell me more about your sister. What did you say her name was?" Palemon broke a small crust of bread and chewed it slowly while he waited for their answer.

"Lealor," Seren answered, taking another bite of cheese.

"Did she wander into the hills or woods by herself?" Palemon's shrewd eyes watched the boys in turn. "Or did someone take her away?"

"If she wandered off, we probably could have found her ourselves," Argen said.

"Sure," Seren put in with his mouth half full of food.

"Was Lealor taken away in a boat?"

"Not exactly. She rested quietly, locked in a box, the last time we saw her."

"Locked in a box? The last time you saw her?" Palemon frowned. "Boys, if I am to help you, I must hear the story in full. Something tells me you are not trusting me with the whole tale."

Should they trust Palemon? He seemed all right. Argen looked at Seren, who shrugged.

"It's clear we have to have help from someone, Palemon. The box Lealor entered was magic."

"There was a sphinx, too," Seren added, trying to be helpful.

"A sphinx, you say?" Palemon looked surprised. "It's not often that ordinary mortals get to see magical beasts."

Seren raised his head quickly at that.

"We're not really so ordinary, Palemon," Argen explained.

"And would it be those dragon bracelets you wear that make you different?" the old man asked.

Argen waited a moment to see if Nyct or Soladon would forbid talking of them, but nothing happened. "Yes, sir. The name of my talisman is Nyct."

Nyct raised his head and bowed to Palemon.

"Mine is Soladon," Seren said.

Soladon repeated Nyct's gesture of respect for Palemon.

"They remind me of a powerful dragon mage named Wyrd," Palemon said after looking carefully at the dragons.

"He is our father, sir," Nyct spoke directly to Palemon.

"Indeed." Palemon ran his long-fingered hand down his

snowy white beard while he considered that piece of information.

Argen felt himself relax. Here was someone he was sure would really help them—or put them in contact with someone who could. For the first time since his adventure on Achaea began, he felt safe.

"Do you know about the gates?" Argen asked.

Palemon nodded.

"Our mother, Mirza, came from our world, Realm, to Achaea through your gate. It's quite possible that someone— we think it is a wizard called the Shadowlord—is tampering with the gate. That's why your sun is acting so strangely. There's a creature that lives inside it called a Bright One. The Bright One in Achaeasun is young. If it gets disturbed enough, it will—" Argen paused. What did Bright Ones do that exploded their suns? He had never thought to wonder before. When he got back to the library—if I ever do, he thought—he wanted to ask Librisald. If Librisald didn't know himself, he could tell Argen where to look, or who knew the answer.

"Yes?" Palemon's soft voice urged Argen to continue his tale.

"Argen's always drifting off like that, sir," Seren explained. "He's not weird. Honestly. My dad says that he thinks long thoughts sometimes, that's all."

Palemon struggled to repress a smile. He understood Argen and Seren far better than either knew.

"Sorry, sir," Argen grinned, looking sheepish. His father would tell him to get to the point, he knew.

"Go on," Palemon suggested.

"Well, when a Bright One gets disturbed enough, it does something and the sun explodes."

Palemon raised his eyebrows.

"Yes, sir. It's true. I swear," Seren put in.

"Your sun brightens and dims like it does is because the Bright One is roused. I don't know how much longer it will wait. So it's really important that somebody stop whoever is tampering with the gate. Before we were born, our mother and father saved the sun of Realm. That's why our mother is here. Our father came after her. We were to stay on Realm and wait for them to return."

Seren rushed in with the rest of the story. "But Lealor, our sister, climbed in this box and a sphinx closed it on her and they disappeared. We think Lealor is here on Achaea someplace. That's why we need to speak to the gods."

"Indeed," Palemon said. "Your cause is worthy. Shall we go to the Hall of the Oracle?"

"Oracles are pretty weird, aren't they?" Seren asked.

"Sometimes, my boy. Sometimes. When they are not entranced to see the future, they can be relatively normal, like anyone you might meet." Palemon rose from the table.

"Shouldn't we help with the dishes or anything?" Argen asked.

"No," Palemon smiled. "A serving girl from the village in the next valley will come up later to cook my evening meal and she will clean up then."

He walked slowly from the room and the boys followed him to a huge hall with a hole in the center of the floor. A three-legged stool sat next to the opening. The hall was open on two sides, but Argen and Seren could see some vapor coming from the hole. The gentle breeze dissipated the fumes, but Argen wrinkled his nose.

"Smells like sewer gas to me," Seren said sotto voce.

"Shhh!" Argen hissed, sounding like his bracelet. "Sir," he said aloud to Palemon, "where is the oracle?"

Palemon's answer was to sit on the stool and smile at the boys.

"You?" Seren managed.

"You're the oracle?" Argen asked.

Palemon nodded and, bending low over the vent in the floor, began to breathe deeply.

CHAPTER
TWENTY-TWO

Jarl trudged toward the mountain that loomed over the plain. It was as if there were a perpetual eclipse. In the half twilight, Jarl peered upward for a glimpse of the sun. Surely Achaea-sun had not actually dimmed to this extent? If so, he was probably almost too late to rescue Mirza and confront the Shadowlord before the sun went nova. Jarl felt a moment's pity for the small Bright One who would probably end up destroyed or at least deformed by the tampering the Shadow-lord was doing. He shrugged. No sense worrying about things he couldn't change.

He looked down at his bracelet. "Wyrd," he thought as strongly as he could, "would you please give me a hint as to where this Graiae is?" Jarl fully expected no answer, but to his surprise, Wyrd raised his dragon head and nodded to the mountain. "You mean that's where I must go?"

An almost imperceptible nod was his answer.

"Thanks," Jarl breathed, wondering if Hades and Persephone were both watching in the magic mirror.

Distances were deceiving on the plain. After only a few minutes' walk, Jarl found himself looking upward at a cave large enough to contain two good-sized barns. The ledge outside the cave was so wide that Jarl was unable to see inside. Wyrd's whispered, "Here," told him he had at last reached the dwelling place of the Graiae. The name seemed familiar, but he couldn't quite remember where he had heard it before.

After all, those Greek names could be confusing. No wonder people back on Earth said, "It's Greek to me," when they didn't understand.

Jarl checked his sword before starting to climb the short incline to the cave. He felt prepared for any kind of monster Achaea could throw at him. He didn't put it past Hades to send him on this quest just to keep Persephone amused. His sense of being watched formed cold prickles at the back of his neck. One of the side benefits of being reunited with Mirza was the idea that Persephone's mirror would stop operating at that point. At least, it would if Hades kept his word. Somehow, the idea didn't reassure Jarl much. There were many cases where gods had broken promises to mortals. In fact, the only god who always told the truth was Apollo.

For a moment, Jarl wished Apollo had told him about the Graiae. Then he remembered what happened to Cassandra. Why couldn't Mirza have adventures at home, on Realm, where things were normal? Jarl heaved himself onto the ledge with a smile on his lips. Normal? A place which dripped magic from every bough? He had come a long way in his beliefs when he could regard Realm as normal!

A strange rock formation blocked his way into the cave. He would have to work his way around it. He checked his sword for the second time. There was enough room along the ledge for Jarl to stand comfortably without fearing the edge. It was as if the rock was a marker for a hiding place. It was easy for Jarl to peer around the edge and look for the Graiae. When he did, he sheepishly took his hand from his sword. Three little old ladies with gray hair sat in rocking chairs, busily knitting.

"Same old thing, dears," said the tallest of the women. "The gods are busy partying, the peasants are working, and those strange people on the Isle of Atlan are making weird thingamabobs and doohickeys or whatever you want to call them."

"Whatchamacallits, Deino," said the oldest looking of the three. Her hooked nose reached almost to her chin. "Whatchamacallits is what I call 'em."

"That's nice, Pephredo. Whatever you do, don't fuss," said the third old lady with a smile.

"Any why shouldn't I raise a ruckus? It's my turn to see

now. Deino always wants to have more than her share of time, and you always take her part. I'm the oldest and so I ought to have the longest turn with the eye." Her long fingers scratched the wart on the end of her nose.

"Oh, very well. You can be so hard to get along with. Now, Enyo is always so charming, I'm glad to relinquish our eye to her." The tall woman's hand reached up and removed her eye from its socket. She carefully placed it in the hand of the old crone, who almost snatched it from her. Her shaky fingers pushed the eye into place.

"Now, that's more like it," she said. Her head moved from side to side as she peered into the distance. "I can see so many more interesting things than you two," she said. "I'm always glad to have my turn so we can get some real news of the world. Times aren't what they were in our girlhood, I can tell you. Did you notice, sisters, that even the light seems to come and go out there? Didn't used to do that in my day, I can tell you! Crops are all in. Looks like it's been a good year. Cattle have increased, too. Say, girls, do you remember that rich farmer outside of Delphi?" She glanced to each side, making sure her sisters were paying proper attention. "Well, he's got himself a new wife. Pretty little thing, she is. New coat of whitewash on the house and all. That must be in her honor. He's still got her working, though. She's milking the goats. Bet she's going to make some of that goat's cheese—you know, the soft kind I like best. Haven't had any in centuries, seems like."

"Well, it's your own fault. When Daddy had us placed here, he told us to ask for any supplies we wanted. You never thought to ask for a goat!" Deino rocked back and forth. "I, however, did remember to ask for fruit trees and berry bushes."

"Don't be pompous, my dear," Enyo warned. "None of us could know that we'd be waiting here forever, you know."

"Should have known, should have known," Pephredo muttered, intent on her watching.

"We were remarkably silly when we were girls, weren't we?" Enyo said. "Father thought he was doing the best for us all, I'm sure."

Deino sniffed. "You don't have a cross bone in your body.

You should have taken the offer that old shepherd made for you. Daddy would have been happy to see at least one of us married."

"We'd have been in a fine pickle, if she had."

"Oh, surely Daddy wouldn't have made us marry one of those sea monsters. He was just threatening us to make us consider some of our offers."

"But, sisters, although it's hard to remember, we were born looking old. What personable men were going to offer for our hands? It must have been such an embarrassment to Daddy. Even offering the best of dowries, he couldn't interest any young men. And there were so many handsome ones." A tear rolled down Enyo's cheek at the memory.

"Don't sit there blubbering," Pephredo's harsh voice said. "Won't change a thing. Why, we've been sitting here in this blasted cave longer than some mountain ranges have existed." She cackled briefly. "It's far too late for us. Lucky we weren't spring chickens. If we'd have married, we'd have gone to Hades realm by now. Yes, long gone by now, dead and buried."

"Can't you tell us what's happening out there instead of doddering on?" Deino's sharp voice broke the brief silence. "You're supposed to tell us what's going on. That was our bargain when Zeus gave us the eye. With only one eye and one tooth between us we have to share."

"That's so, sister. If we had married, though, perhaps we might have had children."

"Well, I've always thought we were most fortunate. We were never subservient to any man—except Father, of course," Deino said.

"Well, you were too proud to wed and I never took any man's fancy. Daughters of Phorcys and Ceto, we were. Sea gods don't find it easy to marry off their girls to mortals—and we all had human shapes right from the start."

"You're keeping the eye far too long. It's Enyo's turn now, I'm sure."

"She hasn't said anything, has she? Let her ask for it when she thinks it's her turn. At least she never rushes me for her time with the eye." Pephredo rocked and looked, making no attempt to pass on the eye.

"If I wasn't here to encourage you to pass it on, she'd probably never get a turn."

"You just can't resist a chance to harp, can you?"

"Harp? Well I never! Phredo, you always were a pig!"

"Don't call me Phredo! You know I hate it."

"Oh, my dears, don't fuss so. You know it always upsets me when you argue."

Pephredo glanced at her sister's agitated face. "Now, Enyo, you know we don't mean it. Here, it's your turn. Take the eye and see what you can find to tell us about." Her aged hand removed the eye and passed it to her sister.

"About time," Deino muttered, but so softly that only Pephredo could hear.

"Oh, how wonderful it is to see! I love to hear you both telling about all the things you see, but being able to see oneself is so much nicer."

"No argument there," Pephredo said, rocking back and forth as her hands resumed their knitting. "I suppose now we're going to get the latest report on all our little feathered and furred friends," she sighed.

"Of course we are," Deino put in. "If ever the Fates slipped up, it was when they made Enyo our sister. She should have been a nature goddess. Then she'd have been happy."

"The Fates don't often ask a body what they want to be. And as for being happy—" Pephredo snorted. "Hah! Just look at all the miserable mortals the Fates bedevil."

"And not just mortals. Consider the plight of our sister, Medusa, poor girl."

"Yes, she's a good case in point. Why, on that miserable little ball of dirt—what was its name? Earth, I think they called it—the Fates actually let one of those mortal heroes kill our sister."

"Wouldn't you rather hear about all the lovely animals in the woods?" Enyo asked. "You do want me to tell you about the animals, don't you?"

"What I wish we had was some of that goat's cheese," Pephredo said.

"What I wish is that we could have an adventure ourselves. Why, the last important thing that actually happened to us was that time when Perseus came to us for help. Since we moved back home to Achaea, we haven't had one hero come to visit us. Those were the days." Deino sighed.

"Oh, I wish you could see! There's the cutest little squirrel. His cheeks are full of nuts and he's carrying them into his tree home." Enyo smiled happily, but neither of her sisters saw her look of joy.

"How exciting," Deino said, not meaning a word of it.

"Don't be snippy, sister dear," Pephredo said. "It will be your turn for the eye soon enough."

"I can't get used to it, sitting here day by day. Somehow, I still wish I could play a part—even if it was a small one—in the real happenings on Achaea." Deino sighed again.

"Fat chance," Pephredo answered. "No one even remembers us except the gods. Even the gods forget us. Only Hades comes to visit once in a great while."

"And I'm sure he only remembers us because we will never enter into his kingdom. It's no fun being a symbol of old age."

"Excuse me, ladies," Jarl said in his politest voice, "but I would like to have some information." He stood directly in front of Enyo, who still retained possession of the eye.

"Oh, my dears, if you could only see what I see!" Enyo's mouth dropped open as Jarl bowed to her. "Oh, my. And so handsome, too," she breathed, as if she was afraid she would scare Jarl away.

"Who spoke?" Deino commanded.

"Who, indeed," echoed Pephredo. "Give me the eye, sister." She fumbled for it, but Enyo made no effort to remove it from her socket.

"Give me!" Pephredo commanded.

"No, wait," Deino said. "Remember what happened the last time we tried to pass the eye with a stranger present?"

"Indeed I do," Enyo said. "We all sat here blind, having to bargain with that handsome young man—what was his name? Pericles? Persuit? Persimmon?" Her murmurs fell away as Pephredo broke in.

"Perseus, that was it."

"Well, whoever, we mustn't trust this one," Deino said.

"Weren't you just wishing to have part in an adventure?"

Pephredo chuckled softly. "There speaks an adventurous spirit."

"He looks perfectly lovely, sisters," Enyo assured them. "Quite trustworthy."

"I'll believe that when I can see him myself. How can we be sure it's safe to pass the eye?"

"Let me assure you I have no desire for your eye, being fortunate enough to possess two myself."

Deino said acidly, "We supposed as much when Enyo didn't introduce you as a cyclops."

"What if you get ready to transfer your eye and then I walk way over there near the edge while you change?" Jarl offered.

"That sounds fair," Pephredo said. "If we don't trade the eye, I won't get a chance to see him, sisters."

"Very well," Deino grudgingly agreed.

Enyo took one last look at Jarl and handed the eye to her sister.

"Well, for once, Enyo, I agree with you. He is a very comely mortal."

"Deino, give me a quick turn with the eye. I want to see him too."

"Only if you promise to return the eye to me after you look. You always want to have the longest turn."

Pephredo reached out with her scrawny hand. "I promise. I promise," she said. "One quick peek and then I'll give it back."

Deino handed the orb to her sister, who popped it in and then looked at Jarl. "Fine-looking fellow, sisters. Now, we'd like to know what you are doing here. I'm sure you didn't make this visit because you know us. Someone must have sent you. Who was it? Why have you come?" She leaned forward in her chair, peering at Jarl.

"Sister, you promised," Deino interjected.

'Oh, indeed I did. Here." Pephredo reluctantly removed the eye and give it to Deino.

"Now, that's better," she said, positioning the eye in its socket. "Did someone send you?"

"If I may have your permission to approach," Jarl began.

"I wish I could still see him. How polite he is!" Enyo said, rocking very fast in her excitement at the thought of an actual visitor.

"Come closer," Deino commanded.

Jarl obeyed. He took off his sword and shield. Turning his shield upside down, he sat on its padded interior. The shield made a noise as he sat upon it.

"Oh," Enyo said, jumping at the sound.

"What was that?" Pephredo asked suspiciously.

"Nothing, sisters. Our visitor just sat on his shield. I must say he certainly isn't acting much like a heroic type." Then she turned to Jarl. "Don't you know you should be ready to fight at all times? Who knows what kind of a monster might materialize any moment?"

"I rather hope not," Jarl said. "I've been very busy ever since I arrived on Achaea, so I could use a little rest."

"You've not told us yet who sent you."

Jarl found it interesting. Whoever had the eye seemed to be the spokeswoman for all three sisters. "Hades sent me."

"Hades? Whatever for?" The other two old ladies rocked and nodded their agreement to the question.

"He told me to find the Graiae. That is you, isn't it?"

"Grey women, that's us." Pephredo chuckled.

Deino cast her a look. "I was talking with this hero, sister."

"Humph. Doesn't mean the rest of us have to sit dumb as stones, does it?"

"Well, no," Deino admitted. "I do have the eye."

"Don't have to be able to see to speak," Pephredo said with some logic.

Enyo said, "Sisters, we are ignoring our guest to bicker among ourselves. He will think us rude," she added gently.

"No," Jarl told her with a smile. "I can understand it's quite upsetting to have a stranger pop up on your doorstep as I did."

"Quite right," Pephredo said.

"So Hades told you to find us, did he? And why would you come on such a quest?"

"My wife has disappeared. I know she is somewhere on Achaea."

"And you want us to help you locate her? How romantic!" Enyo sighed.

"That's it," Jarl confirmed.

"Why did Hades send you to find us? It can't have been very easy. Hades knows where we are. Why didn't he come and ask us himself?"

"His wife wanted to watch me find Mirza, so he created a magic mirror for her."

"You mean she's watching us now?" Enyo's hand went up to smooth a stray curl back from her forehead.

"Yes, I think so," Jarl told her.

"Oh, dear me."

"Don't fuss so, sister. What if she is watching? You know yourself, looking can't change things. If it could, we'd have some soft goat's cheese here every time I wore the eye. Maybe Persephone will take the hint and send us some, now that she knows."

"He didn't say she could hear, sister. Only see."

"Hearing is part of the enchantment. Perhaps I have some cheese in my pouch, here." Jarl rummaged in the magic provender bag Cibby had given him and found a neatly wrapped parcel of the cheese. He offered it to Pephredo, putting it in her hands.

"What's this?" Her hand patted the package, then unwrapped it. She lifted it to her nose. "Goat cheese, as I live and breathe!" She pulled off a morsel. "Thank you, stranger," she said before putting a piece in her mouth.

"Tell us what you want. Giving us gifts won't gain you our good will." Deino frowned slightly.

"Gained him mine!" Pephredo contradicted, chewing busily.

"My name is Jarl. I've already told you I'm searching for my wife. I know she is being held a prisoner against her will. She has long red hair," he continued.

"Ha! We already know where she is!" Pephredo said.

"You do?"

"Yes, indeed," Deino added. "Our sister Medusa is her warder."

"Then you did see her with the eye!"

"Of course," Enyo said, nodding. "She's a very beautiful woman. No wonder you search for her."

"Wonderful! Tell me where I can find Medusa."

All three shook their heads.

"You can't tell me where she is?" Jarl was thunderstruck. "Yet you have seen her?"

"Yes, Jarl, we have," Deino said. "But we won't tell you where to find our sister Medusa."

"We've sworn a pact," Enyo said.

"We won't tell," Pephredo added. "Does this mean I've got to return the rest of your cheese?" she asked sadly. "We'll never tell."

CHAPTER TWENTY-THREE

"What do you mean, you'll never tell! I can't find my wife unless I find Medusa."

"It's the fault of that Persimmon person," Pephredo explained, still clutching the package of cheese. "We'd tell you except for our oath." She held out the package to Jarl. "Here's your cheese," she said gruffly.

"Oh, keep that," Jarl told the old woman. "What I'd like to know about is this Persimmon."

"Not Persimmon. Perseus," Deino told him.

"Oh. I've heard about him. He killed Medusa."

"Yes. And you would do the same if you saw her."

"Just a minute," Jarl said. "If Perseus killed Medusa, how can she be alive here to hold my wife captive?" He looked at the three old women, awaiting an answer.

"The gods restored her when we left Earth," Enyo offered.

"Then why are you worrying? Besides, I won't hurt her."

"It was a terrible experience. Imagine having your head

lopped off when you really hadn't done anything wrong."
Enyo shook her head sadly, unable to understand such wick-
edness.

"She was the only mortal sister, you see," Pephredo said.
"She was young and beautiful when she offended Athena.
Always a mistake to offend a goddess, mortal. Remember
that!" She rocked silently a moment before adding, "Must be
getting old. Giving free advice when it's not wanted."

"You may be sure I will remember what you have said. It
rings true." Jarl sat, perplexed. How was he going to get these
old women to tell him what he wanted to know?

"It was so sad," Enyo told him. "She had the most beautiful
curly black hair."

"Down to her waist, it was," Pephredo nodded. "Some
goddesses can't stand to see a lovely mortal. That flame-
haired woman of yours had better be very careful."

Jarl's heart skipped a beat. He had not thought that Mirza
might excite the envy of any goddess, although she was strik-
ingly attractive. He remembered the first time he had seen
her. One glance and he loved her. Looks like hers might well
attract the attention of one of the philandering gods. Then
what would he do?

"Alas!" Deino rocked back and forth, her old hands clasp-
ing the wool she was knitting. "Athena turned her hair to
snakes, ugly repulsive things that writhed and hissed when
anyone approached."

"Medusa almost went mad the first few days. She stayed in
her room, moaning and carrying on. Not that she didn't have
reason, you understand."

"Pephredo, it was a fortunate thing that she did. Remember
that shepherd boy who saw her out on the hill the next morning?"

"That I do, Deino. That I do. His blood froze up in him.
Stone cold, that's what he was."

"No, sister," Enyo's gentle tone broke into the discussion.
"Cold stone. The boy turned to stone."

"Yes, I remember. We covered her head, but it was so awkward. And when the neighbors came, wanting to see her, she
sometimes took off the covering."

"Right. Got so statues of horrified neighbors covered the

place. So father sent her off to live with her sisters, Stheno and Euryale on the shores of Oceanus, near—"

"Pephredo!" Deino warned. "You almost gave away Medusa's location."

"Ladies, knowing my wife's location is much more important than simply finding her. There is a sorcerer called the Shadowlord. He is trying to force a gate from this world to others. My wife and I stopped him on Realm, where we come from. He must be vastly more powerful now than he was years ago when we first encountered him. Already this tampering with a gate disturbs the Bright One in your sun. The light elsewhere on your world dims and returns. When this has happened often enough, your sun will become a nova and explode, destroying everything on this planet. I'm not sure how far the process has gone since I began talking to you. Believe me, it is important I find my wife as soon as possible."

Deino, who had the eye at the time, said, "He looks like he's telling the truth, sisters."

"Could I please see," Enyo asked, holding out her hand.

"Very well," Deino said, passing her the eye.

Enyo's hand shook, and the eye rolled from her fingers onto the floor. "Oh, dear," she said softly.

"Well, what do you think?" Pephredo asked.

Tears rolled from Enyo's empty sockets. "Sisters, I fear to tell you, but—"

Jarl found the eye and pressed it firmly into her hand. She gave him a radiant smile. "I think, sisters, that we can trust him."

"Well, let me see as well," Pephredo grumbled. "Have to be last all the time. Well?" Her voice cut the air like a knife. "Well?"

"I just wanted to make sure I didn't drop it, sister."

"All right." Pephredo fitted the eye in her socket. "He does look like an honest sort. Are we agreed? Shall we tell him where Medusa lives?"

Deino said, "But our oath, what about that?"

Jarl could feel time rushing by. How many minutes had he wasted with these three already. "What exactly did you swear?"

"That we would never tell another hero where Medusa was so he could go and hurt her."

"And if I promised not to hurt her?"

"How can we be sure?"

"I can make you a promise."

"We never had suitors, but we know how easy it is for a mortal man to break his word when he wants something," Pephredo said.

Deadlock!

Jarl stared at the Graiae. They gazed back at him with their five empty sockets and the eye.

Enyo offered timidly, "Do you suppose—" then she paused. "No, I guess not."

Jarl was ready to try anything at this point. "What?" he coaxed.

"If you would leave your shield and sword with us . . ."

"Good idea, sister." Pephredo turned to Jarl. "Leave us your sword and shield, and we will tell you."

"Agreed." Jarl placed his sword and shield at their feet. He hoped Hades would not be angry, and he also hoped he didn't meet anything he couldn't talk into a reasonable frame of mind. He decided he'd worry about how to handle Medusa when he came to her.

"Sisters," Enyo said. "We are not being quite fair."

"Not fair!" Pephredo said. "Remember what happened the last time we dealt with a mortal—that Per—what's his name?"

"Perseus," Deino corrected.

"Can't we allow him at least his shield? He cannot hurt Medusa with that, but it might protect him. Remember, he cannot look at her without turning to stone."

"Very well," Pephredo agreed.

"We must keep the sword," Deino said, having the last word.

"Now, where is Medusa?"

"You will find her near Tartarus, on the shores of Oceanus."

"Which direction would that be?"

Three arms raised, fingers pointing south.

"And how long will it take me to make the journey?"

"Many days."

"I don't have that kind of time!" Jarl was ready to swear from frustration. Wyrd would refuse to zap him there, he was sure. Lealor's rejection of Wyrd's gift was costing her father dearly. "How am I to get there? I wish Faf were here."

Jarl spun around at the slight "pop" behind him.

"Did someone mention my name, Uncle Jarl?"

Jarl was so happy to see the small dragon that he didn't even bother to correct him for saying "Uncle Jarl."

Pephredo had the eye at the time. "Aha! So you finally come to see us again, Little One."

Faf reached under a wing tip and pulled out a bag, which he gave her. "I thought you might like these," he said.

"What is it, sister?" Enyo asked. "I love surprises."

Pephredo opened the bag. "More of that steakfruit. Good stuff," she said, taking one and passing the bag to Enyo.

Jarl's stomach heaved at the thought of riding with Faf, but he had no choice. "Can you take me to where Medusa lives?"

"Sure, but why do you want to go there?"

"That's where Mirza is."

"I think I've got the time. I can't stay, you know. My mother will be checking on my studies any minute. Besides, I just brought your—"

"Later. Just get me there. Then you can go," interrupted Jarl. He turned to offer a courteous goodbye to the Graiae, but Faf wasted no time. He grabbed Jarl by the belt and popped them to the shores of Oceanus.

"Where's Medusa?" Jarl tried to ignore the queasy feeling in his stomach.

"I didn't think you wanted to drop in on her literally," Faf said. "You'd better figure out how you're going to talk to her without looking at her. You turn to stone if you look her in the face, you know. She's up the beach in a cave." One talon pointed the direction. "Gotta go, Uncle Jarl." With a cheery wave of his talons, Faf disappeared with a faint pop.

Jarl walked slowly in the direction the dragon indicated, holding his shield ready. If he thought Medusa was near, he planned to use the shield like a mirror. The conversation of the Graiae had reminded him of the story of Perseus, who used his shield in the same way Jarl planned.

The sun shone brightly on the golden sands. The waves curled in to the shore. A surfer would be in ecstasy in a place like this, Jarl thought. Ahead a cliff face that jutted out into the sand interrupted the strand, almost obliterating the beach. Jarl hoped he wouldn't have to swim. He didn't think he could and still carry the shield. And that shield was one thing he definitely wanted with him when he found Mirza.

When Jarl actually reached the narrowed part of the beach, he found a three-foot clearance between the cliff face and the water. If he were careful, he wouldn't even have to get his feet wet. He had no idea what was on the other side of the cliff, so he stopped and listened. He couldn't hear anything except the sound of the water against the shore. To be on the safe side, he positioned the shield and advanced, looking into it. If Medusa awaited him, he wasn't going to look at her by accident.

The bronze shield does not make the best of reflective surfaces—even if it is a magical gift from Hades, Jarl thought. He saw movement above the cliff face. Was it Medusa? The wildly flowing locks might be snakes; however, he was too far away and the shield simply wasn't a good enough mirror.

"Jarl!" the figure shouted.

He recognized Mirza's voice. The figure was his wife, not Medusa. His happiness at being reunited with her almost made him cast his shield aside, but common sense triumphed. He clutched it awkwardly as she ran into his arms.

She leaned against him with her head fitting into the curve under his chin. "Where have you been? I sensed you a long time ago. It's the Shadowlord again," she said calmly. "What took you so long?" She planted a kiss on his chin by way of apology for her questions.

"I went through hell to get here," Jarl told her, not aware of his pun. Mirza was certainly taking it calmly, he thought. But then, who else would tamper with the gate system? Everyone had been so sure it would take the Shadowlord years to recover from his defeat on Realm. The power being used here was tremendous. It made the Shadowlord's former abilities seem almost insignificant by comparison.

"Do you mean it was hard to find me or that you actually went to the Land of the Dead?" she asked with a twinkle in her eyes.

"Both," he offered, hugging her.

"Tell me. Tell me," she teased him as Lealor often did when she wanted a story.

"Very well. We missed you on Realm. The opened *Book of the Worlds* was left turned to the page about Achaea, and that was our only clue. The Bright One in this sun is in a disturbed condition. I couldn't use the gate, so Faf brought me. I mistakenly wandered into Hades and Cerberus wouldn't let me out, so I begged my freedom from Hades himself. Either he didn't know where you were, or he wanted to use my odyssey in search of you as entertainment for Persephone."

"How could that be?"

"He created a magic mirror for her. It was like a handheld television."

"You mean she's watching us now?" Mirza looked around as if she could locate the video camera she suspected was taking pictures of them.

"Not now. Hades promised me Persephone would only watch until I found you."

"Did you come by boat or did you walk?"

"Part of the way I walked, but this last part of my trip I came by Air Fafnir."

"What's Old Fafnir got to do with this? There's no way he could have made the trip."

"Not Old Fafnir—young Fafnir."

"Young Fafnir? Who's that?"

"First Egg," Jarl explained. "He's decided to be an adult and Fafnir is the name he chose for himself."

"But I thought there had to be a ceremony and a horde of gold, and—"

"Faf has cut most of that short with my blundering aid. I gave him a piece of gold. When he arrived back home—by the way, dear, the refrigerator and freezer are empty and the pantry is pretty well decimated, too—he intended to remove all the gold he could carry from Fort Knox. He thought there were mountains of the stuff stored inside and that humans wouldn't notice if he took enough to start his hoard. I convinced him to return to Realm with me. We'll have to replace the gold piece in Seren's coin collection."

"You old softy, you gave it to Faf, didn't you?"

"Well, how was I to know that was the official start of his hoard? I'm lucky Ebony and Fafnoddle didn't roast me for it."

"They're pretty understanding, for dragons. If more dragons had adventures with humans, they'd all come around to more sensible positions."

"Speaking of sensible positions, where is Medusa? I had to promise I wouldn't hurt her and give up my sword to find out where this place was."

"She's resting at the back of the cave." Mirza brushed her long hair away from Jarl's face. The snappy breeze off the water cooled the air.

"Then why didn't you run away from her?" Jarl asked.

"I dare not leave. Sometimes I see her watching me in the evening when I comb my hair. Those snakes are truly hideous. She has such an ugly expression on her face, sort of soured."

"Well, I can understand why. You weren't very happy when the Shadowlord placed that enchantment on you—remember?"

"Yes." Mirza shuddered.

"Why haven't you left already? Or is there some reason you won't help me foil the Shadowlord again?"

"No matter what the danger, I must help you, but I am afraid.

"You're afraid of Medusa?"

"No, it's not her. She's only guarding me so the Shadowlord will remove the snakes. No one else on Achaea would dare the wrath of Athena. Poor Medusa."

"Poor Medusa indeed! And how is it you've stayed with her for days and not turned to stone?"

"Oh, remember the spell of the Green Lady protects me, plus I always carry a little moley with me—in case of unicorns, you know." Mirza reached into her pocket and pulled out a small sprig.

Jarl took the few leaves she offered and put them in his shirt pocket, which he firmly buttoned. "Okay. Now what?"

"The minute we leave here, we put Lealor in danger."

"Lealor? She's back on Realm with a guardian bracelet!"

"Not now. She was enticed into a magic casket by a sphinx and the Shadowlord has her."

"Then what are we waiting for? We'll go to wherever he's holding her—"

"No, Jarl. I have probed the magic of the Shadowlord while I waited for you. I was planning to try something—anything —if you did not come, and I needed to know his real power. It is tremendous. He can actually tap Achaeasun itself. All my instincts tell me to try to rescue Lealor right away, but I know we cannot succeed unless we have the power of the gods to aid us. Even then, defeat is a real possibility."

Jarl saw the shimmer of tears in Mirza's eyes. Mirza never cried, but now she seemed ready to weep like any silly heroine.

"How much time have we? Will Medusa report immediately to the Shadowlord?"

"Well, I told Medusa all about the Bright One. She's agreed to let me go because I've promised to take her to Realm and use the waters of the healing spring on her."

"Oh, I almost forgot. Persephone sent this for you." Jarl handed Mirza the opaline box. "Maybe Medusa won't have to wait."

Mirza opened it curiously. The salve within emitted a flowery scent. "What is it?"

"Persephone said it was some kind of magical beauty cream," Jarl began, but Mirza was already running to the path up the cliff.

"I'll be right back." The words drifted over her shoulder to the astounded Jarl. "I want Medusa to try this. Persephone is so thoughtful!"

Mirza disappeared above. Jarl knew all about beauty routines. He found a dry patch of sand shaded by the cliff and stretched out for a nap. Mirza would return when she wanted him. He wondered how much time they would have to rescue the Bright One. Mirza hadn't seemed worried about the time element at all. Jarl couldn't really blame her. His concern about Lealor wasn't allowing any sleep or rest. Rescuing the Bright One just might have to wait.

At that moment, the sun dimmed ominously.

CHAPTER TWENTY-FOUR

Jarl jerked upright. The dimness seemed to last fractionally longer than before. How were they to stop the Shadowlord? His power had definitely grown in the years while Jarl and Mirza reared their children. He remembered the prophecy which said it would take the combined powers of them all to stop the Shadowlord. This time it was crucial he not escape.

He rose and started up the path Mirza had taken so short a time before. When he came to the opening in the cliff, he set down his provender bag and debated whether to trust the moley's power or not. Then, too, he had Wyrd. Even if he was still sulking, he probably wouldn't want Jarl to turn to stone. He felt like such a fool maneuvering the shield. With a shrug, he placed the shield over the provender bag and entered Medusa's home.

The absence of light almost blinded him. He stood in the dimness and waited for his eyes to adjust. He could hear Mirza's voice within the cave. The beauty preparations were at a critical point, he could tell. The next few moments would be crucial. The possible nova would have to wait. He preferred facing it to facing Mirza if his interruption caused Medusa to refuse to try the cream that Persephone had sent.

"Well, just hold still a moment. I need to cream this around your hairline. Do you suppose you could hold the snakes off your neck for me?"

Jarl shuddered. He imagined Mirza carefully creaming away the snakes from Medusa's scalp. She had a much stronger stomach than he did.

"There. That's done. Don't you feel much better now? Let me put a little on your face. Hold still. I don't want to waste any. Now rub it well to be sure you get the full benefit of the cream," Mirza advised.

"Am I really going to look the way I did before Athena punished me?"

Jarl listened carefully. The second voice must be Medusa's. It didn't sound as if she were a horrible monster. The tone of her voice was remarkably similar to Enyo's, even gentle. It wasn't so surprising. They were reputed to be sisters, after all. Phorcys and Ceto were supposed to be the parents of the gorgons and the Graiae. He wondered if they had any normal children. Ceto, their mother, must have been a really brave goddess. Who knew what the next batch of children would turn out to be or look like? Jarl's blood ran cold. Maybe it wasn't bravery after all. He had married a shape-shifting witch and never given a thought as to what kind of children he and Mirza might have. Neither of the boys had showed much magical aptitude so far, but Lealor was already demonstrating witchly powers. That of healcraft for animals, for instance. The sound of someone approaching drew him from his thoughts.

"Jarl, dear, I want you to meet Medusa."

Jarl turned. Leave it to Mirza to be cordial to her jailer. The tall, curly-headed young woman next to her was lovely. Her black hair had a sheen that was spectacular. Her facial features were regular and her complexion was radiant. That beauty cream Persephone sent much have worked, he thought.

"I am most happy to meet you," Medusa said in quiet tones.

"And I you," Jarl answered, bowing. He hesitated to offer his hand because of the snakes that were wound around her arms.

"Do not be afraid of my companions," Medusa said. "We

have been together so many centuries. I have not the heart to abandon them."

Jarl decided Medusa really wasn't monster material. Perseus must have stretched the truth a great deal when he retold his adventures. And didn't drops of blood from her severed head form Pegasus? Surely a truly evil monster couldn't produce such a wondrous creature. Perhaps the gods had engineered the whole thing. Hadn't Pegasus helped another hero kill the Chimera, the lion-snake-goat mixture of myth?

Mirza gave the gorgon a hug, snakes and all. "Jarl and I must go now. I hope shortly to have the Shadowlord so busy that he will not have the time to seek you out. If he should send a messenger to see how I am, just say I refuse to join him and am staying with you. I bet no one will enter the cave to check. Just stay in the shadows yourself. In a few days, I hope this whole adventure will be over for everyone."

"Thank you, my friend. May you have success in your enterprise." Medusa glided the few short steps to the opening in the rocks and waved as Mirza and Jarl descended the path.

"Isn't she lovely now? I don't know how long we can keep the news of my escape from the Shadowlord, but we really must get working on this." Mirza's hand sketched a gesture toward the sun. "That poor little Bright One."

"That poor little Bright One that has the power to destroy the entire sun to escape the machinations of the Shadowlord," Jarl muttered. Why was it that when he was with Mirza he was unable to worry effectively? Was it because they had come through all kinds of scrapes in the past? He knew he didn't trust Wyrd's powers nearly as much as he did those of his wife. She often assured him that he was her equal in power, but he knew he was not yet her equal in knowledge. Power without the knowledge of how best to use it was almost worthless. Together, however, they made a formidable team. Why then was he so concerned over the increase in the Shadowlord's powers?

"Now to begin," Mirza said.

"You mean we're going to start the battle here? Now?" Jarl's voice rose in spite of his efforts to keep calm.

"Of course not," Mirza said. "First you have to get us to Olympus."

"Olympus?" Jarl swallowed. "What makes you think I can get us there?"

"Not you. Him." Mirza's finger pointed to a spot over Jarl's left shoulder.

Jarl turned to see what or whom she pointed to. Shades of the three o'clock monster movie! Winged sandals, funny hat, and caduceus, a staff with two snakes curled around it. Why, he thought to himself, do I have to get involved in so many adventures with snakes? I hate the loathsome things. However, he did recognize the god. Hermes, the messenger of the gods, always carried the caduceus.

"Are you looking for us?" Mirza asked the god.

"If you be Mirza, I seek you."

"Are you here to transport us to Olympus, or do you only bear a message for us?"

"I bear a message."

The god's, admiring eyes made Jarl nervous. He wracked his brain to remember all the stories of Hermes he had ever heard—he was a trickster, a messenger, and insatiably curious about everything. The memory of a bubble gum wrapper he had collected as a child came to mind. The Greeks worshiped Hermes because he was the god of speed and gamblers. Not one of Jarl's recollections showed Hermes to be a womanizer. Probably, he didn't stay around long enough in one place to attract feminine attention. Jarl hoped this was so. How was a mere mortal to compete with a god if the god decided he liked the mortal's wife? Remembering some of the stories about Zeus, Jarl rather hoped Mirza wouldn't get to meet him on this trip to Achaea.

"Well, don't you think you'd better tell us what the message is?" Mirza smiled.

"Gladly will I tell if you will but answer me a question first." Hermes zipped over to a rock in the shade and sat. He reminded Jarl of a hummingbird. Holding still seemed to be an unnatural thing for him to do.

"Of course I will. You have only to ask," Mirza said.

Mirza was being her usual charming self. Jarl was busy

wishing she was worn from her captivity. She looked ravishing to Jarl. Perhaps she had dabbed on a little of Persephone's magic beauty salve. Medusa hadn't said a word if she had. Even women born under different suns ganged up on men when it came to beauty secrets.

"Are you immortal that you dare to undo a spell placed by Athena? When she finds out how fine Medusa is looking these days she will probably be quite put out, you know. You are the most courageous being I have met in quite some time."

"Pooh. There's no courage required. I didn't do anything, or use one speck of magic. Persephone sent Jarl, my husband, with the magical beauty salve. Could I do any less than share it with Medusa, who, you must admit, had suffered long and had a great need for the properties of the salve? Now how can Athena be angry with me? Medusa endured the punishment for centuries. I'm sure wise Athena can judge the measure of the gorgon's suffering. Why should her punishment continue? To dwell on the past would be less than wise—and I'm sure Athena sees no necessity for that."

Hermes watched Mirza with a grin. "Well said, My Lady," he agreed. "You are as clever verbally as you are in other ways. I can see that having you on Olympus is going to prove to be quite entertaining. I was planning on delivering my message and running off in search of some excitement. Your arrival, however, may engender more adventure than that hidebound band of old fuddy-duddies cares for."

"And have you the power to take us there with you?"

"Or course. There is one little problem . . ."

"And that is?" Jarl put in. No matter how interesting the conversation was, he wanted to get on with the matter of the Shadowlord. Saving Lealor and the Bright One were his only two priorities. He would feel much better when he started the preliminary steps to curb the power of the Shadowlord.

Hermes shifted his attention to Jarl from Mirza. For a moment, Jarl felt very much like an ant at a picnic.

"What is the problem?" Mirza asked impatiently.

"I am not commanded to take you two with me, only to tell you to come to the meeting place of the gods. . . ." Hermes considered the situation.

"Oh, come," Mirza said. "Are you not the god of gamblers? Are you not willing to trust to chance and take us with you?"

"Well said. Well said. I admit that what you say is true. With the possibility that Athena is angry or at least annoyed with you, is it worth bringing you unannounced before Zeus? I, naturally, will be on your side. We can count on Hera as well. Apollo will be glad to have help to straighten out our sun. I can't really speak for any of the others. You start your travels, and I'll just check back to make sure it's safe to bring you. Then I'll return." Hermes stood, raised the caduceus, and disappeared in a flash. Literally.

"Well, now what? We don't seem to have made any progress there," Jarl said.

"Will Faf be popping in again?" Mirza looked at her thin sandals. They were not what she would have chosen for a long walk.

"Who knows?" Jarl's exasperation showed in his voice. "Too bad Hermes didn't leave us a little of that luck he's supposed to spread around. We have certainly had our share of unlucky happenings."

"What do you mean by that?" Mirza asked. "I thought you were pretty lucky to find me so fast."

The sun dimmed, brightened, and dimmed again.

"Do you know something about the Bright One that I don't?" He gazed skyward with his eyebrows raised. "Like, for instance, how long it is until Achaeasun goes nova?"

Mirza felt the strange rippling effect in her mind. What could it be? Was her trip through the flawed gate going to cause her permanent brain damage? She frowned at the thought.

"You may well frown." Jarl wiped his eyes tiredly. "You can't work magic for fear of offending the gods. Wyrd promised Hades not to help us until we actually face the Shadowlord. Lealor waits imprisoned in a casket. Faf is unreliable about arriving, and we can't be sure what kind of time frame we've got before it's too late to stop the Shadowlord."

"We are in a pickle, aren't we?" Mirza laid her head on Jarl's shoulder.

"Did someone mention pickles?" a voice asked. "I'm quite hungry."

As Jarl started to turn, he and Mirza disappeared.

"Uh, oh!" said the little dragon, scratching his head. "How did they do that? Maybe it's time for a father and son talk." A large pop indicated a hurried departure.

CHAPTER TWENTY-FIVE

"Weird," said Seren, watching the oracle inhale the vapors from the opening in the floor.

"Wyrd rests, storing energy," Palemon said in a voice that raised the hairs on the back of Seren's neck.

"Lealor, our sister. Where is Lealor?" Argen asked.

"In a box."

"He isn't wasting any words, is he?" Seren looked skeptical. "I could have told us that!"

"That's the way an oracle works," Argen explained, trying to decide how to frame his next question.

"Where, exactly, is she?" Seren asked.

"In a box in the main audience hall of the Shadowlord's castle."

"Where is the castle?" Argen asked.

"On Atlan."

"Is Atlan another world?" Argen asked, hoping it was. If Lealor was on another world, she would be safe if this one blew up.

"Atlan is an island on Achaea." The voice of Palemon sounded dead, somehow. Both boys could hear the strangeness.

It was as if the Palemon they knew, the kind old man, had left, and something or someone quite different inhabited his body.

"Can I rescue her?" Seren asked.

"You can retrieve the box. With help."

"Who will help me?" Seren asked.

"Call on the gods."

"Can you summon the gods for us?" Argen asked.

"They come not at mortal summoning," Palemon intoned.

"Oh, great!" Seren broke into the conversation.

Argen gave him his dirtiest look. "How then are we to get the help of the gods? How can we win their favor?"

"They come not at mortal summoning," Palemon repeated, "but they are here." And with those words, Palemon fell from the stool.

Argen and Seren both rushed to help the old man up, but a luminous figure in a white robe materialized beside him. "Rise, faithful servant."

It was the most powerful voice the boys had ever heard in their lives. They couldn't have told what made them believe implicitly in the power of the figure, but there was no doubt of who was boss in the room.

Seren and Argen looked around them. A number of the luminous figures stood in a half-circle behind them.

Argen murmured, "Hera."

One of the beings smiled.

"Ares."

The well-muscled warrior set his spear on the floor sharply in answer.

"Artemis, the huntress."

Another silent smile.

"Athena, the grey-eyed."

A nod.

"Hephaestus, master artificer."

The figure shifted slightly. The boys could see he was lame.

Seren looked in awe at the beautiful woman who stood next. He burst out, "I know her! Aphrodite!"

Seren felt a warm glow from the figure. It felt almost like a hug.

The next luminous figure stood with a small puddle of water beneath his feet. The air smelled faintly of seaweed.

"Poseidon, the Earth Shaker," Argen said.

"And I?" the hollow voice of Hades echoed in the room.

"Great Hades, Ruler of the Underworld."

Seren wondered where his brother found the courage to speak to the King of the Dead. In fact, he wondered how he found the courage to speak at all. The room was filled with power; he could almost feel the electricity in the air. He had always wanted to meet a Bright One, because they were reputed to be the most powerful creatures on this plane of being. After seeing the gods, Seren decided to give up his wish. This was about as much as he could handle.

Palemon stood beside the awesome figure of the silver-haired god.

"And Father Zeus," Argen concluded. If anyone could save Lealor, it was this group. In fact, any one of them could probably transfer Lealor, box and all, to this place with a raised eyebrow. A light sweat covered Argen's forehead. If only Seren didn't put his foot in it. He understood Faf's worry about being turned into a coralberry crumpet now. He and Seren could become grains of sand on the beach, for all these magnificent beings might care.

"We heard," Zeus said.

Argen felt relief. The tone of voice was mighty, but not unfriendly. Perhaps the gods would help them.

"Let us destroy this Shadowlord, brothers," Poseidon said.

"Not without a battle, surely," Ares said.

Hades looked at the God of War. Argen was very glad he had not received that look.

"Yes. He deserves severe punishment," Zeus said.

"Impertinent mortal." Hera's cool tones made Seren feel as if he was standing in a draft.

"I agree," Athena said.

"That's a first," Hera said. Argen stifled a smile. So the old tales about the infighting among the gods were true!

"Are we not all forgetting about the innocent maiden in the box?" Artemis said. "I would not have one of my creatures trapped so."

"Bring the box," Hera commanded.

"I will," answered Venus. She raised her hand in a commanding gesture, but nothing happened.

"Well?" Athena asked.

"Gods, the box is strangely heavy. It refuses to come at my command." A slight frown marred her perfect visage before she remembered about wrinkles and ceased.

Seren looked stunned. What kind of force did the Shadowlord have at his disposal to thwart the wishes of a goddess?

"Let me try," said Hera. After a few seconds, her face fell.

"I shall bring the box," Ares said. At his command, a short buzzing noise sounded. He winced. "It bit me!" He pouted.

"No, it only resisted your command," Zeus said. "Let us play no more. All lend your will. Let us show this upstart mortal the power of the immortal gods! At my command," he said, looking at the luminous figures around the room. "Now!"

The surge of force reminded Argen of an electrical storm. His skin crawled. He wanted this to be a bad dream so he could wake up. He glanced at his brother. Seren stood calmly, but Argen knew his brother very well. He could see the pounding of his heart at his throat where his open-necked shirt lay unbuttoned.

The box appeared in the room, first as a shimmering outline, then in reality. Seren hurried up and looked within. "Yes," he said. "She's in there, all right."

"We thank you all," Argen said, half-afraid of what Seren might blurt out in his happiness.

"May I open the box?" Seren asked, surprising Argen. Maybe Seren did understand the danger of alienating the gods.

"If you can," Zeus said.

Seren took hold of the handle and tugged, but the lid remained immovable. The gods watched silently as he tried.

"Argen, come here and give me a hand," he commanded.

The combined efforts of both boys did not budge the lid.

"What's the matter? The sphinx just flipped the lid down. Soladon told me," he explained to Argen.

"Then why can't we open it?" Argen asked reasonably.

"A strange force—what you humans would call magic—binds the box from within and without," Zeus explained.

"From within, we understand," Nyct said, speaking for the first time.

"Ah," said Zeus. "Do I not recognize the form of my old friend Wyrd?"

"We are the children of Wyrd, created to protect these three young ones," Soladon offered. "Our sister, Myst, is under a vow of silence," Soladon continued. "We know that she locked the box with dragon magic from the inside."

"She is willing to release her magic, mighty Zeus," Nyct said, "but she does not know where the second spell came from. Since it intended no harm, and was meant to protect, she did not even know it was there until Argen and Seren tried to open the box."

"It is the outer force that holds the box immobile. Is one of you responsible?" Zeus asked.

"Lovely as she is, I did not bespell the box," Aphrodite said.

"Although I rejoice that the little maiden is unharmed, it is not my will which holds the lid shut," Artemis said. She pulled an arrow from her quiver. "Shall I shoot at the lock?"

Zeus smiled. "No. Pure force is not the answer. What we need is the magical herb, long gone from Achaea, called moley."

"We have lots of that on Realm," Seren said.

"Yes, on Realm, but we are here, and have no way to get any," Argen reminded his brother. Argen felt frustrated. "I bet anything she's got a pocket that's full of the stuff, seeds and all," he said, kicking the heavy box with his foot.

The small thud of a book falling from pocket was his only answer.

"By the Bright Ones," Seren said, "couldn't you even come here without a book to read?"

Palemon said softly, "The youth seeks wisdom."

Seren bent down to pick up the book. "Hey, look. Something fell out."

Argen snatched it from the floor. "It's the twig I stuck in to mark my place before I started my adventure with Kiron the Centaur."

"And it's moley," Seren said jubilantly. He grabbed it from his brother and handed it to Zeus. "Is this what you need?"

The other gods gathered round to touch it.

"Link with me and the magical moley," Zeus commanded. "We will shatter the spell together."

"Beware, sister," Nyct called out.

"Protect Lealor as you were bid," Soladon advice.

Myst's head shot up at an indignant angle. It was just as if she said, "I know what to do."

Seren and Argen privately worried at the idea of their sister at the nexus of the force which the gods commanded. There was nothing for it now but to hope that Myst knew what she was doing.

The room filled with a strange green glow as the gods used the moley to focus their powers on the lock. With a small ping, it flew to pieces. The lid raised of its own accord at the will of the gods.

At a nod from Zeus, the boys went to the side of the box.

Argen called softly, "Lealor, are you all right?"

Lealor's chest rose and fell, but there was no answer.

Seren said loudly, "Wake up, Lealor!" It was the same tone he used when she didn't get up in the morning for school.

Lealor's eyes fluttered. Her small hand rubbed across her eyes. "Do I have to?" she asked Argen. "I was having the most wonderful dream about a sphinx . . ."

Then she noticed the faces around her. "Where am I? This isn't my bedroom back on Realm."

"Don't be afraid. We're here to protect you," Seren said, just as he always did when he thought she was scared.

"Okay," she said, sitting up. "I'm not scared, am I, Argen? Not with the two bravest brothers in the whole world to protect me."

The adults in the room hid their amusement as best they could. The little maiden was unharmed.

"Now that item is complete," Athena said, "should we not do something about our sun?"

Hermes sped through the door. "Oh, Zeus, I have done as you commanded and watched Jarl and Mirza. They are free, having turned Medusa into an ally, and can come at your command."

"All is well, then." Zeus raised his hand and pointed to a spot on the floor where no one stood. A strange shimmer, like the heat on an asphalt road, began to form. Within seconds, Mirza and Jarl stood in the room.

"Faf?" Jarl said.

"No, dear, the immortal gods of Achaea," Mirza corrected him. "And look, they have saved Lealor for us!"

Jarl strode across the room and lifted Lealor from the box. She clung to him tightly.

"We are greatly in your debt," Mirza told the gods, addressing her words to Zeus. Her happiness at being reunited with her family was almost palpable.

A soft, silvery glow formed in the center of the room. Both gods and mortals looked at it in wonder.

"Is there a god missing?" Seren hissed to his brother.

"There's a bunch, so don't ask me. I don't know everything," Argen whispered back.

As they watched, the silver light slowly coalesced into the slender figure of a woman. It was the Lady, Mirza's special benefactress.

Mirza smiled. "You are most welcome here, my Lady."

"I thank you." Then she turned to Zeus. "O, Zeus, I greet you in the name of the Old Ones."

Zeus astounded Seren and Argen by inclining his head in greeting. "And what happening of great moment has caused you to appear before us, O, Silver Watcher?"

"Two things. First you broke my spell on the casket which alerted me to your involvement and Oron's growing anger. You were but young when first you knew Oron, Guardian of the Bright Ones' children."

"I remember him well. He wanted to destroy mortal man many times, but we stood as their protectors," Zeus said.

"Oron is vastly angered by the disturbance of the Bright One in Achaeasun," the Lady informed them all.

"Let him be! What business is it of his?" Ares said.

Zeus gave him a look that Argen wished he could learn to use on Seren when he was being especially exasperating.

The Lady answered, "If there is more disturbance to the Bright One, Oron has sworn to cast this world and Realm into the Black Universe!" Jarl held Lealor more tightly. Mirza moved to his side. The twins stood awed by the pallor on the faces of the gods.

"This Oron must be some powerful guy," Seren whispered to Argen.

Argen swallowed and nodded. He had a much better idea of the power such a feat would require than did his brother. The term "guy" seemed ludicrous for so mighty a being. Not for the first time, Argen wished this was all a dream so he could wake up.

"You have little time to act. We who favor men have done all we can to restrain Oron. Now, unless you act in concert, you will disappear from this universe forever!"

"All of us?" Poseidon asked.

The Lady nodded. "Mortals and gods, Wyrd and his children."

Lealor wriggled and Jarl set her down on the floor. She approached the Lady and looked up. The Lady raised her hand and placed it on her head. A shower of silvery motes bathed Lealor from head to foot.

"Oh," Lealor breathed softly. "And am I to help, too?"

"Yes, my child."

The Silver Watcher sketched an ancient sign of blessing over them all and faded into an argent haze which the breeze blew away.

"Surely not the children," Mirza burst out.

"Yesss," Wyrd answered. "The Shadowlord is more powerful than any mortal has ever been before. Every hour that passes increases his strength, for he is tapping Achaeasun for power. It is his drain on the sun which causes the dimming. I fear the Bright One cannot last long under such a strain."

CHAPTER
TWENTY-SIX

The Shadowlord stood in his workroom, putting the finishing touches on a strange collection of wires. "There, now, that corrected Mirza's officious meddling. The power of Achaeasun is mine for the taking." Soon, very soon, he would create a gate that the Old Ones had considered impossible. He allowed himself a small feeling of satisfaction. All the years of sacrifice had been worth it. Those who thought him unfit to wield the power of the gates would bow before him. Perhaps he would destroy the Old Ones' gates, leaving his gates as the only access between worlds. His grandiose plans were interrupted by a knock on the door.

"Come in," the Shadowlord commanded.

His voice sounded so pleasant that it frightened the messenger who had been present when the genial tones of the Shadowlord ordered unspeakable magical acts performed. He, however, found himself committed to delivering the message, so he opened the door and spoke when commanded by the Shadowlord.

"O, Great One, a kraken has come to the undersea gate and we believe it wishes to speak with you."

The wizard moved to the door, saying nothing. The messenger hastily stepped back. There was something strange about being in close proximity to the Shadowlord. Whatever the sensation was, it went far beyond simple fear. Some of the workers swore the hair on their necks stood up when they approached too closely. The messenger heaved a sigh of relief as he exited the room. He, at least, had escaped the wrath of his master.

Far beneath the magical tower where the Shadowlord worked his arcane spells lay the seagate entrance to Atlan. In the past it had allowed whole ships to pass inside the walls of the fortress. With the arrival of the Shadowlord, however, stranger visitors than the ships of those from the far reaches of the sea entered silently and left, bearing various commissions from the master of the fortress.

The guards were all gathered near the door with weapons at the ready. They saluted as they moved aside to allow their master passage. The surface of the water was calm and inky black. Here and there the golden light of torches glimmered on the water, but many were close to burning out.

At the Shadowlord's command, the neglected torches sprang to new light, seemingly burning the very air that surrounded them. The wizard turned to his men and commanded, "Bring me two prisoners." Then he turned his back to them and faced the dark waters.

Those who watched later swore that the wizard listened and spoke softly to the water itself. No sign of the giant sea creature was evident. When the soldiers arrived with the two prisoners, the Shadowlord gestured for them to hurl the wretches into the water. That one of the prisoners was fair and female made no difference in his command. The soldiers hesitated, knowing what lay in wait beneath the surface. The Shadowlord made a sweeping motion of his hand. Lightning crackled, forcing the two hapless humans into the dark sea. The soldiers watched as the waters writhed and turned. Each imagined the horror of what must be happening beneath the waves. One young soldier turned a pale green, visible even beneath the light of the torches. His commander put a steadying hand on his shoulder, as if to warn him that the sea could hold three as easily as two.

After a time the movement ceased. The slap of the water against the stony walls of the manmade cavern stretched the courage of the soldiers to the breaking point. One veteran made up his mind to retire should he survive whatever was to happen next. As they watched, a giant eye slowly rose until it lay upon the surface. It filled the watery area.

Undaunted, the Shadowlord commanded, "Show!" and the eye of the kraken became a mirror of the events the monster had witnessed. Thus the Shadowlord saw the joyous reunion of Mirza and Jarl, the visit of Hermes, and the departure of Mirza and Jarl. For a second, it was as if the heartbeat of the world stopped. The soldiers cringed from the anger of their master.

His raised hand gathered power from the air and cast it in the form of a fireball at the eye of the watery messenger. The vitreous fluid of the eye seethed, forming steam that carried the strong odor of sea wrack. The very stones of the fortress trembled. A miniature seaquake disrupted the area, dislodging stones, as the huge beast withdrew from the wrath of the incensed mage.

"How dare she escape!" The voice of the Shadowlord filled the area as if Stentor himself spoke. Stones loosed by the passage of the monster fell into the water propelled by the sound waves the voice of the foiled lord created. A crack of lightning hurt the eyes of the terrified soldiers who watched helplessly, fearing their doom would be next. When a few blinks had restored their eyes, they looked in vain for the Shadowlord. He had disappeared.

The frustrated mage reappeared in the audience hall. The strong smell of ozone alerted the guard. One of them opened the door to check the room. The Shadowlord vaporized him before he could even ask if everything was all right. The door slammed in the face of the remaining guard.

The Shadowlord picked up the container which held the green liquid that would turn Lealor into a monster. With the speed of a striking bushmaster, he glided to the curtain that hid her box and disintegrated it with one wave of his hand. Nonplussed, he stared at the empty spot! Lealor and the casket were gone!

The guard outside the door did not repeat the error of the first. He stood at attention, jumping slightly as he heard the various crashes and tinkles of the Shadowlord's ire. Retorts flew from tables and crashed against the wall, spraying assorted contents all over the room. Some splashes ate the stones they hit; others ran down to the floor and writhed with pseudolife. Metal containers were squashed flat before disappearing, contents and all. Wood vanished in a puff of flame. The very air shimmered with the force the Shadowlord called upon as he flew from one area of the room to another. The wizard who wanted to control the vast system of the Old Ones' gates could not control himself. The Shadowlord was throwing a tantrum.

After a time, the audience hall lay bare. Nothing remained but the walls, ceiling, and floor. At this point, the Shadowlord conjured a chair and sat. His sobs were too quiet for anyone to hear. Then a long period of silence fell. Finally the Shadowlord rose and paced the room. His mind, which had been overwhelmed by the force of his anger, began working once more. Mirza was no longer his goal. He wanted Lealor. A child would be more malleable. Then the Shadowlord did something no one ever saw him do. He smiled. What better way to make Mirza pay than by taking her child?

They would see, he told himself. First he would locate Lealor. . . .

"We must act quickly," Mirza said, hugging Lealor tightly.

"I'll shake the earth under Atlan," Poseidon offered.

"And what will happen to the innocent humans who live near the shore? The tidal waves will kill many and destroy the fishing. You are as rash as ever," Athena told him.

"She is correct," Zeus said.

"What do you want us to do to help?" Jarl asked, not at all sorry that Zeus was to be in charge of the battle.

"First, we must move to the site," Zeus said. "Poseidon, raise up a promontory where we may stand and see the Island of Atlan, but not be on it."

"I obey, brother," Poseidon said.

"Now we must travel there," Zeus said.

"Won't that take too long?" Seren asked before he was aware he spoke out loud.

"No, child. I will take us." And with those words, the walls of the room disappeared.

They stood upon an upthrust of rock on the coast. In the distance, a dark spot upon the blue water, lay the island where the Shadowlord made his headquarters.

Zeus turned to Jarl. "Your child is safe from the Shadowlord. Are you willing to help us in repayment?"

Mirza looked at Zeus. His question surprised her. The gods asked for their help? How could that be?

"You may well wonder how it can be that we need your aid. In our arrogance—" Zeus looked at the other gods "—all of us ignored the danger to our sun. It has been many centuries since anything threatened the peace of Achaea. We came to believe that never again would evil lodge here, on our world. When we chose to return home from Earth all those centuries ago, we swore not to advance man further, to allow him to live peacefully, without the growth that brought the beginning of science and the end of magic to Earth. That result was a surprise, and not desirable. Why, mankind even denied our existence once he embraced science."

"And we have kept our vow," Athena said as the others added words of agreement to her statement.

"What do you know of the Shadowlord, this upstart mortal who somehow developed such power?"

Zeus naturally looked to Jarl for information. Mirza held her tongue. They would turn to her if Jarl could not furnish the facts they needed.

"He is a powerful sorcerer. He seeks power over others without counting the cost. Both my wife and my daughter have been his prisoners. He uses a mixture of machines and magic. Realm was the first place he tried to gain control of a gate. Now he not only seeks to be able to travel from place to place, but also from time to time. Isn't that right, Mirza?"

"Yes. He calls his gate a universal gate. If he should succeed, there is no place and no time that will be safe from him."

"Oh, Mother," Lealor said, standing as close to the edge of the promontory as she could. "Feel the pretty light!"

In the wink of an eye, a long, golden cone of force arrowed across the waves and homed in on Myst. In that brief instant, Mirza intuitively sensed the danger to her child, but quick as she was, Lealor and Myst vanished before their eyes.

"The little maiden," Artemis gasped.

"Gone!" said Ares, stamping his foot in anger.

"How dare he!" Hera said, her regal eyes widened in shock.

"Because he can," Zeus answered her, "and his powers appear to be greater than ours."

Mirza turned to Jarl, who placed his arm around her shoulders.

"We're not going to let the Shadowlord get away with that,

are we, Father?" Seren asked. He couldn't believe there was any situation his father could not handle with the assistance of Wyrd.

"Not if we can help it, son," Jarl answered.

"Now we have no time to waste," Mirza told Zeus urgently. "He knows I am working against him and he promised he would enchant Lealor with an evil potion that will slowly turn her into a monster. We must not give him time to do that."

"Mortal woman, we will plan carefully," Zeus began.

Then the sun dimmed again. It was a bare outline in the sky. The darkness was greater than that of a total eclipse. The gods themselves stared in wonder at the sight.

Wyrd's voice hissed painfully through their minds. "Mirza is right," he said. "The Shadowlord is now at the most crucial point in his manipulations. If he can succeed in channeling the power he has amassed, the sun and the Bright One within will release all their power at once in one great explosion which the Shadowlord hopes to form into a gate."

"How do you know this?" Athena asked.

"Because he has been studying my notes, which I thought were destroyed all those centuries ago." There was sadness in Wyrd's voice.

"Why weren't they at the library at Realmgate?" Argen asked.

"I hid them at Fellkeep, deep within the earth under the castle, ensorcelled with the strongest magics at my command."

"And he found them?" Mirza asked.

Wyrd nodded. The sun became even dimmer. "He may have too much power now for me to contain him," Wyrd said, "yet I must make the effort. Goodbye, Jarl, my friend."

And with these words, Wyrd uncoiled from Jarl's wrist and flew toward the island. As he flew, he grew larger and larger, until he was bigger than the island itself.

Jarl, Mirza and the children stared. Jarl tried to understand how a creature that huge could have coiled about his wrist for so many years. He hadn't known the immensity of the being who had voluntarily chosen to make himself a servant of an ordinary mortal.

"Not ordinary, Jarl," Wyrd spoke within Jarl's mind. "You

have the potential to become what I am over the centuries of
life that I have granted you."

"Centuries?" Jarl repeated.

"Ask my children," Wyrd commanded. "No time remains
for pleasantries." Wyrd's mental voice grew until it commanded all who stood on the rock. "Form into a circle of
power, hand in hand. I will endeavor to send Lealor to you,"
Wyrd said.

CHAPTER
TWENTY-SEVEN

On the island, Lealor stood before the Shadowlord, firmly
held between two guards. She looked at him, wide-eyed.
"Why did you bring me here?" she asked.

"You are to help me since your mother declined," the Shadowlord told her.

"I won't," Lealor said at her most stubborn. "And you can't
make me," she added for good measure.

"You certainly are your mother's daughter," the Shadowlord commented.

"What an odd thing to say. Of course I'm my mother's
daughter," Lealor said, not understanding. "And tell these
nasty men to let me go," she commanded imperiously, stamping her foot. "They're hurting me."

The door swung open and a harried man rushed into the
room. "Master, we have a problem with—"

"I know," the Shadowlord said, already on his way out of

the room. "I'll return shortly to deal with you, miss," he told Lealor over his shoulder.

As soon as the door swung shut behind them, Lealor shifted into dragon form. Her captors were so astounded, they let her free. She turned to face them, blowing fire in their direction. They turned and fled the room.

"Good," Lealor said, with no small satisfaction. "Now, what can I do to spoil the Shadowlord's plans?"

A red light blinked atop a mass of wires. Lealor scattered the wires with one blow of her talons. An intricate group of candles that burned on a table caught her attention next. One hot breath, and the candles melted. She charred an open book and many of the papers which lay out as if the Shadowlord studied them. Feeling she was getting into the spirit of the thing, she swung her tail and brought down two tables holding retorts and vials. The weak sunlight illuminated a metallic device in the corner. Lealor sensed power there, so she approached warily. The cone pointed straight up. She exhaled on it. Several of the small wires at the top drooped. The sunlight seemed a little brighter, so she drew back, inhaled, and prepared to incinerate the entire contraption. It was difficult holding a dragon shape and burning things. Her flame was almost nonexistent, but she tried. A few more wires drooped. She was almost ready to charge the corner and risk the power, when the Shadowlord entered the room.

"You little monster!" he said in a voice that gave Lealor goose bumps under her scales.

Lealor agreed; he was right. A dragon was a kind of monster, she supposed.

With a wave of his hand, he returned her to her human form. Then he stood over her, radiating anger. "If ever again you attempt to turn yourself into another form than the one that is honestly yours, you will stay in that form forever. Do you understand?"

Lealor understood. Even though it was fun to take the shape of other things, there was no other form she preferred to her own. Her heart beat fast.

"Well?" the Shadowlord thundered.

"Yes, I understand," Lealor said.

"And now, you must promise not to try to shape-shift again, for even I cannot remove the spell I have laid on you," he said.

"I promise," Lealor said.

"And you must never tell anyone else about this, either," he went on inexorably.

"I promise," the frightened Lealor told him.

"Sit," the Shadowlord commanded.

"May I sit by the window?"

"Yes, but do not be so foolish as to try to escape. A sheer drop to the sea lies below."

"That was nice of you to care," Lealor said.

"You would be of no use to me dead. You do not yet realize it, but you have a marvelous gift."

"A gift? Where is it?" Lealor looked around the room.

"Where all the important gifts are, inside you."

"Inside me?" Lealor cocked her head like a little sparrow.

"When you are around magic, you steal bits and snippets for yourself."

"I do not!"

The Shadowlord chuckled, a rusty sound. "Well, then, let us say your gift is to gather extra bits of magic and add them to your magical store."

"Why are you so mean all the time?" Lealor asked.

"Mean, do you call it?" The Shadowlord glanced at the girl before returning to his work. He was trying to replace the delicate wires she had ruined.

"Yes," Lealor replied, undaunted. "When you were nice and let me sit by the window, I could see how pretty you could be."

"Pretty?" The Shadowlord gave a thin laugh.

"You don't laugh enough, either. When you do that, it lightens you."

"Child, I am the same grey old—man I've always been for as long as I can remember."

"No, I don't think you are a man. Or if you are, you surely are different from all the others I met on Earth and Realm," she told him. "Inside, you're half sparkly and half dim. You know, shadowy." A smile lit her face. "I bet that's why they call you the Shadowlord!" Lealor was proud of herself. She felt she had figured out the riddle of his name.

"Hmph, sparkly, indeed. There's not a spark of light about me."

"Oh, no, Shadowlord. You're wrong."

The sorcerer turned to her and held out his hand. He pulled back his robe so she could see it clearly. It was old, wrinkled, and covered with age spots. "See, child, there are no sparkles there. So long as I can remember, I have been old and ugly."

"No," Lealor insisted. "I can feel inside you somehow. Inside, you are half sparkly and half shadows. When you were little, you didn't have all those wrinkles and funny brown spots, I bet."

"I don't remember," he said gruffly.

Lealor sat quietly, deep in thought. Then she said, "I know what must have happened! When you were just a little, little baby, someone must have magicked you into an old man. No wonder you're so unhappy. My mother says when we're unhappy, we like to see others miserable, so we mustn't let ourselves be grumpy."

"Enough!" the Shadowlord commanded, returning to his work.

"When you talked with me, you were getting more and more sparkly," Lealor insisted.

"Enough! Or I shall—"

Lealor gasped. The Shadowlord kept working feverishly, and did not turn again. He thought he had frightened her into stillness with his partial threat, but Lealor was not looking at him. She was watching the form of Wyrd grow larger as he approached the island. She sat quite still and gazed.

When Wyrd's magic pulled her through the window and hurled her onto the promontory, she shuddered as first fear, and then surprise washed over her.

"Oh, Mother," she said, safe in Mirza's arms. Then Mirza firmly put her to one side. "We are all holding hands to call power to help Wyrd," her mother told her. "You must be part of the circle."

"All right." Lealor happily stood between her mother and Artemis, who smiled down at her.

A little of the light had returned to the sun, but it was still dark enough to look at without hurting the eyes.

The oddly assorted bunch of gods, mortals, and children stood and waited for Wyrd's next command.

CHAPTER
TWENTY-EIGHT

Wyrd hovered above the island, blocking out the light of the pale sun. He could feel the power of the sun being drawn down to Atlan through his body. His dragonsensory perception searched the building for the wizard, even as he broadcast a warning to the people of Atlan. If they heeded him, they would escape. When he finally became aware of the Shadowlord's whereabouts, he made a discovery. The girl-child had been right. The being all had assumed to be a mortal was not. He was the Bright One that Wyrd had searched for after his experiment had failed so many centuries before. Wyrd felt a pang at the thought of how the young Bright One must have suffered, hiding all these centuries as a decrepit old human. If only he had thought to check the Shadowlord when they battled on Realm! His search over the long years, with no clue to prove the Bright One's survival, had made him careless. He no longer expected to find the Bright One whose sun-nest he had made uninhabitable. At last he could right the wrong he had committed by telling the Shadowlord who he really was.

Wyrd sent out tendrils of thought and spoke gently to the flawed Bright One the humans knew as the Shadowlord. He tried to reason with him "The child is right, you know."

"Right about what?" the Shadowlord replied, making a few delicate adjustments to his apparatus.

"You are not a man," Wyrd said.

186

"That's what everyone has always said. No one wanted me as part of their group."

"I mean that you are a Bright One."

The Shadowlord laughed. "A Bright One, indeed. Why, then, do I stand here, old and misshapen?"

"Because you were flawed when I tried the experiment you are trying now," Wyrd told him.

"Lies, all lies," the Shadowlord said. "If I were a Bright One, I'd throw every world I could into the Black Universe!"

"Why?" Wyrd asked, trying to understand the warped creature that stood before him.

"Because of the centuries I have spent like this!"

"What is a few centuries compared to millennia?" Wyrd asked.

"Lies!" The Shadowlord almost howled the word. "You think to make me stop or falter so that those overgrown gods can help the Koenigs save the Bright One in Achaeasun."

"Do not twist that last wire," Wyrd warned.

The Shadowlord reached out defiantly and adjusted the last small wire. Before he could even begin the chant to liberate the power, a fine humming began.

Back on the promontory, those in the circle channeled their power into the rapidly disappearing sun at Wyrd's command. Then, with no further warning from Wyrd, a vast shimmering area began to grow where the island rested in the sea.

Sweat formed on Jarl's brow. Mirza gritted her teeth. Lealor's grave frown of concentration showed her participation. Seren and Argen held hands even tighter.

The sorrowful voice of Zeus said, "We have no more power to give. Look!"

Out on the water, a great gate was forming. Through it the watchers could see scenes of life on many worlds, a kaleidoscope of shapes and events, swirling too fast to make coherent sense.

"Try harder, everyone," Mirza called in desperation. "We must help Wyrd!"

Jarl remembered calling heroes to fight the Shadowlord on Realm. Wyrd said he had powers of his own. So Jarl decided

to try to call the mightiest hero he could think of—Paul Bun-
yan—to their aid. Jarl concentrated on the magic and the
great woodsman appeared in the center of their circle.

"Hey, Jarl," his great voice boomed in greeting. "What did
you call me for?"

"Paul, I want you to join in this circle and help call up
power for Wyrd to tap. Come next to me and I'll let you in."

"Sorry, Jarl. Me and my buddies won't be of any help in this
battle. Now, if you needed someone to bash a few heads, why,
I'm your man, but this heavy thinking isn't anything I do well."

Jarl received Paul's words with despair. He hadn't stopped to
think that this was a mental, not a physical battle. All the heroes
who helped on Realm were physical types. Paul was right.

Mirza squeezed Jarl's hand in sympathy. She understood
what he attempted. She wished they could call on the wyverns
for help, but she knew they would never leave Realm. This
wasn't their fight.

"Can I go now, Jarl?" Paul asked.

Jarl nodded, and Paul faded from sight. They would have to
fight the Shadowlord with the magic power on Achaea—and
they had it all through the presence of the gods. He knew that all
the power at their command was barely maintaining Wyrd.
When Wyrd needed more power, as he was sure to do, they
would fail.

Young Faf popped in. "Oh, is this a game?" When he attempted to enter the circle, he fell to the ground with a thud. He
was, after all, a young dragon, in spite of his size. The young
dragon's arrival was a hindrance, rather than a help, because his
plight distracted Seren. Jarl could almost feel the power level
fall.

"Where is Faf?" Fafnoddle roared as he arrived, hot on his
son's trail. He took one look around and joined the circle.
"Shadowlord, eh?" he muttered, before concentrating and
adding to the power being hoarded for Wyrd.

"Maybe you'd better check on first Egg, Faf," Mirza said.

"Later," Faf growled. "If we succeed in defeating the Shadowlord, we'll have all the time in Achaea to help him. If not—"
Faf rippled his scales in the dragonly equivalent of a shrug.

If the prone form had been one of his children, Jarl knew he would not have been so calm. Dragons really were cold-blooded creatures, he decided.

Jarl assessed the power now present and calculated how much would be needed to assist Wyrd. Even with Faf's self-less help, they were still far short of success. Gods, humans, and dragon knew they would fail. There was no further power supply to call upon. The white faces of the gods and humans showed the strain.

Tears rolled down Lealor's face. Seren looked surprised. He had never considered that his father and Wyrd could fail. Argen looked years older than his age. He, too, understood they would be defeated.

Suddenly, a tremendous river of force poured into each of them. It was almost painful in its intensity. With a tremendous explosion, the gate flew apart. Wyrd spread his giant wings over the island in an effort to isolate the effects of the Shadowlord's magic. The second explosion was even louder. Wyrd, the Island of Atlan, and everything on it disappeared in a flash.

"Oh, my goodness," Lealor said, recovering her voice.

"Wow!" Seren added enthusiastically.

"Did we really defeat the Shadowlord?" Argen asked Hades as he dropped his hand.

"Yes," Hades answered. "My halls just filled with the newly arrived. I must go." He gave them a small bow and disappeared.

"We thank you," Zeus intoned.

"Was the Shadowlord really destroyed this time?" Mirza asked hopefully.

"Well, if not, it will take him some time to get up to more mischief, although Wyrd appears to be gone for good. The essence of his lifeform disappeared in the explosion," replied Zeus.

"If we destroyed the Shadowlord, Wyrd's demise would not be so painful," whispered Jarl. "The Shadowlord and Wyrd—both destroyed."

"Not the Shadowlord, Father," Lealor contradicted. "He went all silvery and slid through the gate as it disappeared."

"And how do you know that?" Zeus asked.

"Well, sometimes I can see inside people. He was all spar-kles and shadows usually, but when all that power poured through us, he used it to change somehow."

"What I would like to know is where that river of power came from," Mirza said to try and change the subject to ease the despair Jarl showed on his face.

"It was me," a mental voice blasted in to the minds of everyone.

Lealor put her hands over her ears. Seren and Argen made faces. The mind shout made everyone most uncomfortable.

"Easy there. We hear you," Jarl said.

"Don't deafen us. It hurts our heads," Mirza explained.

"I'm sorry," a quieter thought reached them.

"Who are you?" Lealor asked.

"Yes, who are you?" Mirza echoed her daughter's question.

"You know. You saw me a lullaby."

"Sang," Mirza corrected automatically.

"Well, then, you sang me a lullaby and made those bad things stop squeezing me so tight. I'm Sweet Baloo."

"Sweet Baloo?" Mirza gasped.

"Who is Sweet Baloo?" Jarl asked.

"It must be the infant Bright One," Mirza said.

"Can I come out and play?"

"Not yet," Jarl said.

"Pretty please?"

"No," Zeus said firmly.

Everyone felt the sob.

"Where did he learn to speak?" Jarl asked.

"Probably from me," Mirza told him. "All during my stay here, I've felt watched. Sometimes I'd have an odd riffling feeling in my mind. I guessed it had something to do with the mess the gate was in when I arrived. I never thought it was the Bright One."

"My name's Sweet Baloo," a petulant thought reached them.

"Now it is time for you to go to sleep," Mirza said. "You have many more years to sleep and grow. When you wake up the next time, you'll find yourself more stable and then you may come out to play—but only if you are very careful not to hurt Achaea and all the things upon it," Mirza warned.

"But—"

"Promise me," Mirza said.

"Oh, I promise."

"Then good night," Mirza told Baloo.

"Good night."

The faint tingles of power which had swirled around them ceased and Achaeasun returned to its former brightness. Then Mirza knew the Bright One had returned to sleep.

"Mother," Argen said, "you'd better check on Lealor."

Lealor stood in the center of a group of goddesses, explaining. "So then I just melted the funny wires. I'd have done more, but I got tired and the Shadowlord came and made me stop."

"You are a brave child," Aphrodite said, "therefore, I give you the gift of beauty."

"And I," said Artemis, "give you the gifts of nature and the ability to understand animals."

"I give the gift of hearth and home," Hera said.

"I give wisdom," Athena said.

Before another goddess could say anything, Mirza stopped them. "Please," she said, "she is such a little girl. These gifts are much too grand for a child. She will not be able to grow up normally if so many wonderful presents mask her true potential."

"We cannot take back our gifts," Hera said.

"Could you sort of see she comes into them gradually, then?"

"We might manage that," Athena said.

"Done," said Aphrodite.

"Thank you all," Mirza said, relieved that she had not needed a major confrontation with the goddesses to make them see sense.

A sound caused Mirza to turn. Fafnoddle had revived his son, who seemed fine.

"Have I missed all the fun? I still haven't found where you store your gold. Seren, have you seen any gold?" he asked, looking around for his friend.

"By what right do you visit here on Achaea and look for gold without our permission?" Zeus asked.

Argen shuddered. One dragon wisecrack and they might all become coralberry crumpets.

"I didn't know I had to have permission," Young Faf said. "My friends were here and Uncle Jarl and Aunty Mirza—"

The gods had a sense of humor, but they tried to hide their smiles at the idea of a mortal being related to a dragon. Zeus was getting ready to speak again when an additional sauroid form materialized on the promontory.

"And is this how you study dragon history?" she hissed, ignoring everyone but her son.

"Study history? Why, Mother, we made history right here," Young Faf told her.

"I was hard put to trace you," she scolded. "If it hadn't been for your father following you, I might never have reached wherever this is."

"Achaea," Seren put in, anxious to help his friend.

"First Egg," Ebony said, ignoring Seren and shaking an admonitory talon, "how dare you sneak away from your studies!"

"Not First Egg, Mother," Young Faf said in a conciliatory tone, noticing the haze of smoke coming from his irate parent's nostrils.

"Ebony, my dear, we have enough problems without—" Fafnoddle told his mate.

"Oh, Ebony, how glad I am to see you!" Mirza said, effectively distracting the black dragon from her wrath.

"Is this where you have been?" Ebony asked, looking around her in some disdain.

"It was the Shadowlord again. Your son and his father have been a great help."

"Well, that puts a different complexion on matters," Ebony snorted, partially mollified.

"Allow me to present you to the gods who rule Achaea," Mirza said.

Ebony nodded her head, as did Fafnoddle. "I remember that a great-aunt of mine, thrice removed, knew some of you," she said regally.

"Will any more of you be dropping through the skies?" Zeus asked.

"No, this is all of us," Ebony said.

Jarl sighed in relief. Old Fafnir wouldn't be coming, then. He asked Fafnoddle quietly, "Where's your father?"

"Oh, he's keeping watch on our egg, taking my turn. She's due to hatch soon," the dragon told him.

A ponderous thump punctuated his remark. There at the edge of the rocks sat the old dragon Fafnir.

"Father, what in the name of dragon lore are you doing here?"

"Hi, Granddragon," said Young Faf.

"Fafnir! Why have you come? It's dangerous for you at your age!" Ebony said.

"Expected me to sit home like some overgrown lizard, watching that egg of yours hatch, did you? I'll have you know I was flaming cities and carrying off young maidens when you weren't even a twinkle in your father's eye!" the old saurian roared.

"My egg! Is it hatching?"

"Why else would I come rushing off at my age?" Fafnir growled.

"I must go!"

Mirza raised a hand. "Please, may Lealor and I come with you? I'm not too sure how safe the gate may be."

Seren sprang on young Faf's back and let out a shouted, "Wahoo! Dragonback, the only way to travel!"

Mirza said, "Jarl, do you think letting Faf take him is a good idea?"

"Don't fuss," Jarl said. "He brought both boys, but I wouldn't listen when he tried to tell me."

Argen was considering his choices. He remembered all too well his last ride. Which dragon would he have to ride?

"Come on, boy. I'll take you," the old dragon said.

Argen climbed on Fafnir's back. "My name's Argen," he said.

"Don't you worry. I'll have you back on Realm in no time," Fafnir promised.

"Don't just stand there, Jarl," Fafnoddle said. "We don't want to be last off." He lowered his head so Jarl could walk up his neck to a seat on his shoulders.

"Last off, is it?" Old Fafnir said. "Humph!" And with no further warning he—and Argen—disappeared.

"Oh, dear," Mirza said as Ebony puffed them out of sight.

"It wasn't very fair of Fafnir to take off without giving us a chance, was it?" Seren said.

"Well, no, but it will do him good to win for once," Faf said, lowering his head politely to the thunderstruck gods the humans had totally forgotten. "I'll not visit again without permission, sir," he told Zeus.

"Well, see that you don't," Zeus told him.

"Ta ta, then!" Faf said jauntily and disappeared with Seren.

Jarl stood there among the gods looking down at them. "I thank you for your aid and hospitality. I'm sorry that the Shadowlord intruded upon you."

Athena spoke. "No, it has been most diverting. Your little maiden was right, you know. He whom you call the Shadowlord did disappear, and his is more than man—a great deal more."

The other gods and goddesses nodded their agreement.

"We'll keep watch for him," Jarl promised.

"Our world has fared ill because of him. The Island of Atlan is gone and with it, all the islands that were like it, and the allies of the Shadowlord's forbidden magic."

"What do you mean, and "all the islands that were like it?"

"He had recruited many times and many places, islands like this on our sister worlds on this plane," Zeus explained.

"Atlan—Atlantis?" Jarl breathed.

"On your world so was this island called," Athena told him.

"The power—" Jarl said.

"Tremendous, as we saw," Hera said.

"This Lord of Shadows," Artemis said, "will try his evil again, I fear. You will protect the little maiden, will you not? I have a great fondness for her. Give her this as a token of my friendship," Artemis said, taking an arrowhead from a small pouch and tossing it up to Jarl.

Jarl bowed his head.

Zeus said, "You have our leave to go."

"Thank you—" Jarl began, but he never finished, for Fafnoddle said, "I need to be at home!" and transported them back to Realm.

"Interesting creatures, aren't they?" Hermes commented.

"Yes, in the centuries, I had forgotten," Athena said.

"Perhaps it would be worth watching them—" Hera began, then stopped and amended her statement at the look Zeus gave her—"without their knowledge, of course."

"And no interference, mind," Zeus said.

The others all agreed.

"Leave!" Zeus commanded.

The forms of the gods and goddesses dimmed and disappeared.

Zeus stood alone. "Mortals ... worth watching indeed ..." he murmured as he formed a bag of gold. A wave of his hand sent it to Realm. Then he, too, returned to Olympus.

EPILOGUE

Jarl sat alone in the dark hours of the night. No matter how hard he tried, he could not get over missing Wyrd. Everyone else was back to normal—or as normal as they ever got, but Jarl missed the companionship of his magic bracelet. The silver moon shone through a window. Even the peace of the night was no consolation.

Jarl jumped as he heard a slight thump. Rory sat at the foot of the moonbeams, irate as usual.

"Meddlesome old witches," he muttered. "How is an innocent leprechaun going to get any rest? Dragonyoung and ancient crones be damned!" The curse lost some of its force because Rory was rubbing his backside. Evidently, moonbeam riding resulted in a hard landing.

"Rory?" Jarl asked, unable to believe his eyes.

"And how many other leprechauns do you know well enough to call friend?" Rory said irascibly.

"Why are you here now? It must be two or three in the morning."

"That's it exactly. I'm here because you're not in bed, sleeping like any decent human."

Jarl just stared. In all the years he had known Rory the leprechaun had never made him a visit without a reason.

"I'm here with a message."

"A message?"

"Wyrd says—"

"You have heard from Wyrd?"

"Not me. Cibby. Wyrd says not to be sitting around mop-

196

ing. There are things you have to do, but he will see you again, after you have learned to do without him."

"If it were only that easy." Jarl ran his hand through his bronze hair.

"You think you've got problems?" Rory spluttered. "I just wish I knew how to get rid of a pesky dragon."

"What are you talking about? You're not making any sense."

"Young Fafnir, that's who. A leprechaun's gold isn't safe anywhere on Realm. Ever since Zeus sent him that bag of gold—what a waste! A dragon just hoards gold, you know."

"I know," Jarl answered sympathetically. "What do leprechauns do with it?"

"Why, any fool knows that! They buy sweepstakes tickets, my boy."

"Oh," Jarl said weakly.

"To get back to my problem—that overgrown lizard has been popping in and out and round about trying to find out where I've got my gold hidden! It's all I can do to stay one pop ahead of him. Not a moment's peace. If it weren't for my leprechaun perceptions, he might catch me. And then where'd I be? A pauper in my declining years, that's where. Any moment he'll be here, I suppose. So I'd better be going. Remember now, stop moping— grow!"

A whisker from Rory's brilliant red beard made a soft spronging sound.

"There's my alarm. Faf's near my gold again! He'll not get away with it!" And with these words, Rory disappeared.

"Poor Rory," Mirza said, spoiling the sympathy of her tone with a silvery laugh as she entered the room. She held out her hand to her husband. "Come, am I not enough?" Jarl rose from his chair. As he took Mirza's hand, he realized she and the children were more than enough to replace Wyrd until they should meet again as promised.

Wyrd stretched luxuriously. It was a relief to be able to extend himself fully. His mammoth form almost completely covered the huge ledge before his cave. He watched the shimmering energy forms that advanced across the broad valley below his mountain. He knew they came to greet him, for he had been absent a long time. He doubted he would ever become a part of the human plane again, now that his children shared his fascination for humankind. In time, they would help Jarl's children as he had helped Jarl. They had done well for beings so young. Myst, especially, had succeeded in spite of the handicap Lealor had caused her to have. Wyrd's eyes clouded as he envisioned the future. Yes, when Lealor faced the Shadowlord for the final time, she would need all the help she could summon.